CHANGE
OF HEART

by Clare Lydon

custard
books

First Edition October 2021
Published by Custard Books
Copyright © 2021 Clare Lydon
ISBN: 978-1-912019-16-8

Cover Design: Rachel Lawston
Editor: Cheyenne Blue
Typesetting: Adrian McLaughlin

Find out more at: www.clarelydon.co.uk
Follow me on Twitter: @clarelydon
Follow me on Instagram: @clarefic

This is a work of fiction. All characters and happenings
in this publication are fictitious and any resemblance
to real persons (living or dead), locales or events
is purely coincidental.

Also by Clare Lydon

Other Novels
A Taste Of Love
Before You Say I Do
Christmas In Mistletoe
Nothing To Lose: A Lesbian Romance
Once Upon A Princess
One Golden Summer
The Long Weekend
Twice In A Lifetime
You're My Kind

London Romance Series
London Calling (Book One)
This London Love (Book Two)
A Girl Called London (Book Three)
The London Of Us (Book Four)
London, Actually (Book Five)
Made In London (Book Six)
Hot London Nights (Book Seven)
Big London Dreams (Book Eight)

All I Want Series
All I Want For Christmas (Book One)
All I Want For Valentine's (Book Two)
All I Want For Spring (Book Three)
All I Want For Summer (Book Four)
All I Want For Autumn (Book Five)
All I Want Forever (Book Six)

Prologue

Twenty years earlier…

Steph opened her eyes and took a moment to remember where she was. Slatted light from the half-open dusty blinds laddered the opposite wall.

A woman in a white coat stood beside the bed, clipboard in hand, the scratch of her pen almost drowned out by the beep of the monitors. "You're awake again." The doctor's voice was muffled.

Steph's mind cranked slowly, trying to locate the doctor's name. Teresa? Tracey? Trudi? She was pretty sure it began with 'T', but her brain was slow since the procedure.

"How are you feeling?"

Steph went to nod, but her head was a dead weight. She forced a swallow through her dry throat. She really wanted to brush her teeth.

"Okay," she croaked. At least, Steph hoped she would be okay. After six years of living between very tight lines, she hoped this marked a new beginning for her. The start of a new life. It was three days since her operation. She had tubes coming out of her body, she'd been cracked open and stitched up, but she was alive.

The doctor stared, then gave a nod. "Just remember, you're not going to feel great for a while. Take it easy, and be kind to yourself. Don't overdo it. You've got the rest of your life to do that. No lifting heavy weights, no running, no jumping."

Chance would be a fine thing.

The doctor squeezed her arm. "I'll see you later. Get some rest." She closed the door with a quiet click.

Steph adjusted her bum in the bed. Pinpoints of pain flared in her bones. Her molars ached, her chest clenched, and her eyelids flickered shut. She breathed in, then grimaced. She wanted to fold in half, roll into the smallest ball. Anything to soothe the constant aches.

But it was all going to be worth it. Soon, her days of hospital wards and waiting rooms would be over. In time, she might even be able to run. No more calculating the risk in her every step. Steph was going to live as normal a life as the next person, the doctor had promised. "But it will be a slow road for the first few months. You're going to have to be patient."

It was a skill she'd perfected.

"You'll get through this. You're my little warrior." That's what her mum always said.

Steph had joked that this time next year, she was going to sky dive to celebrate her one-year anniversary. Her mum had told her she would do no such thing. Maybe she wouldn't. She didn't want to cause her mum anxiety. Perhaps she'd take it easy, and just do normal things. Stuff that everyone else took for granted.

Like sprinting for a bus. Dancing like a loon. Maybe she'd even finally kiss a girl. She allowed herself a tiny smile, even though her cheekbones panged. That would be *huge*. Plus, perhaps she could finally pursue her dream of becoming an actor. Apply to drama school just as she'd always promised herself. She could hardly believe it was within her grasp.

Steph had been given a second chance and she wasn't going to blow it. She'd lived the last six years of her life as a sluggish caterpillar. Now, she was ready to burst out of her shell and become the butterfly she was always meant to be.

Steph could dare to dream.

Chapter One

Present Day

"I'm not going." Erin slurped the last of the marmalade gin from her wide-rimmed glass, then sat back and closed her eyes.

"You're not going? To your own parents' 40th wedding anniversary party?" Morag's face was stencilled with disbelief. "I'm bloody going, even if you're not. Your parents throw a mean party. Remember your mum's 60th with the vodka ice sculpture and the live-band karaoke?" She waved her arm, the sleeve of her baby-pink batwing jumper catching on the open packet of crisps, making them spin on the table. Morag caught them before they cascaded to the floor and into the grateful mouth of the pub dog, a chocolate Labrador named Freddo.

Erin did remember. She'd drunk far too much ice-cold vodka, got pissed and tripped off the stage in the middle of a rousing rendition of Chesney Hawkes' 'The One And Only'. But she'd styled it out like a pro and gone around the crowd with her cordless mic. Relatives still brought it up to this day.

"I also recall thinking then it was a bit tragic I didn't have a partner to go with."

Morag's face dropped. "You had me!" Her full, round mouth turned down at the corners, her curly red hair outraged on her behalf.

Erin screwed up her forehead and patted her best friend's arm. "I know, and you're the best. But back then, I was only 27. If you're single in your twenties, that's okay. But ten years on, nothing's changed. I can't face all the questions from my extended family about my single status. It gets worse every year. Plus, you know how things are with my parents. They're so relentlessly chirpy and determined to show that everything is fine. So yes, I'm going away." But where to? She decided in an instant. "I'll go to the Seychelles. Just me, the sun, and my lonely heart. I'm not going to be the 37-year-old curiosity at my parents' party."

This time, Morag threw her head back and chuckled loudly. The Falcon, their local, was crowded. Two women in their 50s wearing hiking apparel at the next table turned to look at them, and Morag gave them a wave.

Erin covered her face. Morag had always been embarrassing.

"Shall I get you another drink or will you get even more maudlin?" Morag secured a fistful of curls behind her right ear. She got up, not waiting for an answer, then turned to Erin before she left. "Gin and tonic with extra bitters for the drama queen?"

Erin filled her cheeks with air, then blew out a raspberry. "Normal gin, please. That marmalade-flavoured one made me crave tea and toast." Her shoulders slumped. "I know I have to go, but I don't want to. Why don't you come and pretend to be my girlfriend?"

Morag baulked. "If Patsy and Duncan don't invite me purely for my sparkling personality, I'm going to be mortally offended." She paused. "And while your plan is a great one, your friends and family all know me. They also all know I'm straight. I'm hardly going to suddenly find you delectable after all these years, am I?"

Erin would go to the party. She was just venting, and Morag knew that. But why was her relationship status such essential news? She was successful in every other aspect of her life, wasn't that enough? Not according to her grandmother. "It's my dying wish to see you settled," she'd told her last time they'd met. If Morag wanted dramatic, Erin had learned from the best. Her gran was fit as a fiddle with not even one foot in the grave.

Morag arrived back with their drinks—gin for Erin, sauvignon blanc for her. She gave Erin an eyebrow raise as she sat.

Erin's Spidey-sense tingled. That look on Morag's face normally spelt trouble.

"You know, what you just said made me think. About me pretending to be your date."

Erin blinked. "You're going to do it?"

"Course I'm bloody not. For a start, what would Tim say?"

"You've only been out a few times."

"I'm not being your date."

"Spoilsport."

"No, it made me think about this podcast I heard recently. The one about relationships." Morag ploughed on. "They had this guy on—I forget his name. He was talking about this agency he's set up for people who need a friend or a date."

"I'm not hiring a hooker for my parents' party." Erin had standards, and that was a non-negotiable. She wasn't Richard Gere.

"I'm not talking about a hooker!" Morag sipped her drink. "Also, who calls them hookers anymore? They're escorts these days." She tapped the table. "Back to my point."

"Of telling me to hire a hooker?"

"No! This bloke runs an agency where you can hire a professional actor for just such an occasion to be your pretend girlfriend. No strings attached. It's not an escort agency. These are out-of-work actors who're tired of being extras in *EastEnders*. You don't have to sleep with her, you don't even have to kiss her. She'll just turn up and be your pretend-girlfriend for the whole weekend. It's perfect when you think about it."

"It's desperate when you think about it."

Morag gave her a pointed look.

Erin blinked, then puckered her brow. "I am *not* desperate!"

Their outdoorsy table neighbours turned their heads again. Was it Erin's imagination, or did they lean in this time?

Morag snorted. "No, the whole pub believes you. You did just shout it at them, which is always the best way to convince people."

Erin rolled her eyes. "Even if I did hire an actor, how on earth would I get my parents to believe it? We speak every week." They were used to her being single. She couldn't just spring a woman on them.

"You tell them you've met someone a month or so earlier. It's not like you live around the corner from them, is it? They live in the Highlands; the last time we drove there it took us four hours. Unless they've got cameras in your flat, they will not know you're *not* humping a new woman 24/7."

Erin considered it, then made a face. "It's not happening. We've got too much on to even consider it." Their Edinburgh decorating company, Female Flecks, was booked solid for months. Home improvements were something that never went out of fashion, and a female-run decorating company was different enough to score a steady stream of clients. "Plus, it's not just my parents. What about Alex? I'd have to lie to him, too."

"So? He and Wendy are far too busy running after their triplets to worry about your dating life. Plus, they'd probably feast on the distraction. Something shiny and new to talk about that doesn't involve potty training or toddler tantrums."

That was true. Erin always felt in her brother's shadow because he had a grown-up job as a doctor, along with a wife and kids. It didn't matter that she ran her own company. In her head, Alex always trumped her.

Then, of course, there was Nadia.

"I know they'd be happy for me, but that might make it worse knowing it's all a lie." She stuffed a couple of cheese-and-onion crisps into her mouth while her mind buzzed with possibility. "I'm always the odd one out. Mum and Dad, Alex and Wendy. Even the triplets have got each other."

"So change the narrative. What's the harm? You've never taken anyone home. Make this time different."

Erin always thought she would have met someone by now. Introduced them to her family. But she hadn't exactly sieved the city in her search for true love. Would hiring someone to play her girlfriend be any worse than turning up on her own? Plus, the family tensions always ramped up around special occasions. All the things left unsaid. Maybe a new person would shift the spotlight.

"How about if I look into it? Speak to this bloke or someone he works with. Find out the details." Morag tilted her head. "It's not like you can't afford it. You're always telling me you have money to spend, but you've nothing to spend it on. Why don't you consider this an act of self-care? Some people meditate, some go on a spa weekend. You can hire yourself a gorgeous girlfriend for the weekend, just to take the pressure off and make the whole thing more bearable."

Erin pictured the scene in her head. Walking into the party with someone on her arm, instead of being alone. In her stomach, the pit of despair warmed. It would be nice. Heck, it would be a huge sea change, and it would mean her Aunt Helena wouldn't come up to her and pat her arm conspiratorially, telling her there was nothing wrong with being a loner, just like her.

She sat up. Perhaps hiring someone would be better all round. No feelings to navigate. The woman would do what Erin wanted. She'd have complete control, something she'd been striving for ever since... Well, ever since her life changed.

Plus, Morag was right. She could afford it.

"Fine. Look into it. But I can't see it happening. For one thing, whoever I hired would have to be queer. Or else, a very good actor."

Her best friend frowned. "You want a *queer* fake girlfriend? Did you not hear the part about them being an actor?"

Erin squeezed her shoulder blades together. "I know that. It would just make things easier if they were queer. They'd know about family pressure."

Morag gave her another pointed look. "The pressure you're under from your family is all in your mind. Your brother loves you. So do your parents." She paused. "I know this is about Nadia, too…"

"Stop." Erin sat up. Her heart thumped in her chest. It still happened, even so many years on. "This is about me and my inability to have a relationship." She snagged Morag's gaze. "But you're right, walking in with someone would be nice. Look into it and see what you come up with."

Chapter Two

"Steph, catch!"

Steph looked up just in time to see a can of gold Elnette sailing towards her head, but not quite quick enough to stop the can hitting her cheekbone with a satisfying clunk.

"Fuck, Jody!" Steph retrieved the can from the dusty dressing room floor. She rubbed her face as she stood up. "Why the hell are you throwing a can of hairspray at me?" She glanced down at her costume. A lurid green bodysuit, green rope around her waist, and fake leaves covering her from shoulder to toe. It wasn't a look she intended to replicate for a night out anytime soon.

"Because you need it to complete the full beanstalk *ensemble*." She said the last word like they were about to take to the runway at Paris fashion week. "Plus, I was more throwing it *to* you rather than *at* you." Jody stood in front of her, dressed as a Christmas bauble. Her six-foot frame was subsumed by a cylindrical shiny robin-red sphere, her face and hair were painted gold and fairy lights blinked on top of her head. She looked, frankly, ridiculous.

"Also, can I just say, I'm two inches taller than you and *still* cannot believe I didn't get the beanstalk gig." Outrage streaked across Jody's face.

"What can I say? I've got beanstalk experience."

Jody gave her a grin. "You need to redo the top of your hair green before you use that hairspray, too."

Steph patted her hair, knowing Jody was right. Steph's acting career had arrived at the point where she was in the chorus of the Jack and the Beanstalk pantomime in Croydon, playing three different parts including villager, cow, and the wise, talking beanstalk. They were about to head into the first big group song of the second half, and this was the beanstalk's big moment. On stage, Jack was singing about being lost and not knowing which way to turn. Steph glanced in a nearby mirror. She understood his plight.

"Are you coming to drinks at mine tonight?"

Steph nodded. "I am. Michael's coming and he says he has a job for me."

Jody raised a heavily caked eyebrow. "I still can't believe he gave up acting."

Steph, Michael, and Jody had all met at drama school. Jody's and Steph's careers had been glued together ever since, but Michael had grown tired of the job insecurity and started his own business, renting out actor friends to people who needed a pretend date. She hadn't seen him for a few months, but judging from his Instagram profile, his new business was going well. Tonight, Michael was coming to see her with "an offer she couldn't refuse". She'd see about that. He'd tried to offer her jobs before, but their schedules had never worked. Plus, Steph didn't consider what Michael was doing *proper* acting. Sure, this pantomime might not be where she'd imagined herself at 37, but at least she was still on stage and had an equity card. Wasn't Michael's business little more than an expensive escort service? She wasn't quite that desperate yet.

She was still in the game.

Better that than *on* the game.

"I'm not sure what he's got in store, but he was very insistent. Maybe he's got the role that will be my big break. Maybe it's my time to shine."

As Jody nodded, her costume jingled. "It's definitely my time to shine!" She pressed a button on her thigh and the lights covering her body blinked way too fast.

Steph turned her head. She was glad she didn't suffer with migraines. Her mum did: she'd never cope in panto.

"Places everyone!" That was Ron, the stage manager. He had a thick head of hair, the colour of the carrot juice Steph loved, but could seldom afford. He also had a wrinkle so deep between his eyebrows, he must have come out of the womb in frown pose. "Your audience loved the first half judging by the amount of happy ice cream being eaten out there right now. They've sold out of chocolate and vanilla. A first in this run!"

Something to be proud of at last.

He turned to Steph, waving a hand up and down her costume. "You need more leaves. Did you lose some in the first half?"

She nodded. Ron also had a terrible memory. This happened every night. "They fall off in the big group number. Too much twirling."

The wrinkle twitched on his face. "And your hair needs to be greener." He looked around. "Marion! We need to make Steph so green, the Martians can see her from space!"

Marion appeared with more leaves which she jabbed on

Steph's body in the manner of an amateur boxer. Then she grabbed the Elnette, covered Steph's eyes and sprayed, before topping up her stacked hair with extra green. She stood back, added a little more, then gave Steph a broad smile. "Martian ready."

"You're the sexiest beanstalk I've ever laid eyes on," Jody told her as she walked by with her fellow baubles. "Remember: tequila at mine later!"

Steph nodded, as two human Christmas trees ran past. Then Harry, who played Jack, appeared at her side, still doing up his shorts after a quick trip to the loo.

Steph averted her eyes.

"Three-minute call, everyone!" Ron shouted. "Get in position!" He pointed at Steph, then Harry. "Good, you two are together. Stay that way, okay?"

Steph's mind wandered to what Michael wanted to speak to her about later. Whatever it was, it had to be better than playing a beanstalk for the third year in a row. Yes, she was five foot ten, but that was verging on being typecast.

"Have I told you green's my favourite colour?" Harry asked. They waited in the wings, the rest of the cast already front and centre, singing and dancing their hearts out.

"Every night for the past 33," Steph replied. He was sweet, but tiring.

"Jack and the beanstalk, ready?" Ron whispered from behind, making Steph leap in the air. A few leaves fluttered to the floor. Within seconds, Marion appeared and stuck them back on in record time.

Ron gave them a thumbs-up, followed by a wide grin.

Show time.

* * *

Steph saw Michael as soon as she walked into the party. He wasn't hard to spot being six foot three, Malaysian and ripped. As well as starting his own acting agency with a difference, Michael had also installed a gym in his house. Now, every spare 15 minutes was spent pumping iron, and it showed. He was never short of male attention, even if the men he saw never seemed to stick around too long.

She walked over and gave him a hug. After the night she'd had, where she'd slipped on some water and nearly fallen into the orchestra pit, it was great to see a familiar face. Although, sadly, not as familiar as she'd like. That was the trouble with theatre work. Whenever Steph was off, her friends were working, and vice versa. Michael knew all about that, having trodden the same path himself until two years earlier.

"Just the woman I want to see!" Michael kissed her cheek, then held out a strand of her once-chestnut hair. "Your hair's still green, by the way."

"Hazard of the job."

He smelt of expensive cologne and smoke, and kissing his cheek felt like she'd just run her face down a sheet of sandpaper. Steph had no idea how people coped kissing men.

"How's my favourite beanstalk?"

"Extra stalky." Steph took his hand and pulled him towards the kitchen. Once there, she greeted a few people, as did Michael, grabbed two bottles of Sol from an ice bucket on the counter, and headed into the garden. Even though it was December, the fresh air was welcome. Steph sucked it in, staring up into the inky sky. If only there was a magic, wise beanstalk she could turn to for advice and life therapy. Michael was as near as she got. They walked over to a row of old railway sleepers that lined a wall of flowerbeds and perched on the edge.

"Tell me again there's life after acting." She popped the tops on the bottles and gave Michael his.

He took a swig before he replied. "I tell you that every time I see you, but you're determined to make it work. I admire that. It's a good quality. But sometimes you have to know when to cut and run. Try something new. Like my agency." He produced a packet of Marlboro Gold from his pocket, lit a cigarette and inhaled. "Which is why I want to talk to you." For someone obsessed with fitness, smoking seemed to have fallen down the back of his regime.

"You were very cryptic on the phone."

"I've had a very specific request come in. A client needs someone to act as her girlfriend for a long weekend for her parents' wedding anniversary. She's 37, a successful business owner. The specific thing is she's gay, and she's requested a queer actor if possible." He licked his lips. "I can't ask the actors on my books to state their sexuality, and I'm not about to ring around to find out. But then you sprang to mind."

"I'm not on your books."

"I know. But you said yourself acting is terribly paid, and my agency is not. I quoted this woman a higher price if I could find a queer actor, and she didn't flinch. She said yes. Well, her friend who was ringing on her behalf did." He held up a hand. "I know you've turned me down before, but this is different. You would be doing me a personal favour. Plus, I would pay you well for your trouble. You'd earn in five days what it would take you two months to earn on the stage."

Steph's ears perked up. "Two months? No wonder I'm hearing so much about your service from our peers."

Michael gave her a knowing look. "Life's all about trying new things."

"I don't know." Was she at the point where she really wanted to give up? Yes, she said it all the time, but it had been her lifetime dream. "I've got no experience of this kind of work."

"You're great at improv, that's all you need. Remember that time when you creamed all those guys at the improv challenge? Plus, you even tried your hand at stand-up, and you were great. You should do that again."

"And get kicked by life a little more? Being a stand-up is hard. Especially a female stand-up."

"And being an actor is a breeze?"

He had a point.

Something tickled Steph's neck, and she jumped up, slapping the back of it with her hand and spinning around. A shiver ran up her spine.

Michael tilted his head and gave her an amused look.

"Can you stop grinning and check I don't have a killer spider on my back?" She wriggled her shoulders and shook her hips like she was twirling a hula-hoop.

Michael rose and brushed her back. "You're fine. Nothing there."

Steph checked with her palm one more time, then they sat back down.

"I wouldn't ask if I didn't think you could do it." Michael

gave her a pleading look. "It's five days pretending to be someone you're not. You've been in training your whole life. You did a degree in acting. And you're gay! Plus, I've seen a photo of this woman, and she's easy on the eye. Pretending to be her girlfriend for five days is not going to be hard. Pretending to look at her like you want to jump her bones? A cinch."

Steph frowned. "Why does she want a gay actor, though? Straight people can play gay, too. Look at Suranne Jones in *Gentleman Jack*." She put a hand on her hip. "She doesn't expect me to sleep with her, does she?"

"Of course not! I told you, this is purely an acting gig. I think she just wants someone who understands the pressures of being gay and dealing with family."

Steph chewed on that for a moment. "Just to be doubly clear, though. I'm *not* sleeping with her." She'd always had a suspicion that it was part of the deal.

Michael rolled his eyes. "I'm not hiring you to be a prostitute, okay? It's an acting job and you're a highly experienced actor. Plus, we all know you can't sleep with anyone without falling for them, so I'm begging you not to for everyone's sake."

Steph snorted. "I can do casual sex without falling in love!" She was lying, and they both knew it.

Michael's laughter pierced the air. "Sure you can." He took a swig of his beer. "Anyway, what work have you got lined up?"

"I'm in that new play at the Old Vic from February, a week after panto finishes. That runs until April. Then I've signed up to do a school run around the country that I really don't want to do from May 10th for two months. A play on sexual health aimed at teenagers. But the pay was above normal, and I panicked. I'm trying to forget the fact I play Chlamydia." It truly was what she'd trained for four years in drama school to do. Not.

Michael snorted a little more. "That is trying new things, but sometimes, your life choices make me howl." He caught her eye. "This job is for the start of May, so our calendars have aligned. It's like it's written in the stars." He stabbed a finger her way. "I guarantee you it's better than playing Chlamydia. You want to know the other huge selling point? Apart from the pay?"

"Tell me."

"It's in the Scottish Highlands."

Steph gulped. Michael knew what the area meant to her. He knew the connection. "The Highlands." Something fluttered against her ribcage.

He nodded. "Lochcarron to be precise. Remember when we went?"

Steph smiled. "How could I forget?" They'd gone up in the summer of their second year at drama school and camped their way around the coast. They'd got bitten to death by midges, and suffered food from the fifties. Steph's mum had done the trip a few years ago and had told her the food situation was much improved, and the scenery just as spectacular. Steph had always wanted to go back, but she'd never found the right moment. Now it was being put in her hands.

She took a deep breath. She could act for five days, then hire a car and go on a trip of her own. Visit the place that meant so much. She was part-Scottish, after all.

"I can't remember Lochcarron precisely, can you? All the

place names are a bit of a blur. I remember Skye, and Ullapool, but not much more."

He shook his head. "It was almost 20 years ago. But I'm sure it will all come flooding back when you get there."

"I haven't agreed yet." But she knew she would. So did Michael from the smile on his face.

"It's Scotland, it pays well, and you get free food and drink all weekend. And whatever happens, it can't be as bad as when you met Andrea's parents, can it?"

Steph sucked in a breath. Even three years on, meeting her ex's parents still had that effect on her. "No, you're right, it can't be." She ground her teeth together, then came to a decision. "All right, you're on. Where does this woman live?"

Michael gave her his winning grin, then picked her up and spun her around. "I knew you were my best friend for a reason." He put Steph down. "From what I know, she lives in Edinburgh. You'll have to arrive together, so you have the drive from Edinburgh to Lochcarron to firm up your stories at least. Not that the queen of improv needs much preparation, of course."

"You should come up afterwards and meet me. We could redo our Scottish trip."

"That's a great idea. So long as you don't fall in a loch again."

Steph laughed at the memory. It had been fucking cold. "I did do that, didn't I?" She paused. "I nearly fell in the orchestra pit tonight, too."

"Can I ask that you try not to fall over or break anything on this job? Only then will I come to meet you."

"I'll try my best."

"And can we stay in hotels and not tents this time?"

"So long as you're paying."

He smiled, then bowed. "It would be my pleasure, madam."

Chapter Three

Erin crouched and rubbed the sandpaper rigorously over the skirting board. She'd decided she needed to work with her hands, to take her mind off the impending party that loomed large this weekend. The woman she'd hired to play her girlfriend arrived in Edinburgh tonight, and they were meeting for dinner. Erin had spent the past 24 hours worrying about what to wear and what to say. She kept having to remind herself this was *not* a date. Rather, it was a business dinner. She could do business, it was her thing. She'd set up her own successful company and dealt with clients every day. Only this time, she was the client. Erin just had to imagine her fake date wanted the whole of her downstairs painted, woodwork included. She smirked. Was it just her or did that sound rude?

When Erin had found out her fake date's name, she'd Googled her, of course. Checked out her IMDB page. Stephanie Mitchell had been in quite a few plays and TV shows, but never had her big break. However, she was a proper actor with real credentials. Why had she taken this job? Her pickings must be slim right now, but that was Erin's gain. That she was tall, brunette and easy on the eye hadn't snuck past Erin either. But that was neither here nor there. This was a business deal, the result being her family saw she could find love, too. Even for just a short time.

Erin leaned down and blew some dust from her arm, which also had a yellowish bruise from two weeks ago. She'd had a fight with a hammer, and the hammer had won. She ran her index finger along the woodwork. One more rub down, and the skirting would be ready for primer.

Footsteps coming down the stairs made her look up. Morag wore her usual white T-shirt and blue overalls combo. She had three sets, which, in her words, saved having to worry about what to wear to work. Her head was adorned with a navy-blue baseball cap with NYC on the front. She'd bought it when she visited the Big Apple two years earlier. She looked like an extra from Glee.

"Cuppa?" Morag filled the kettle from the fancy bendy tap that used to only be in industrial kitchens, but now were in every other house they painted. Decoration was the final stage of this house's renovation, and then the family could move back in. For now, it was just Morag and Erin sanding and painting in an empty shell.

Erin nodded. "Please."

The gentle glug of the water heating filled the air. Morag walked to the patio doors at the end of the large open-plan kitchen-diner-lounge space and flung one open. The rain had stopped, and the earth's natural petrichor filled the air.

Morag breathed it in.

"That's better. Much as I love the smell of paint, the scent of wet soil and natural chemicals is much better." She returned to the kitchen and made their tea. Then she offered Erin a bright orange Le Creuset mug, and leaned on the counter-top as Erin slotted in beside her. The counters were made of Italian marble, which showed the Hayne family were made of money.

"How's the panic going?" Morag gave her a sly grin.

Erin played dumb. "Panic?"

Morag wrinkled her forehead. "You haven't given a second thought to your first date later?" The tone of her voice told Erin she didn't believe that at all.

"It's not a first date."

Morag grinned, took a sip of her tea, then put it on the counter. "Not a first date, got it."

"You told her my name was Erin Brown, right? I don't want her knowing who I really am just in case things go wrong."

Her friend nodded. "The guy who runs the agency promised she wouldn't know. You're Erin Brown and not Erin Stewart for the weekend."

Erin exhaled. She didn't want to be tracked down before or after the event. She was already uncomfortable enough letting a stranger into her life temporarily.

"Have you told your parents you're seeing someone?"

Erin fiddled with a button on her overalls, then nodded. "A couple of weeks ago." Not being used to revealing much to her parents, telling her mum had been excruciating. "I was very vague, but they know she's coming to the party. The celebration on the other end of the line was something special. Mum and Dad always say they don't care that I don't have a partner, but their reaction would suggest otherwise."

"They just want you to be happy."

"I know." She sipped her tea. "Anyway, the ball is rolling, I've paid half the money so backing out now would be costly, and she's on the train as we speak." Erin's stomach dropped through the floor, and then through to the basement right below. Fear gripped her. What had she done? She should have been stronger when Morag had talked her into this.

"What kind of woman has to hire a girlfriend? You know I'm blaming you when this all goes wrong."

Morag poked her in the arm with her index finger. "What about the other option? That this all goes right? Then you'll be thanking me. Who knows, it might give you a taste of what having a girlfriend might be like. You haven't had one since Michelle and that was over a decade ago. She broke your heart, but that's a rite of passage. You have to get back on the horse. Maybe actor lady can help. What's her name?"

"Steph." Erin swallowed hard.

"Steph. That's a nice name." Morag clicked her tongue. "Steph," she repeated. "Erin and Steph. Steph and Erin. Got a nice ring to it, slips off the tongue, don't you think?"

Erin rolled her eyes. "It's a business deal, that's all. Hopefully it will slip off my tongue for a whole five days at least." Erin paused. "The email from the bloke at the agency told me she's actually been to Lochcarron before, and the Highlands. What are the chances?"

"A wee English lassie who loves the lochs and glens! Maybe this could be a match."

"She lives in London. I live in Edinburgh. Plus, we've never met. I don't think your crazy rom-com notions are about to come true." Although Erin would admit, it was nice that Steph knew the Highlands. She was proud of where she was from, even if the rest of the UK had no idea where it was. The Highlands were a secret hiding in plain sight, and Erin was keen to keep it that way.

"What time are you meeting?"

"Seven o'clock at the Malmaison in Leith. Dinner, a glass of wine. Maybe two if she's a gobshite. What if she's like that client we had from Portobello? I can't spend five days with someone who sets my teeth on edge every time she opens her mouth."

"That woman was crazy! Plus, you're the client this time around. You get to be crazy, and she has to put up with it."

"I'm crossing my fingers she's got a sense of humour at least."

"Have you seen what she looks like? You were going to do some research when you got her name last week."

Erin kept her features neutral. "She won't scare the horses, let's put it that way."

Morag raised an eyebrow. "This is all about you getting back on the horse. If Steph doesn't scare them in the first place, I'd say we're off to a good start."

* * *

Erin put her navy shirt into her suitcase, then went into her drawer and pulled out five pairs of underwear. Then she added another. She'd never needed an extra pair of knickers in her entire life, but she always packed one extra "just in case". She glanced at her thong, bought for a wedding when she wore skin-tight trousers and no visible panty line would do. She wasn't taking that.

She tucked her underwear into the gap at the top of her case just as her phone lit up. Mum. Did she have a sixth sense Erin was on a time-sensitive schedule today?

"Hello you!" Patricia Stewart — Patsy to her mates — was

always chirpy, and today was no exception. "How's my big-city daughter?" Her mum had once said 'favourite daughter', and it had made them both stop in their tracks. She hadn't said it since.

"I'm good. Just packing."

She could almost feel her mum's smile down the phone. "Have I told you how excited we are to have you all home? All the family together, all my children in one place." That, at least, was the truth.

"You might have mentioned it once or twice."

"And you bringing someone, too. Your dad and I are so excited to meet her. She must be quite the woman if you're actually introducing her to the family."

Erin winced. Yes, she wanted to show her parents she could do relationships like normal people, but she knew there would be fallout, too. This was a temporary thing. A stop-gap. But at least they wouldn't think she was someone who couldn't attract anyone, *ever*. That was important. Plus, it was a great distraction. Something else to focus on that wasn't the elephant in the room. She wanted this whole charade to go well, and she'd deal with the aftermath when it happened. By the time it did, she'd be tucked back into her Edinburgh life.

"She's an actress, too. Very glamorous."

"It's actor these days," Erin corrected.

"I can't keep up!"

Erin could picture her mum, stood by the window, looking out over the gardens and the pool.

"So long as she treats you right, that's the main thing. Is she hoping to get some acting work locally when her run has finished?"

"That's the plan. But enough about me. How are the preparations? Is the marquee up and standing?"

Her parents were hosting their party in their garden, and had hired a marquee, a caterer and a bar for the occasion. You couldn't ask for a prettier backdrop than the one they had naturally, overlooking the village, the loch, and the glens beyond. Erin never tired of it.

The Highlands were a hug of reliable hills, a sweet coffee overlooking the loch, the crackle of a log fire on a winter's day. The burn of an Islay on a long summer night, the kiss of the sea on a sandy beach. She'd always be pulled back there, despite it all. A constant hook in her splintered life.

"It's up, but it still needs decorating, of course. It's all hands to the pump once you get here."

Last time she'd spoken to her dad, he'd told her all about the marquee's gutters and draining system. It'd been thrilling. Erin had hoped she'd escape the decoration, but they were waiting for her. Deep joy.

"I'm sure Steph can help, too. Many hands and all of that." Her mum paused. "She's part of the family now, seeing as she's with you. I'm so happy you've met someone. We all are. I just want you to be happy."

A lump formed in Erin's throat. Dammit, her mum getting emotional always got to her. She found it easier on the phone than face to face.

The underlying meaning was implicit.

Nadia would be happy, too.

However, the swell of love was quickly followed by a swell of guilt. Erin pushed it down, the way she'd learnt to for years. The next five days were all about family, love, and a celebration of the two. Yes, she'd hired help, but so had her parents. Their help was serving up the food and drink to their guests. Erin's help was serving up smiles and a warm body to stand beside her the whole weekend.

There was hardly a jot of difference.

"Anyway, I have to go, I'm meeting Steph for dinner. Her train gets in about now." Erin blinked. She surprised herself how easy she'd slipped into this deception.

"Say hello and tell her we're all looking forward to meeting her."

That makes two of us.

Chapter Four

The train journey brought back so many memories of her trip with Michael all those years ago. Not least the rolling green as the train slid into Scotland, particularly when it got so close to the glittering blue of the North Sea, Steph felt she might fall in.

Why hadn't she come up to Scotland more in the intervening years? Money and time. Right at this moment, she was glad she'd agreed to this job, even if she was about to enter into the most bizarre weekend she'd ever agreed to.

She arrived early at the airy, tall-ceilinged hotel restaurant. An ocean of shiny glassware caught the evening sun, and graphic art hung on its bare brick walls. At nearly seven on a Wednesday evening in May, it was already busy. Groups of casually dressed friends laughed together, while a knot of colleagues in suits and ties were more likely congratulating each other on getting to the hump day of the working week. The smell of fish stained the air, reminding Steph of her mum enjoying a plate of salmon on her birthday this year. She was about to meet someone else's mum this week. She pressed down a flicker of fear.

Nerves were good. They were all part of acting. The job started now.

The waiter led Steph to her table, where a woman was already seated. The tops of Steph's ears burned as she approached Erin. Her client had her head in the menu, but looked up when the waiter cleared his throat.

"Madam, your guest has arrived." He gave them both a nod, before leaving them to it.

Erin rose to her feet and held out a hand, accompanied by a nervous smile.

Steph was glad she wasn't the only one. "Nice to meet you. I'm Steph." Her voice cracked as she spoke. She cleared her throat and her teeth banged together.

Erin's grip was firm and sure. It threw Steph off a little. Did she do this all the time? Was she expecting Steph to put out? Suddenly, this felt a little *too* real.

On stage, she had lines, make-up, and a director. She needed Ron beside her to gee her up, tell her what to do next. But for the next few days, she was on her own. There was nobody to put words into her mouth or tell her how to say them.

Erin was not what Steph had expected. In the back of her mind, she'd thought that a woman who hired a date for a family party must be undatable. Erin seemed anything but. Steph studied her high cheekbones, her ever-so-slightly sloped nose. The beauty spot on her left cheek, which was *very* Marilyn Monroe.

Steph loved Marilyn Monroe. She'd spent a great deal of her teenage years obsessed with her beauty spot.

"Erin," her client replied. She flicked her gaze up and down Steph's body. "Wow, you're taller than I expected."

Maybe she wasn't *quite* so sure of herself. Even so, Steph

was enchanted by her soft Scottish burr. She'd always been a sucker for it.

Erin blushed bright pink. "Sorry, that was meant to stay inside my head." She poked her tongue into the inside of her cheek. "How was your journey?"

"Smooth sailing. Thanks for the first-class ticket." When Steph had got that, she'd wondered if Erin would be unbearably rich and posh. First impressions suggested otherwise. What should she say next? While this wasn't a date, it *was* an interview for her to be Erin's date. Sort of. If things didn't go well today, Erin might call the whole thing off. Steph couldn't have that happen. First, she needed the money. Second, she *really* wanted the trip that came afterwards.

The onus was on Steph to get on with Erin, make her feel at ease. To ask questions and be charming. Michael had rammed that point home enough times.

She refocused. Erin's denim shirt was open *just* enough to make you look. Steph took in Erin's cropped hair, the colour of ink. She'd always admired women who had the guts to cut their hair that short. She'd never done it, as she was convinced her face would look weird.

The waiter came back, and they ordered house gin and tonics. When they arrived, Steph took a gulp, then exhaled. She could do this.

"You live in Edinburgh?" Small talk. That was needed to ease them in.

Erin nodded, her fingers caressing her glass. "I run a decorating and DIY business here with my best friend."

Steph's ears pinged. "So you own a toolbelt?" It was out of her mouth before she could grab it and stuff it back in.

Ruddy hell.

"I do, I even have one for my paint brushes," Erin said. "I've lived here for years, but I'm originally from the Highlands. It's where my parents' 40th anniversary party is being held." She paused. "You've read the details, right?"

Steph tapped the side of her forehead. "Memorised on the train, and all stored up here. It's like learning lines, so I'm used to it. Your parents are Patsy and Duncan. Your brother Alex is married to Wendy, and they have three kids: Kay, Elise, and Haley. How am I doing?"

Erin laughed, but gave her an appreciative nod. "You've passed the first test, well done." She scratched her ear, then sat forward. "I should tell you, this wasn't my idea. My best friend put me up to it. In theory it's great, and I'm sure you're lovely. But this is odd, right? I'm 37 years old, I should be able to get my own date without hiring someone."

Steph let out a snort as her muscles relaxed. Maybe this could work. She'd been worried she might be put with a control freak who she couldn't get on with. But someone who was a mass of self-doubt and whose life choices were made by their best friends? She understood that more than anything in the world.

She sat up and leaned forward. "If it helps you, my best friend, Michael, talked me into this, too."

Erin frowned. "He did?"

Steph nodded. "He runs the agency. We went to drama school together, but he got tired of the acting life, so he set up Rock Your Date. When your request for a queer woman came in, he asked me directly. Plus, he knows I love Scotland, so the two married up. If you're worried we might not have anything in common, we have pushy best friends for a start."

Erin's shoulders lowered, and she gave her first genuine smile. It curved around her face like a sunrise. "Okay, that makes me feel more at ease."

Steph nodded at Erin's drink. "And we both like gin."

"I'm amazed we haven't met already."

Steph guffawed. Erin had a sense of humour. Maybe this wouldn't be so bad. Now she'd met her, Steph wanted to make this the best acting job of her life. A standing ovation every night.

"I'll let you in on another secret, as I think it's best to be honest from the start." She rested her elbows on the table and steepled her fingers. "This is my first time doing this. But if it works, it could be the start of a new career." Michael would probably kill her for this—but he didn't have to know everything.

"You've never done this before? Neither have I." Erin's face paled and she sat back. "Oh jeez. I was hoping I'd have you to steer me right."

Maybe honesty wasn't *always* the best policy. Steph rallied. "The good news is I've been an actor for the past 15 years and counting. I'm known for my improv skills. So I'm looking at this as an extended improv play that lasts five days. You should, too."

"I've never done improv in my life." Erin looked like she'd swallowed a frog.

"Just follow my lead."

The waiter arrived to take their order.

Steph ordered the salmon, Erin the sea bass.

"We both love fish, too." Steph tilted her head. "We're off to a flying start."

Erin still didn't look convinced, so Steph decided to take charge.

"I know your family's names, but feel free to fill me in on the details and anything else you think would help." Steph paused. "Michael told me this meeting is like a first date on steroids. So tell me about your life and what I need to know, stuff that would normally leak out naturally over the course of however long we've been together. If you were on a real first date, of course, you'd never spill your family secrets because you don't want to scare the person off. But this time, I can't be scared off. I'm paid to be here. So hit me."

Erin sat forward, her cleavage winking.

Steph averted her eyes. Not safe for work.

"This weekend is a celebration of my parents' 40th wedding anniversary, as I think you know. Tomorrow, we're driving to Lochcarron, where they live, and we'll have dinner with my immediate family. Friday, it's a case of getting the marquee ready, which you're already roped into. Saturday's the party with all my extended family, and then Sunday will be a lazy family day, maybe lunch out."

Erin furrowed her brow, and her gaze slid away from Steph, then back. A flicker of something passed over her face, but then her smile clicked back in. "Then Monday is the final lunch before you're free to go. You might be chomping at the bit to get out by then." She gave a forced laugh. "My parents are very proud of their Scottish roots, so it's good you like Scotland. My brother Alex is a bit of a know-it-all, but his heart's in the right place. His wife, Wendy, is a sweetheart. Their triplets have just turned two, so I suspect part of the weekend will be making sure they don't fall in the pool."

"I didn't know there was a pool. Your parents have a pool?"

Erin nodded. "So my mum didn't have to keep trekking to the local loch to swim. It's not huge, but it's heated and has an amazing outlook over the village and the loch. There's hammocks and a bar on one side."

"I think I've found my perfect job."

Erin laughed. "Did you bring a swimsuit?"

Steph shook her head. "It's May and it's Scotland; it wasn't top of my packing list."

"You might be surprised. Sometimes, you can get hot weather in Scotland, too."

"Last time I came it rained every day. I still loved it. I did a tour of the Highlands when I was 19. But now I'm 37 and I haven't been back since. It's about time, isn't it?"

"You've definitely stayed away too long." Erin paused. "I have to say, you're not what I expected."

"What were you expecting?"

"I'm not sure, but not someone so... normal. Maybe an actor with a voice that had no dimmer switch."

"I can get louder if you like," Steph said in a raised voice, then she lowered it to her normal level. "If it helps, you seem sane, too. I had my fingers crossed we'd get on, so this is a good start."

"It is," Erin agreed. Then she flashed her smile again.

It meant that Steph couldn't look away.

"I want to be honest with you this weekend. If something irks me, I'll tell you, and vice versa. This is a business arrangement. My friend thinks we're going to fall madly in love and sail off into the sunset, but we're not. This is a job,

I'll pay you, we'll shake hands and swap Instagram handles at best." She held up her gin. "Can we drink to that?"

Steph blinked. Erin was a woman who knew what she wanted. She'd been right with her first impression.

She tapped her glass to Erin's. "Five days, and you never have to give me another thought. Here's to a successful mission pretending to be madly in love."

* * *

"How did we meet?" Steph asked.

Their first evening together was going surprisingly well. Dinner had turned into dessert, and now they were in the hotel bar overlooking the port, the sun setting on the water. As romantic spots went, it was right up there. But this was very much work. As if Steph was doing a read-through of a play, but the script had got waylaid. Instead, they were laying the groundwork, filling in the gaps.

"I told my parents we met in a bar after a play you starred in. I chose an all-female version of Hamlet because it was the only one I could think of on the spur of the moment. I really did see it last year, too. It was also my favourite Shakespeare play at school."

"I've actually done that, so you chose well. I played Horatio. Which theatre was it at?"

"Edinburgh Playhouse, of course. You live in Edinburgh, but you're staying with friends in London while you complete your most recent play. It was just bad timing we met when we did."

"You've got this shit all figured out, haven't you?" Steph was pleased she didn't have to fill in all the blanks. Erin was more than playing her part.

"I try my best."

"Who approached who?"

"I don't think we need that level of detail."

"It might help you to picture it, though." Steph looked around the modern bar, with its rows of spirits on display, mirrored backdrop and a neon sign overhead that proclaimed, 'Don't Worry, Help Is On Its Way'. "Imagine this is the theatre bar. Let's say I approached you."

Steph got up and walked to the end of the bar. She flicked her hair, cleared her throat, then turned back and walked up to Erin with what she hoped was a high level of strut.

"Hi." Steph's voice dropped an octave. "I couldn't help notice you from over the other side of the room. It was your killer smile." She wasn't lying there. "Could I buy you a drink?"

Erin's cheeks turned bright-red and she didn't hold Steph's gaze. "I g-guess you can." She looked anywhere but straight ahead.

Steph sucked through her teeth. Wow. She'd been burned by her past, but she'd never been as bad at taking a compliment as Erin. If nothing else, Steph was going to spend this weekend buffing up Erin's self-esteem. It had clearly taken a battering.

Steph sat down. "That's where you say yes, then I spend the next hour charming you, and you become dazzled. I'm pretty sure that's the way it happened."

"If you say so." Erin fiddled with her coaster.

"If you don't mind me asking, why are you doing this? I'm just surprised that an attractive, easy-going woman like you doesn't have a line of people who want to date her."

"Maybe there's a line in some other imaginary universe.

Morag—the one who put me up to this—says I'm too focused on our business to go out and date."

"Does she have a point?"

"Maybe."

"When was the last time you went out with the thought you might meet someone?"

Erin put a hand to her face, and her eyes took on a faraway look. "It's been ages." She gave a small shrug. "I'm a disaster when it comes to love. My last meaningful relationship was 12 years ago. I prefer fixing houses, fitting a kitchen, or painting a lounge. There's a process, a method, and it works every time. If there are issues along the way, I can deal with them. I can't say that about my adventures in dating. Things always go wrong, and I'm never quite sure how to fix them. No amount of Polyfilla or superglue works." Her shoulders deflated. "Which is why I find myself here, buying a date." She shook her head. "It's so tragic when I say it out loud. If my brother ever found out, he'd never let me hear the end of it. As for my parents—"

"—They're never going to know." If nothing else, Steph could guarantee that. "The good thing is, you've told them I've been working away. There's a reason we're not that established yet. So this isn't much of an acting gig to pull off. We'll use the car journey tomorrow to fill in any gaps. Like which relative I need to be most wary of. I may not have done this professionally before, but I've met other people's families." Andrea's acidic Aunt Karen sprang to mind. "So which member of your family do I need to look out for most?"

Erin thought for a moment, then shook her head. "None. They're all lovely. Apart from Uncle David, but the only harm he might do is chew your ear off about how we were all better off in the 1930s. He's a bit of a vintage bore."

"What about friends? Any exes lurking in the Scottish glens?"

Erin shook her head. "Morag will be there, who signed me up for this. But honestly, my relationships and any subsequent hook-ups all happened in the big city. In my twenties, I liked to keep my love life and my family separate. Now that I'm ready for them to meet someone, there's nobody on the horizon. Sod's law, isn't it?"

Steph blinked. "Have you introduced them to anyone before?"

Erin gulped, then shook her head. "You're the first."

Chapter Five

"Calm down and breathe, then tell me again exactly what the problem is. Because as far as I can tell, there isn't actually one."

Erin glared at her phone. Sometimes Morag was wilfully obtuse.

"Of course there's an issue! The main one being that I let you talk me into this hare-brained idea in the first place. I'm driving to the Highlands tomorrow with a woman I've only just met, and she's going to pretend to be my girlfriend in front of my tinderbox of a family."

Morag didn't say anything in response.

"What if she bludgeons me to death on the side of the A835? Highland roads aren't like Edinburgh roads. If she uses the right implement at the right angle, I could be dead in seconds and then left on the side of the road for hours before someone comes. I might get eaten by foxes, or worse."

"Killer hedgehogs? Crazed sheep?" Morag paused. "Did she seem like an axe murderer to you?"

"They never do, do they? It's the quiet ones you have to watch out for."

"Was she quiet?"

"That's beside the point."

"We've been through this. Taking someone home might make it fun." Her friend paused. "Take my advice and go into this with a positive attitude. You're paying for her company, so try to enjoy it. Was she as hot in real life at least?"

Erin couldn't deny that. With her long legs and heart-shaped face, Steph had a classic beauty about her. Plus, she'd seemed kind. That counted for a lot.

"I don't want to objectify her."

"Oh please. Give it a shot."

"Okay, yes. Sure. She was hot. She was also tall enough that she looked like she'd have worn a Goal Attack bib for an opposing netball team and made my life as Goal Defence hell."

"You don't have to play netball with her. You just have to play nice. Plus, Goal Attacks were always the most charismatic. It's like being the star striker on a football team." Morag paused. "Hopefully your family will fall a bit in love with her, even if you have to sleep with one eye open and a baseball bat by your feet."

"Not funny."

"You're being ridiculous, but I'm giving you a pass. She's an actor for hire. She will play a part, and then you'll never see her again."

"I told her that tonight." She'd felt better having got that off her chest, even if she swore she'd seen a flicker of a smile hover over Steph's face when she said it.

"You told her nothing was going to happen?"

"I did."

"Christ. We need to work on your chat-up lines." Morag sighed. "Just be nice to her from now on. Stop being defensive.

It's your natural thing, it's why you never open yourself up to anyone. But you can open yourself up to this woman. It's literally her job to listen."

"She said something similar."

"There you go, then. The agency will not have hired her to kill you. I guarantee it."

"No, but this weekend might kill me instead."

"You're going to have a great time, mainly because you're going to lighten up, Steph will help you, and I'll be there on Saturday night to add to the cheerleading squad. I can pretend to know her, too. How did you meet?"

"In the bar after she was in an all-female version of Hamlet at the Playhouse."

"How fucking queer can you get? I love it, it's perfect," Morag said. "Now stop being a wuss and enjoy having a girlfriend. I want photos please."

Erin dropped her phone on the bed after Morag hung up, then flopped down, the back of her head pressing into the pillow. Was Steph currently doing the same in her room? Was she wondering what the hell she'd got herself into, too? Whatever, they were tied together now, for better for worse.

For the next five days at least, Erin had a girlfriend.

* * *

They'd been driving in Erin's white Toyota Yaris for two hours and so far, Steph had not produced an axe. It looked like Erin wouldn't be left for dead and eaten by badgers after all. A good start. The traffic had been stop-start, so they'd had plenty of time to get to know each other. When the chat had run dry, they'd tuned into Radio One, which, apart from live cricket, was the only station available. Erin had terrible memories of car journeys when she was little, being forced to endure the cricket for hours on end. At least Steph wasn't a cricket fan.

"If this is your first gig being somebody's girlfriend, does that mean your acting career has gone well so far?"

Steph coughed before she replied. Her long legs looked at home in Erin's front seat already. "It really depends on how you define 'going well'. Am I getting jobs on a semi-regular basis? Yes. Are they all stellar jobs? No. Do they pay well? Sometimes. Do I still work in a bar when I need to? Depressingly, yes." She stared out the window briefly before she continued. "But I have been on TV a number of times and my mugshot has been in the *Radio Times*. My mum would say I'm a success. So if you ask her, yes."

"I'm asking you."

"Then not really. I think about ditching it for a steady job at least once a month. But then I remember I'm not really qualified to do anything else. I went to drama school, I was very determined, but all of that means I have no experience doing anything else."

"Determined is not a bad thing. If you still enjoy it and it pays, I'd say stick at it. But if other things are more important to you now, then maybe you need to change it up."

"I do. I have. All the time. I suppose that's the thing. You never want to give up, because what if the next job is the one where you get your big break? The one where you become a household name and get paid enough money finally to buy a home to call your own, rather than renting a room in a house at an age where it's rather unbecoming."

Erin glanced across at her. "I hate to tell you, but this job will not be that one."

Steph let out a hearty laugh. "But it's a new experience, and I like those. I might learn something big."

"Like that you don't want to pretend to be someone's girlfriend ever again?"

Steph sat up straighter and flashed her a smile. "I'm reserving judgement. So far, it's going okay."

Erin pulled up behind a red estate car. "I take it you're single, like me?"

Steph nodded. "There's nobody. There was, a few years ago, but it ended when I realised she didn't have my best interests at heart, and nor did her family. Getting on with people's families is a bigger deal than you might imagine. This whole 'us against the world' ideology is romantic, but it's not real. If the family of the woman you're dating doesn't like you, the relationship is unlikely to last." She cleared her throat and glanced at Erin. "Which is why you better fill me in on your parents and what they like to do before we turn up." She glanced at the sat nav. "Two and a half hours to go."

Erin gripped the steering wheel and focused on the road. What to say about Patsy and Duncan Stewart? They bury their heads in the sand, have no idea how to deal with personal tragedy or emotions, and that keeping up appearances is what she was taught to do, no matter what?

No, a misguided sense of family loyalty dictated she couldn't say that.

"My parents." She drummed her fingers on the steering wheel. "What can I tell you? They met at medical school, and spent their whole lives being the local GPs. Even now they're both retired, people still come to them for advice. They're pillars of the community, they both like to cook and walk, and they love the Highlands as if it were their child."

"Wow, high achievers."

Erin glanced at Steph. She supposed to the naked ear, they were. That was the trouble with achievements. They could mask the truth. "What do your parents do?"

"Parent, singular. My dad left when I was two, and he's never figured in my life. My mum's a nurse, so that's something we have in common. If a lightning bolt strikes and we end up getting married, our parents can talk coughs and colds."

"Don't joke, my friend Morag is banking on us falling instantly in love. You'll meet her on Saturday at the party."

"If she's coming to the party, we can put on a little more of a show, just to wind her up. I mean, there will be holding hands and cute smiles, that's a given, but if you want me to put a hand on your bum or lay a kiss on your lips, just say the word."

It wasn't the worst thought in the world. Erin couldn't help the smile that curled from her lips. "It's been a long time since anyone had their hand on my bum." Was it bad that she couldn't remember the last time? Very probably.

Erin glanced at the clock again. A flash of Steph's lips on hers disappeared as quickly as it came. Butterflies flapped within. "Talking of which, should we lay down some ground rules before we arrive at my parents' house? Like you said, hand holding is permitted, as is arm touching. I'm ruling out bums for now. Anything else you can think of?"

Steph glanced her way, then gave her a sly grin. "If you want me to kiss you, I am a pro. I've literally taken classes on kissing for show." She paused. "We could even practice beforehand."

Was it just her, or was it suddenly a little hot in the car? Erin tugged at her shirt collar, and inhaled. "I'll let you know." Then flicked her eyes back to the road and tried to stop her cheeks burning.

She wasn't sure she was successful.

Chapter Six

Erin was quiet on the final half hour of the drive, but Steph wasn't surprised. She might well be too if she was bringing someone home for the first time in over a decade. At least they were getting on, which was a relief. It could have been so much worse. Erin could have turned up wearing bright red Crocs. Declared a hatred of musicals. Disclosed she was a Tory party member. But she'd done none of those things. Yet.

On top of that, she'd gradually opened up as the drive wore on. Steph was now determined to make this weekend the best it could possibly be for Erin. She'd spoken warmly of her parents, but there was something she wasn't saying, too. Were her parents accepting of Erin being gay? She guessed she was about to find out.

They'd driven through the Cairngorms and across the Moray Firth at Inverness before motoring into the Highlands, and the scenery had catapulted Steph right back to when she was 19. She'd wondered if she'd be as impressed second time around, but the answer was yes. The ever-rolling landscape was like being dropped into a multimedia universe, and she couldn't take her eyes off it. The fact that the sun had shone the entire way helped, too. Everything looked better with a lick of sunshine.

"You know, if I was brought up here, I don't think I'd ever leave."

Erin gave a brief smile. "That's not how it works. You always want something different to what you had. I grew up in the country, and so I wanted to live in the city. Besides, unless you provide an essential service or you want to be a farmer, most people don't have a choice. They go to the city where the jobs are."

"But you do provide an essential service. Don't people in the Highlands need their houses painted, too?"

"Yes, but when I left home after university, it was to do marketing for a big bank." She nodded towards Steph. "That's what I meant about being open to change in your career. The shine of what I was doing wore thin after a while, so I changed up completely. There's not much call for financial services for sheep." She waved her hand to the field full of them on her right, then slowed as they approached a small ramp in the road, alongside a sign indicating roadworks. Her car bumped up the ramp, and a few metres on, they passed a sign that declared they were in Lochcarron.

Erin sat up and shifted in her seat. "Welcome to Lochcarron, home to my parents and another 877 other residents. It's quite a metropolis for the Highlands. We've got a Spar shop, a pub, a garage, a chippy, a primary school and a bistro." She nodded left. "Plus, obviously, one of the most picturesque lochs around."

Steph wasn't going to argue with that. They drove along the side of the loch, that stretched as far as her eye could see, majestic hills applauding in the background. "It's just incredible." She glanced right as they passed the pub. "Do you need to fill me in on tales of teenage Erin getting drunk and snogging boys in the pub car park?"

Erin turned right, then shook her head as she guided them up the single-car road, houses and small bed & breakfasts dotted on either side.

"I'm sure other people like my brother could tell you, but I can't remember anything about those days, which is probably a good thing. My brain protecting me." Erin sucked on her top lip as they climbed the hill, the loch views only getting more impressive as they did. "We moved here when I was 17, and I left for university when I was 18, so there's only a year to pore over anyway."

This was news. "Where did you live before Lochcarron?" They drove past three houses on the right, and two on the left, before they arrived at a driveway signposted 'Loch View House'.

"Still the Highlands." Erin swung her car into the steep driveway and accelerated harder, powering them to the top. She parked outside an imposing white house with a huge pitched slate roof, and cut the engine. To its right, an equally impressive white marquee with see-through windows billowed on the hillside.

It was only then the reality of their situation sunk in. The real performance started now. Could Steph remember everything she'd been told about Erin's life so far? She checked her face in the mirror, ran a hand through her chestnut hair, then turned to Erin, whose face had gone white.

"It's going to be okay, you know. We can do this." She wanted to give her a reassuring pat or squeeze, but she didn't want to overstep. They'd still known each other less than a day. Only, it already felt longer.

Erin gazed at her, then nodded. "If you say so."

Steph stretched as she got out of the car, her shoulder muscles clicking and grinding as she did. Erin's family home sat on top of the hill, and it was spectacular. For the first time, Steph got an inkling of what she was in for this weekend. Erin might come across as unassuming, but her family clearly were not. She had no idea how much property went for in the Highlands, but she knew this wasn't cheap. The house boasted double height floor-to-ceiling windows at the front to take full advantage of the panoramic loch views, and the property went back further than she could see. The car park could easily hold five cars, and a gravel path ran down to a breath-taking stone-lined pool replete with swim-up bar and hammocks to one side. She wasn't coming to just any house in the Highlands. She was at one of the best. She didn't care what Erin said. If she'd grown up here, she'd never have left this pool. After over four sticky hours on the road, she wanted to dive in right away.

The doors to the main house opened as soon as Steph closed hers.

"You're here!"

A woman approached the car and came to greet Erin. She wore what Steph's gran would have called "slacks", along with a floaty linen top. But instead of throwing her arms around Erin as Steph's mum would, the hug she gave could best be described as perfunctory. Distanced. The epitome of a non-hug.

If this was Steph's real girlfriend, she'd mention it later and they'd roll their eyes. But this wasn't real. She had to keep reminding herself. Even though she already felt protective of Erin.

Greeting ticked off the list, Erin's mum turned to Steph. "Welcome, Steph, lovely to meet you!"

Okay, so she didn't have to worry about Erin's family being homophobic. That was a good start. Steph flashed her charming smile, the one she'd practised in the mirror the night before. Then she walked over and held out a hand. "Nice to meet you, Mrs—"

"—Enough of the Mrs! Just call me Patsy."

"Patsy it is." The only other Patsy Steph had encountered had been on *Absolutely Fabulous*. This Patsy's gold hoop earrings glinted in the early evening sun. She had the air of a woman who'd challenge you to a tennis match and not let you leave the court until she'd won.

"You survived the heat, then?"

Steph nodded. "We did. Air-con was our friend." She glanced Erin's way.

Erin was staring like she'd seen a ghost.

"My husband, Duncan, is around here somewhere, but every second of every day seems to be filled with preparation for the party, you know how it is!"

Steph didn't, but she nodded anyway. "I'm very much looking forward to it. I haven't been to this part of the world in nearly 20 years, and it's living up to my memories already."

"It's one of the reasons I love it here." Patsy had a good tan for the Highlands, too. Steph guessed it was from a bottle. "Rain or shine, the loch and the hills are always there. They're reliable. Unlike some children who say they're coming home earlier than they arrive." She gave Erin a look, then shook her head. "But you're here now, and that's what counts. Alex and his brood are getting ready for dinner, so you two take your bags in and get unpacked, then come into the house. I'm sure Steph would like a tour."

"I don't want to be any trouble."

"Nonsense, you're Erin's guest, so no trouble at all."

"Just give us a chance to breathe first, Mum." Erin tried to smile, but failed. "It was a long drive."

"You're in Lodge One. First time Erin's ever stayed there," Patsy told Steph. "It's perfect for a couple, but she's never brought anybody home before. But we're thrilled you're here and it'll give you that little bit of privacy to do whatever you want to do."

Steph blinked, but didn't look at Erin. There were a host of dynamics at work here that she had no idea about.

"Your job is to provide support, whatever happens," Michael had told her. So that's what she was going to do.

"I'm sure it's perfect." Steph walked around to the boot and glanced up at Erin. "Shall we get sorted?" Should she have added a 'honey' or a 'darling' to that sentence?

Satisfied, Patsy gave them a nod, then disappeared.

Erin didn't make eye contact as she collected her bag. She took a deep breath, then led Steph over to the first of two wooden lodges.

They stepped up to its pristine wooden deck, and Steph patted its round table, a log store encased on the far wall.

Erin pointed her finger to the second lodge, a slightly larger version of their one. "My brother and his family are in the two-bedroom next door. Imaginatively named, Lodge Two."

"How many bedrooms does this have?" Steph pushed open the solid wooden door, and lifted her suitcase onto the laminate floor.

"Just one." Erin followed her in, then nodded towards the lounge area, replete with wood burner and stunning loch views. "But don't worry, the sofabed pulls out. I can sleep on that."

Steph shook her head. "No you won't. You're the client, you get the bed."

"Are you sure? Like Mum said, you're the guest."

"Positive. But I'll put my suitcase in the bedroom, so we can keep up appearances in case anybody comes in."

Erin nodded. "Great." She paused. "So that's my mum, Patsy. She who will not be defeated."

Yep, there was definitely a story there. Did Steph need to know it to get through this weekend? "She seemed lovely. You mind if I have a shower before we go to dinner?"

"Of course."

"Is it a dressy affair or can I wear jeans?"

Erin smiled. "Not dressy. No black tie needed. Just come as you are."

* * *

Steph stood up when Erin cleared her throat behind her, but she wasn't prepared for what greeted her. Erin's rendition of 'not dressy' was clearly not hers. Erin wore an olive-green chiffon jump suit that plunged at the cleavage just enough to draw your eye, along with some sparkly silver teardrop earrings, dressed down with some black-and-white Converse.

Steph glanced down at her own black jeans, cream shirt and flowery blazer. Was it enough?

"You look amazing." Even if she was paid to tell Erin that, she meant it. Was this Erin's armour to face her family? Her jet-

55

black hair shone under the kitchen light, and her cheekbones stood proud on her face. Steph followed her jawline, her strong neck. When she went lower, she tore her eyes away from Erin's cleavage. Her heart thumped.

"Thank you, so do you." Erin gave Steph a once over, followed by a tense smile. "Shall we go into the lion's den?"

Steph raised an eyebrow. "Your family don't bite, do they?"

"Only if provoked."

They closed the door on the lodge and walked out into the surprisingly warm evening. The only thoughts going through Steph's mind were 'don't spill anything down your clean shirt'. At 8pm, there was still hours of daylight to come in this part of the world where they had long summer nights. A wistful pink cloud to their right reminded Steph of the blanket her gran knitted when she was a baby.

Erin took a few steps, then turned to her. "Is it okay if I hold your hand? Just to show a togetherness?"

Steph nodded. "Absolutely. It's in our ground rules, right? Although you still need to let me know on the kissing lessons."

Erin's cheeks turned crimson, way darker than the blanket cloud.

Steph held out a hand, just as a deep voice interrupted them.

"Who's giving who kissing lessons?"

Steph jumped apart from Erin.

"Sorry, I didn't mean to startle you!"

Steph turned and a man grinned as he looked from Steph to Erin, then back. "I couldn't help but overhear. I'm guessing you both know how to kiss generally, but I like that you're willing to never stop learning. Are you doing an advanced course? You should offer it online. It's all the rage these days."

The same pair of crystal blue eyes and thick, dark hair Erin owned stared back at Steph. However, this man was taller, and had a stubbled chin, which Erin definitely lacked.

"You're funny." Erin gave him a warm hug, which he returned. Then she stood back. "Steph, this is my idiot brother, Alex."

Alex held out a hand. "The woman who finally conquered my sister's cold, hard heart. And now I know how you did it, with advanced kissing techniques." He gave Steph a handsome grin. "Great to meet you."

Steph shook Alex's hand, immediately warming to him. "You, too." She glanced at Erin, who cleared her throat. They'd got away with the whole kissing conversation, but they'd clearly have to be more careful. This was new territory for both of them. Maybe they'd have to come up with some code words to discuss the trickier elements of their liaison. There was more to this acting job than met the eye.

The threesome walked towards the main house, Alex falling into step beside them.

"Where's Wendy and the kids?"

"I dumped them; they got a bit too much." He grinned. "Or they're already being fussed over by our parents, you choose." The crunch of their feet on the gravel path and the low hum of the swimming pool pump were the only sounds as they walked. Below, the loch sat serene. It would be very easy to lead a contented life here. So far removed from London and the acting world. It would be the easiest thing in the world.

As soon as they walked into the house, however, the noise exploded with the sound of three toddlers and a handful of adults added to the mix.

"Come in, come in!" A man who, by process of elimination, must be Erin's dad approached them. He was a little taller than Steph, and had a kind face, like a train guard who'd let you off if you were short a pound for the fare. He gave Alex a nod, then Erin a non-hug with no squeeze.

Steph was prepared this time. Erin seemed to know it was coming, too.

To Steph, he gave a firm handshake. "We've heard virtually nothing about you because our daughter keeps her cards close to her chest. But you're very welcome!"

"It's great to be here on such an auspicious occasion. Forty years of marriage is quite something, so congratulations." Should she have brought some kind of gift? She hadn't even thought of that. She made a mental note to ask Erin later.

"You get less for murder, right?" He paused, glancing at Erin, then back to Steph. "Now, I hope you like meat, because I've been cooking all day long and nobody's going home until it's all eaten."

Chapter Seven

Erin glanced around the deck outside her brother's lodge. She brushed her arm, checking she hadn't got bitten, but it was just the night-time breeze. No midges yet. Still, Alex was taking no chances. He sprayed some repellent on his skin, and the smell wafted her way. It brought back memories of her childhood so sharply, she could almost feel her mum's hands on her skin. Her, Alex, and Nadia, playing out until late, with no idea what was around the corner. Those were kinder, more innocent days. When the world seemed fair, and everything ran to the right order. Her world had fractured when she was 17, and it had never quite got back on an even keel since. Did Alex have the same memories swirling around his head, or was it just insect repellent to him?

She'd love to ask, but it wasn't what her family did. Plus, she had bigger things to worry about. Like, keeping up appearances with Steph.

That thought brought Erin up short. Was she turning into her parents with this charade? She hadn't considered that. If Patsy and Duncan were uncomfortable with the status quo, they distracted themselves with a shiny new object. A house renovation. The lodge sideline. Lavish parties with endless preparation. A kernel of unrest settled in her stomach. She never wanted to turn into her parents. How Nadia would laugh at the thought.

"Tell us more about the acting life." Wendy clutched her cup of tea, the steam making her nose twitch. Wendy hardly ever drank these days, claiming life with three toddlers was hard enough without a banging headache. After having their first night dinner with them, Erin could relate. "Erin said you met when you were in an all-female version of Hamlet. What part did you play?"

Steph glanced her way, hesitation covering her face. "Horatio."

At exactly the same time, Erin replied, "Mercutio." She froze. *Shit*.

Wendy laughed, then looked from one to the other. "Which one was it?"

"Horatio," Steph said with an assured smile. "But I have played Mercutio in *Romeo and Juliet* before, too. Erin muddles up her Shakespeare on a regular basis."

The blood rushed to Erin's cheeks as she nodded. Damn, Steph was good at this. "It wouldn't be my Mastermind subject," she joked. Crisis averted.

"Anyway, acting isn't half as interesting as hairdressing, I'm sure," Steph added, smoothing things over completely. "Doesn't everyone spill their life stories to you?"

Wendy guffawed. "Hardly. But I can tell you where's good to go for a holiday. Croatia is big right now, as is Sardinia."

She and Alex met in Durham, where he went to university. He'd needed a haircut, Wendy had been his hairdresser, and he'd asked her out on the spot. Alex left his degree with a first in medicine, a fiancée, and free haircuts for life. Wendy was *so* not who Erin had expected Alex to end up with, but she was absolutely perfect. She was street-smart, which Alex never had been, so they were an ideal balance.

"But I still want to know about acting. Have you worked with anyone famous?"

At least Steph didn't have to fake this part.

"I have, but I need more wine to spill any secrets." Steph twirled her wine glass in her hands. "What's being an actor like? It's a rollercoaster ride, but when it goes well, it's the best job in the world."

"What was your most recent part?"

Steph tipped her gaze to Erin, her brown eyes luminous. "My most recent was a little different. A two-header, just me and another actor. It was intense, but rewarding. I was a little worried at first as the other actor was a rookie, but after a stuttering start, she turned out to be a dream to work with."

Erin gave Steph a warm smile as a blush worked its way to her cheeks. She hadn't done much apart from turn up, but tonight *had* gone well. Even with Steph nearly calling her mum Mrs Brown earlier. Maybe she should have hired a girlfriend sooner. It definitely gave her the same endorphins as a real one. It felt like Steph *was* her girlfriend, and Erin kept reminding herself of the truth. But it wasn't easy. Steph was so simple to be with, with her smooth chat, full lips, and stunning eyes that gave glimpses of who she was. She looked inviting, like something Erin wanted to sink into.

Erin gulped, then her body stiffened. She had to remember where she was and what this was. Did she want it to be more?

Now wasn't the time to think about that.

Alex grabbed her glass and took a swig of her Merlot.

Grateful for the distraction, Erin slapped his hand. She pushed her thoughts to one side, then rolled her eyes at her brother. "Get your own!"

Wendy wasn't done with Steph. "Was acting always your dream?"

"It was. I grew up in Sussex, but I had health issues when I was a kid which meant I was up and down to specialist hospitals in London all the time."

Erin twisted her head. Steph hadn't told her this. What had Steph been like as a child? Smaller, cuter, adorable. The image made Erin smile. Then she realised what she was doing, and straightened up her face. Luckily, nobody had noticed.

Wendy winced. "I'm sorry to hear that."

Steph shook her head. "Don't be. But it was because of my condition I wanted to become an actor in the first place. After each appointment, my mum would give me a treat to reward me for being so brave. 'Her little warrior' as she always told me. Sometimes that treat was a milkshake, or a trip to the Tower Of London. But she also took me to see a show every now and again. It was after seeing 'Blood Brothers' on the West End that I decided I wanted to act. I loved everything about the theatre, even the foyers gave me chills. Plus, when I eventually landed at drama school in London, it felt like home because I visited so often before."

"That's what I call turning a negative into a positive." Wendy turned to Erin. "I like her, she's the shot of positivity you need in your life." She turned back to Steph, leaning in. "Erin here tends to be a glass-half-empty person."

Erin frowned. "That's because the glass is often empty.

Did you see how Alex just drank my wine?" She drank the rest before he could.

Alex grinned. "I'll get some more in a minute."

But Erin shook her head. "I've had enough tonight. Tomorrow's another day." She glanced at Steph. "Shall we hit the hay?"

Steph nodded, then downed the last of her wine. "See you all tomorrow."

Erin got up and stepped off the deck. "Don't stay up too late, little brother. It's a marathon not a sprint."

Alex rolled his eyes. "Yes, Mum."

When Steph walked around the table, Erin pulled back her shoulders and held out her hand. They hadn't made contact earlier, Alex had interrupted them. This time, she was determined to see it through. She locked her gaze with Steph's, but couldn't read her face.

Steph hesitated for a millisecond, jumped off the deck and wrapped her fingers around Erin's.

A warmth spread through Erin's whole body which only confirmed her earlier thought.

This felt too real.

* * *

Back at the lodge, Erin moved Steph's blazer from the sofa, threw the cushions off and unfurled the sofabed, pulling out the legs and setting it on the laminate floor. Practicality was her speciality. In the bathroom, the splash of water told her Steph was brushing her teeth. What was she thinking? Was she regretting her decision? Would she rather be on stage, where at least she could get away from putting on an act?

What part of this performance was the real Steph, and what part was a charade?

She *really* wanted to know.

Steph had tried so hard tonight, and Erin was grateful. Yes, she knew she was paying her, but it was more than that. Steph had gone the extra mile. Coped with Erin's Shakespeare snafu. Erin's family had liked her. Despite all the odds, Erin liked her, too. She hadn't met a woman she got on with so well in a long time. Steph had made the first night with Erin's family effortless, made it seem like all of her worries about the weekend were unfounded. Like her parents were normal. That was quite some skill. Plus, when they'd walked back to the lodge, Steph's grip on Erin's hand had been watertight.

The bathroom door opened, breaking Erin's thoughts. Steph emerged still in her jeans, but now in a sleeveless charcoal T-shirt, her cream shirt in her hands. Her toned arms were exposed, as were the tops of her shoulders.

Shoulders were Erin's weak spot.

Steph's looked particularly strong.

Erin stared, then swallowed down a breath. It got stuck in her throat. She went to speak, but nothing came out. She rolled her eyes internally. She'd seen shoulders before. She could cope with this.

She tried again. Her mouth opened, but no sounds emerged. Well, one did, but it was a strangled noise, like there was a wasp trapped in her throat.

Steph scrunched her face, her eyes bright, her skin clear. Had Steph even drunk much wine tonight? She'd refused a couple of top-ups at the table.

Perhaps that was the issue with Erin. Too much wine. In contrast, she hadn't refused *anything*.

"Everything okay?"

"Yes, all good." Erin's grin was made of glass. "Just making up your bed."

Steph's brown eyes flickered to the sofabed, then back up to Erin's face.

When they did, a punch of lust hit Erin in the stomach. For fuck's sake, that was all she needed. Steph might be a fake girlfriend, but Erin's body wasn't buying it. It saw an attractive woman in close proximity, and muscle memory took over. That muscle memory was now working its way from her stomach, and further south. It took all her effort to stay upright. She ground her teeth together and tried to get back on an even keel. Back to some sense of normality. Although, she was at her parents' house. Did normality even exist here?

If Steph noticed anything, she was too polite to say. "I took my shirt off in case I spilt toothpaste down it."

"Smart move."

Steph nodded once, twice, three times. She clicked her tongue against the roof of her mouth. "I'll get properly changed in the bedroom." She tilted her head, then disappeared.

Erin waited for the door to close. Then she blew out a long breath and rubbed her face with her palms.

She could do this.

She could be in close proximity with another lesbian and function like a normal adult. Even if her brain had scrambled every thought she'd ever had. She got the white sheet from the carefully concealed wall storage, and fitted it around the thin mattress. She hoped Steph would be comfortable. Then she grabbed the corner of the duvet and fed it into the cream duvet cover. It was a job she detested normally, but today it was good to focus on something other than a semi-naked Steph in the bedroom. She'd be out soon and Erin could wipe that image from her mind.

She was doing up the buttons on the duvet cover when Steph emerged from the bedroom in a pair of chequered pyjama bottoms and the same charcoal T-shirt. Shoulders still on display. Steph threw Erin an unsure smile as she walked over and picked up the other side of the duvet.

"Let me help."

Steph's voice scratched at Erin's thin veneer of respectability.

She began buttoning the other side.

Erin nodded, as her body tightened. She breathed in Steph's clean, minty smell, and tried not to linger on her long, slim fingers. As the buttons slotted into place, they moved closer still, until Steph's tanned right shoulder was inches from hers.

Only then, as Erin grasped the final button, did she raise her head.

Steph reached for it at exactly the same time, and their fingers brushed.

Time froze. The air around them hummed. Her heart thumped. Erin had got through dinner. She'd navigated post-dinner drinks. But just the two of them and Steph's bare shoulders equalled Erin unravelling. She wasn't cut out for pretending. Maybe she wasn't like her parents at all.

When their gazes met, Erin jolted again. My god, was she twelve?

However.

Was it her imagination or did Steph seem tense, too?

Before Erin could process that, Steph cleared her throat and stepped back, letting Erin finish the job.

Erin welcomed the distraction and fluffed up the duvet like she never had before. She smoothed the corners and plumped the pillows like she was the world's best housekeeper. Soon, she could go to bed and close the door on this car crash. That seemed like the best course of action. Shut it down, and when Erin woke up tomorrow, they could go back to being what they were. Client and service provider.

Right now, Steph was providing more of a service to Erin than she could have possibly imagined.

"Thanks again for doing this. You didn't have to."

Erin shook her head, fighting another blush. She shrugged like it was nothing. "I know where everything is, so…"

"It was really lovely meeting your family tonight." Steph's eyes shone as she spoke. "I feel honoured to be playing a part in your weekend, and I'm going to do all I can to make it as smooth as possible for you all."

That pulled Erin up short. Steph was playing a part. Erin needed to remind herself of that every hour, on the hour. Otherwise, an easy weekend might just get complicated.

"You're doing really well, so thanks for today. Only four more days to go." Did that come out more curt than she intended? Perhaps.

Steph frowned. "I didn't mean it to sound so clinical. It's nice being here, too. It's a treat to get out of London, and to be in such a magical place. I might be helping you, but you're helping me, too."

Erin nodded. What had she said? *Shut it down.* And stop staring at Steph's delectable shoulders. "Sleep well."

Steph's big eyes met hers. "You, too."

Chapter Eight

Steph waited until Erin had used the bathroom and disappeared into the bedroom before she fully relaxed. She got into the clean sheets that smelled like her mum's fabric softener, and pressed her head into the pillows. There were four of them, which seemed a little overkill. However, she wasn't complaining. They were far more comfortable than the ones she had at home. She made a mental note to ask Patsy and Duncan where they got them. She hated her own pillows with a passion.

She let her eyes wander the room, taking in the high-spec finish. Apparently, Erin's family rented these out all year round. Steph bet they did a roaring trade. She'd be thrilled to holiday here. The kitchen was so shiny it hurt her eyes, the log burner oozed warmth and style, and the loch was a dark shadow through the floor-to-ceiling windows. Patsy and Duncan had done a great job. Had Erin and her company had anything to do with it? If so, she was impressed.

She lay still, the only sound her breathing. Was Erin already asleep? Was she in bed wondering the same about Steph? She hoped she'd been an attentive girlfriend tonight, asking all the right questions, making the conversation about those around her. That was another tip Michael had given her before she left. She'd tried to follow it to a tee.

She picked up her phone and messaged her friend. It was 11.30. He'd normally still be up. She needed a little reassurance.

He messaged back right away.

Steph slid under the duvet to muffle her voice, and got through on one ring.

"Hello undercover agent," Michael said. "How's Scotland going? I was expecting a freak-out call from you earlier than this."

Steph couldn't help but smile. To be honest, so had she.

"Things are going okay, I think," she whispered. "I have to be quiet as Erin might be asleep."

"First things first. Have you eaten haggis yet?"

"Negative. Tonight's dinner was local beef and lamb, and it was delicious."

"You haven't broken the family's expensive heirloom vase yet?"

Steph laughed. Michael knew her well. "They don't seem to have one, which is disappointing. But I've met the parents, the brother and his wife, and they all seem to believe we're an item so far. To be honest, it's not hard. Erin is beginning to thaw, and she's actually a sweetheart. Also, she owns two toolbelts, so what's not to like?" A vision of Erin standing, Lara Croft-like, in jeans, toolbelt and tight top flashed into Steph's mind. She'd never been out with someone good with their hands. Did that extend to the bedroom, too?

Something inside her stirred. She frowned. This wasn't that sort of weekend. This was work. Although, she'd swear there had been a frisson of something between them tonight. A shared look over wine on the deck. And when they'd held hands...

"A toolbelt? I'm not even going to ask what's on it."

Michael paused. "Just remember, you're working. No seducing the client."

Could Michael read her thoughts?

"You were encouraging me to provide a happy finish when you offered me the job. Make up your mind."

"I believe I said it's not in your make-up."

"Whatever." Steph bristled, but brushed his comments away. "I'm just doing my job, but this place hasn't lost any of its charm. The Scottish Highlands are still amazing. If this job had been in Kettering or Hounslow, my cup might not be so overflowing."

Michael snorted. "But you're being charming and asking questions?"

"As instructed."

"Good. I've done a few jobs myself, and I've become a better friend and potential partner through it."

Steph waited a couple of beats. She had a question bubbling in her head. How could she put it without raising Michael's suspicions?

"You've done a couple of jobs where you've pretended to be someone's boyfriend."

"Uh-huh."

"A man or a woman?"

There was a pause before he replied. "One of each."

She burrowed further under the duvet, just to make sure she was as soundproof as she could be. "And in these jobs, you've held the person's hand, right?"

"Of course. It has to be convincing."

"Okay." She swallowed down. "What about kissing? Have you done that, too?"

"Yes. With both, before you ask."

She hadn't expected that. "And how was it? I mean, with the bloke? Did you fancy him?"

Michael took a breath before he spoke. "He was good looking, yes. But he wasn't very charming. Not at first, anyway. So when we had to kiss for the first time, I had to put all my acting training into practice. You remember the drills, right?"

Steph did. They'd been paired together for fake kissing practice at drama school. They'd both agreed it confirmed their gayness.

"Of course I do, you don't forget snogging your best mate. Especially when he slips his tongue into your mouth." She shuddered just thinking about it. "I still have nightmares."

Michael sniggered. "It was too tempting. Your mouth was open. What's a boy to do?"

"I don't think that defence would hold up in court, by the way."

"But back to your line of questioning. Can I take it you're thinking about kissing Erin?"

"It's going to be required at some point." Her skin tingled at the thought. "Tell me the truth. Did you go any further with your jobs? Slide your tongue anywhere else?"

Steph recalled Erin's glances at dinner. The way she'd checked to make sure she was okay. It was a quality Steph looked for in a partner, fake or not. Plus, there was also Erin's cleavage in that jumpsuit. It was hard to look past. Cleavages were Steph's absolute weakness. Had she thought about reaching over the table, bypassing the Jersey Royals, and what it might be like to run a finger down it?

Steph wriggled her bum.

No, the thought had never crossed her mind.

"A gentleman never licks and tells. Besides, what happens on a job stays on a job. The golden rule is: make sure the customer is happy, but also that you're happy." He paused. "Just don't get too attached. Remember, you don't do casual sex. Lines get blurred very easily on longer jobs like these. It can feel surprisingly real for everyone."

"I can shag someone and walk away!" It was hard to slot indignation into a whisper.

"You can't. You're terrible at it. If you sleep with this woman, you'll have to break the habit of a lifetime and walk away at the end of the five days." He paused. "But who knows, maybe it might be a good learning curve for you. Show that you don't have to find extra meaning in every single hook-up in your life."

Steph wasn't thinking about shagging Erin. Just licking her cleavage. Perhaps a heated snog. They had separate beds and separate lives, and after this weekend, that's how it would stay. Even if she did have a Marilyn Monroe beauty spot, and a neck that cried out to be kissed.

"Fine," she said eventually, shutting down the conversation before Michael really got into his stride. "I just thought you'd appreciate an update."

"I do, and it's always nice to know the client is satisfied. It's all going okay so far, seriously?"

Was it? "I think so." She *hoped* so.

He paused again. "Just let me know if you do see her toolbelt. You don't need to phone. Just send me the Spanish dancing lady emoji if it happens, okay?"

She ignored him. "I'm off to get some sleep before the big day of preparation tomorrow. Everything still on for you joining me on Monday?"

"Try to stop me." He paused. "And don't forget to take your medication. Have you done it tonight?"

Steph smiled. Michael was always hot on that. "I have. But thanks for caring."

She hung up, then lay under the covers for a moment or two more, her phone hot in her hand. Michael was coming on Monday, and this would all be over.

She already knew she'd be sad to say goodbye.

Chapter Nine

Erin woke up, rolled over in her bed, then grabbed her phone. It was a dreadful habit, but what else was a single girl to do? She'd given up having something else to occupy her. Or *someone* else. Her black T-shirt (that declared she was 'Too Damn Hot', a present from Morag, who else?) caught under her as she rolled back. She lifted her bum and arched her back, then pulled it down. Her knickers were up her arse, too. She dreamed of one day waking up serene.

Having Steph here was still strange. It was even stranger that her family had swallowed it without blinking. But now there was another living, breathing person to consider in her personal life. It had been so long since it happened, she'd started to think of relationships as a hobby other people did. Like stand-up paddleboarding or making fluffy cheese soufflés. She liked them in the abstract, but they took up a whole lot of time and energy. She had Morag, of course, but that was different. Morag had been put on this planet purely to wind Erin up.

As if to demonstrate that point, Erin clicked to wake up her phone, and was faced with a text from her best friend.

'You've been suspiciously quiet since you left. I can only assume that means it's so awful, you've thrown your phone in the loch and have barricaded yourself in the bathroom while your date cackles wildly. Or second option: you've been too busy tapping the hired help. Which is it?'

Erin rolled her eyes. Morag wasn't going to let this lie, was she? When she arrived tomorrow, Erin expected the interrogation to reach new heights. However, the hired help, while charming and easy on the eye, was just that. As Steph had said last night, she was honoured to be *playing a part* in Erin's life. No matter how relaxed Erin felt in her company, Steph was an actor. Nothing more, nothing less. Erin had to remember that.

But first, she needed a wee. Why hadn't her parents put in an en-suite? She slipped on some denim shorts, then grabbed the door handle. Should she knock before going into the lounge? No, that would be weird. She didn't want to be weird. Instead, she cleared her throat as she stepped into the lounge, the laminate floor cool beneath her feet. She should have grabbed the slippers from the wardrobe.

Steph rolled over, her long hair tussled. She threw her arms above her head and kicked her foot. The duvet slid down as she cracked open her eyes and yawned. Her T-shirt rode up her body. Erin stared at the glimpse of Steph's smooth torso, feeling her own body thrum to life. Even after the stern talking to she'd given it last night.

She averted her eyes briefly.

"Morning!" Steph sat up as she spoke, pulling the duvet with her. Her eyes scanned Erin. "I like your shorts. Artfully distressed."

Erin tried and failed not to blush. "Thanks."

"They show off your legs well." Steph sat up, then shook her head. "Not that I was looking at your legs…"

Had Steph been looking at her legs? Erin glanced down.

Were her legs *look-worthy*?

When Erin looked back up, Steph's cheeks had gone pink. "I was just lying here thinking I needed to get up, but the bed is too comfortable. It must be the best sofabed in the land."

The need to wee pressed on Erin's bladder. Also, the need to appraise her legs. She hooked her thumb towards the bathroom, like she was hitching a ride.

"I'm just going to the loo."

But before she could do anything, there was a knock on the front door, then some scratching, followed by more knocking.

"Erin, Steph, are you up? The girls wanted to come and say hi!"

Alex.

Shit.

Erin's eyes went wide. She glanced at the blinds, which were thankfully still closed. Nobody could see in to rumble them, but they had to get rid of any evidence. She sprang to Steph's side, who was already up and out of bed, throwing her pillows on the floor.

"You put the bedding into my room, I'll get the bed fixed back to a sofa," she whispered.

Steph nodded, her wonky hair looking like she'd just had a particularly wild morning.

Not helpful, Erin.

Steph grabbed the duvet, Erin yanked the sheet, then she piled Steph high with pillows like she was on a bedding game show. 'How many sets of bedding can she carry from one room to the other in a hurry, folks?!' The sheets were still warm from Steph's body heat.

Erin shook her head to dislodge that thought. "You got it?" she asked, already folding the sofa's metal frame in half.

"Uh-huh," Steph replied.

Only, when she took a step forward, Erin spotted Steph's foot was already tangled in the sheet.

Determined, Steph took another step towards the bedroom, but only succeeded in getting that little bit more caught up. She wobbled, but stayed upright, juggling the bedding in her arms.

"Just coming, Alex!" Erin shouted, then glanced at Steph, lost in the bedding. "Hold on, let me help you," she said.

Too late. Steph took one more step forward, the sheet now too tight under her feet. She wobbled again, let out a small shriek and then toppled forward, her cushioned fall not making a sound.

Oh shit, was she hurt? Luckily, they had three doctors on hand if she was, but Steph smashing her head open wasn't optimal.

"You okay?"

Steph nodded, her face flushed. "No broken bones." She scrambled to her feet, nearly slipped again, but managed to avoid it.

Erin exhaled, then pushed the frame into the base of the sofa. Just as she did, she heard a thud behind her, closely followed by a loud "fuuuck!" from Steph.

When she turned, Steph was on the floor, her face scrunched, cradling her right knee. She looked so soft and vulnerable, Erin wanted to take her in her arms.

But there was no time for that.

Another bang at the door.

Erin's senses scrambled.

"Auntie Erin! Auntie Steph!" Alex used his sing-song voice.

Steph's eyes went wide and she covered her mouth. "Sorry for swearing!" she whispered. "Shit!"

Erin dropped to her knees, trying not to laugh at the absurdity of the situation. "Tell me you haven't broken anything this time."

"Only my pride," Steph said. "And possibly my kneecap."

Erin laid a hand on Steph's elbow, and the effect slid all the way up her arm. When she locked eyes on Steph, her breath stilled, too.

For two whole seconds, time stopped beating.

"Have we come at an inopportune time? I'll take the girls to breakfast and we'll see you there," Alex shouted.

Time sped back up again.

Erin gazed at Steph for a millisecond longer, then jumped to her feet. "Okay, see you there!" She stared at the door, holding her breath. As her brother's and nieces' footsteps retreated on the gravel, she let it out.

On the floor, Steph let out a breath. "Sorry!" she said, her voice creased with pain. "Perhaps we need to work on our lounge clear-up technique."

Erin let out a hoot of laughter, then almost wet herself. She flung the sofa cushions back on, then hotfooted it to the loo.

"I think that might be wise," she said over her shoulder, then turned and walked smack into the bathroom door.

Crunch.

Ohmyfuckingsonofabitch.

Erin clutched her nose and staggered backwards, her whole face pounding. "Fuck-a-doodle-fuck!"

A howl of laughter from the lounge made her smile through the pain.

What a pair they were.

* * *

"Here they are!" Alex flexed his eyebrow in a devilish arch as Erin and Steph rocked up to the open-air breakfast table. Fresh berries, honey and yoghurt, muesli, and a selection of pastries were all on offer, along with orange juice and two cafetieres of fresh coffee. "Did I interrupt earlier?"

Erin put a hand on her hip and narrowed her stare. "No." It was the verbal equivalent of a clip around the ear. "Steph was in the shower, and I was getting dressed."

He returned her look, telling her he didn't believe a word. "Sounded like it."

Erin rolled her eyes, but that only hurt her face, which still throbbed. She waited for the pain to pass and focused on keeping her face still. She wanted to dunk her nose in the pot of fresh yoghurt, but that might not have gone down well. Instead, she turned to look down the hillside at the loch, glinting in the morning haze, then breathed in the fresh Highland air. At least that didn't hurt. It was going to be another scorcher today. The Scottish people would no doubt go into meltdown. Anything over 23 degrees Celsius and the country baulked. Today was set to hit 26. "It's going to be like the sun sat on ya!" as someone on the news had put it this morning.

Alex glanced at the house, then back to Erin. "Careful, Mum's on her way and she's in a flap. The lighting people have had a disaster, so they've called to ask if someone could make it over to Skye to pick up the lights instead of dropping them off."

Erin's stomach dropped at the mere mention of Skye. "Oh." She eyed her brother. The only other person in the world who understood.

He stared right back.

"There you both are! Did you sleep well?"

Erin and Steph both nodded, then sat at the table.

"That's great, I got new pillows in your honour. Memory foam." She paused. "Hot already, isn't it?" She stared upwards. "I'm just glad we're not still in general practice."

Her parents had hated hot weather because it had always meant lines of locals with sunstroke in their surgery. However, that was all behind them now they were retired.

"Has Alex told you about our lighting predicament?"

Erin nodded. "He has." Her stomach churned again. She'd have to go. Mum and Dad hated going, and Alex had the kids today as Wendy had a spa and hair appointment. She took a deep breath. "We can go and get them."

Her mum gave her a look. "Are you sure?"

Erin nodded as her stomach twisted. She wasn't at all sure. She tried to pretend Skye didn't exist. But it never went away.

Steph sat up. "I'd love to go to Skye if the trip's on offer."

Erin blinked. That settled it, then.

"Can you pick up the Pimm's jugs on the way back, too? They're with Aaron Whittard. Remember him? He borrowed them for his wedding and they're in his garage."

What a treat. She'd gone out with Aaron when she was 16. It wasn't even 9am and she'd agreed to go to Skye, then to see an ex-boyfriend. Plus, she'd almost dislocated her nose. What else did today have in store?

Her mum disappeared, then came back with the keys to their Range Rover. Erin took them. Oblivious, Steph grinned, then helped herself to some yoghurt and fruit.

Erin glanced at Alex, then Wendy, then her mum. A learned silent tension settled on them.

She swallowed down some excess saliva, then poured the coffee.

* * *

Her parents' Range Rover was like driving a tank after her own car. Luckily, Erin was used to driving her work van, so bigger vehicles didn't scare her. It was just driving to Skye she wasn't used to.

Her jaw clicked as she pulled into a passing place to let a camper van through. The driver gave her the universal palm in the air as she drove past, and Erin returned it. She was always amazed how quickly she slipped into the rhythm of driving in the Highlands, very different to Edinburgh. Here, the roads were often the width of a single car, with passing places to pull into every 200m.

Beside her, Steph jigged in her seat, sunglasses on, window down. She hardly ever sat still, something Erin had noted on the drive yesterday. Nervous energy. Her long legs twitched, and she had a tidy light purple bruise on her knee from this morning. Erin flipped the visor and checked the mirror. No bruising or black eye for her yet. She really didn't need either for tomorrow's party. She pulled back onto the road.

Steph sang along to the radio as they drove, as if she and Erin had known each other for years. Erin was grateful for the distraction. Anything to take her mind off where she was going. To stop her tasting candyfloss, the taste that was always triggered by certain memories of her sister.

They passed a sign telling them Skye was 20 miles away, and Steph bounced that little bit more.

Erin swallowed what tasted like a lump of coal. A light sweat broke out on her back and she pressed down so hard on her molars, she wondered if they might crack. She was never ready for Skye.

"I told you about how I came to the Highlands when I was 19, right?"

Steph, on the other hand, had exuberance crashing off her in waves. If anyone were to stop the car, they'd be super-confused at the vibe.

"I came with my friend, Michael, and it was a magical time. I'd just got the all-clear healthwise, and it finally felt like I was living. I could never have climbed any hills prior to coming, and these hills are worth the climb for the views."

What exactly had Steph's health issue been? She'd ask this weekend, but not right now. Erin's heart was beating far too fast in her chest to concentrate. Instead, she pressed down her nerves and plugged into Steph's Highlands enthusiasm. It wasn't hard. She brimmed with Highland joy.

"Skye is one of the places I remember, one of the first places we went. Michael's coming to meet me on Monday and we're going to retrace our steps. I can't wait."

Erin remembered the time she used to think Skye was magical, too.

Steph tapped her fingers on the dashboard, then whistled as Erin steered around a corner and another amazing view of lochs and glens glittered before them. She turned to Erin, cleared her throat, then paused.

Erin glanced her way. "Everything okay?"

A quick nod. "It's just…" Steph paused. "Was it just me, or was there some tension around you driving here today?" She sucked on her top lip. "It's a beautiful day, a gorgeous drive, but you seem tense now, too. Is there something I need to know as your fake girlfriend? Anything I've done wrong? If I have, please tell me so I don't do it again."

Erin gripped the steering wheel and focused on the drive. Did Steph need to know? She'd tell a real girlfriend, of course, but maybe not right away. She liked her life to appear normal before dropping that bombshell. Getting the sympathetic looks. It was the same thing that happened every time. She ground her teeth together and put on a smile as fake as their relationship. Maybe she'd tell Steph soon, but not now.

Not on this drive.

It was enough they were doing it in the first place.

"Nothing I haven't already told you," Erin lied.

It came so naturally.

She'd been doing it for years.

* * *

After they got home and unloaded the lights and jugs, Erin left Steph on the sofa, with a mumbled excuse about getting more teabags. She let herself into the main house and held her breath for a second. Nobody came to greet her. Erin moved stealthily across the vast living room, its fireplace standing proud. She pushed the door to what was comically termed the relaxation room. An old rowing machine, a dusty treadmill and a long-forgotten yoga mat greeted her. Erin clicked the door shut, then exhaled. She'd made it. On the shelf in the far corner, she spied what she was looking for.

Erin walked slowly past the lumpy futon sofabed that her mum had declared "a disaster" shortly after she bought it. She stopped at an ancient school photo of the three of them, the only room it was allowed. Both Erin and Nadia wore wide smiles and wonky fringes, the latter commonplace in their childhood. It was something her nieces were never going to suffer from. Alex looked confused, which was standard, too. She stopped and studied Nadia's face as she always did, trying to conjure her voice. She focused hard, but the volume in her head was tinny, like Nadia couldn't quite connect to a speaker. Her voice was muffled, just like Erin's memories.

She reached out an arm and took down the bubble-gum-pink ceramic pot that held Nadia's ashes. A taste of candyfloss flooded her mouth. It always happened when she was in close proximity or when she thought about her; it had been Nadia's favourite fairground treat until the day she died.

Erin had never opened the pot. To her knowledge, nobody had. After the day she'd had, going to Skye, seeing where it happened, she needed to hold her. To be near her.

One minute, her sister had been alive. The next, she was a pile of ashes in a pot.

It still made no sense, even nearly 20 years on.

Erin clutched Nadia in her arms, then sank onto the futon. Her mum was right. It was hellishly uncomfortable. That thought at least made her smile. Nadia would tell her to throw it out. Erin sat up. Suddenly, Nadia was there in Erin's mind's eye, speaking as clearly as if she was standing right in front of her.

"What the hell is this?" she said. "You can't sit on it, and nobody's going to want to sleep on it unless they're really drunk. I mean, just toss it out and get a proper sofabed. One with soft cushions maybe?" Nadia rolled her eyes.

Erin hugged the cool pink pot harder and squeezed her eyes tight shut.

How she missed her sister.

Nadia had been a hilarious blend of no-nonsense practicality mixed with a love of glitter and all things pink. They might have been twins and shared the same sense of humour, but that was where the similarities ended. Nadia had been a girly girl, whereas Erin was not. She still couldn't bring herself to wear Nadia's favourite colour, pink. Her motto had always been, the brighter, the better. At her funeral, her coffin had been studded with pink glitter. Erin still jolted every time she walked past a Claire's Accessories.

Tears leaked out of her eyes and rolled down her cheeks. Erin sniffed but didn't try to stop them. She'd learned over the years that grief hit you at odd times, and you had to let it. She'd tried fighting it, but it got her nowhere. Now, when it overtook her, she let it. Therapy had taught her that. She looked around for a tissue box, but couldn't see one in easy reach, so she used the back of her hand to wipe the end of her nose. She was glad Steph couldn't see her now. She wasn't faking a single thing.

The door opened and her mum walked in. Erin blinked, then sat up. She wiped the back of her hand across the end of her nose again, then loosened her grip on the pot. She wanted to hide it, the way her family always did. She didn't want her mum to see her upset. But she was here now, and there was nothing Erin could do. She sat up a bit more and put the pink pot on the sofa beside her, almost as if it was an afterthought. Like she hadn't been crying and hugging her dead sister's ashes at all.

"I thought I heard you come in. I was just checking we weren't getting burgled." Her mum glanced at the pot, and her eyes flickered to Erin's damp face. "I take it today brought things up?"

She sat beside her and patted Nadia's pot like it was something she just bought at a car boot sale for 50p after bargaining the seller down. Then she reached further and patted Erin's hand, light and quick. "It's natural that might happen, but you have to pull through it. Get on with it. Fight the good fight." She punched the air with little conviction. Like losing her daughter was an inconvenience, but one Patsy Stewart had learned to live with.

Erin knew that was a lie.

Her parents had never dealt with Nadia's death, just as they never had as a family. Why else was Erin in here hiding away, dealing with her grief alone?

"Can I?" Her mum lifted the pink pot without waiting for an answer.

She put it back on the shelf, then sat back down. She avoided Erin's gaze, just as she had ever since it happened.

It was a pattern they were both so used to, a game they both played. But Erin was so tired of it.

In her real life, she dealt with emotions and sat with her feelings. But as soon as she walked through the door of her family home, she was instantly transported back to being a teenager again. Flailing and out of control. She desperately wanted to be an adult with her parents and have an adult conversation about Nadia, but she had no idea how that would happen, how it would start.

Not when her mum always pulled out the military euphemisms when it came to her sister. Encouraged her to "get on with things."

'Stiff upper lip' was a phrase that succinctly described her family.

"I appreciated you going today, I know it's not easy." She crinkled her eyes in a rare show of emotion. At least, it looked like emotion, but Erin couldn't be sure. "Especially when you had to drive so close to where it happened. But I'm sure it was a big help having Steph there. Someone to fall back on, to help you with these tricky times."

Tricky.

Driving close to where her twin sister died, and her mum described it as "tricky". She and Alex had long conversations about their parents' inability to deal with feelings and reality. This was another treasure to regale him with later.

Erin glanced up at the ceramic pot, put back where it belonged. Out of sight, out of mind. Was that why this room wasn't used half as much as it should be? Because Nadia was here?

Her mum jumped up. "There's so much to do, no time to sit around here moping." She clapped her hands and painted on a wide smile.

Grieving wasn't on today's schedule, and Patsy Stewart was a stickler for schedules.

Chapter Ten

Steph leaned down and took the string of LED lights from Duncan. It was the longest string she'd ever seen. The kind her mum would spend hours untangling every Christmas. Steph steadied herself on top of the ladder, then strung them across the marquee. The lights were set to cover great swathes of the marquee's swooped, ruffled cream material ceiling, and they were on the final stretch. Beneath her, Duncan fed Steph the lights with an appreciative nod. He suffered from vertigo, so wasn't keen on the climb. On the other side of the tent, Erin fed matching lights to her brother, at the top of a different ladder.

"We really do appreciate you helping out," Duncan repeated for about the fourth time that day.

Steph gave Duncan a shrug. "I'm happy to help. I'm pleased to know my summers spent doing arts festivals and putting up a gazillion tents have come in handy. I knew they would one day." She raised a single eyebrow. "I won't tell you about the time I undid the wrong guy rope and collapsed a whole tent on top of an audience of people, though."

Duncan laughed like it was a joke. "There will be none of that tomorrow! I had a crew setting this up on Monday. Every screw is tight, and the guttering is state of the art."

89

"I've no doubt."

When they finished, she climbed down and stood beside him. When the marquee was lit tomorrow, it was going to look absolutely magical.

Duncan wiped his hands on his chinos, then glanced around the massive tent. At one end, a candyfloss machine was ready to go, along with a photo booth and a tuck shop.

Steph gave a small wave as Alex and Erin walked over.

"Can I just say, a candyfloss machine is the best news ever!" Steph grinned at Erin and her brother. "I love candyfloss and funfairs, so this is a real treat!"

They both stared at her, and a muscle in the side of Erin's jaw clicked.

When Steph glanced at Duncan, he was looking at the floor. What had she said to elicit that reaction? She was just about to ask, when Duncan jumped in.

"I need your mother to tell us where the tables are going, so we can direct the team where they need to set up. Can one of you go and get her?" He addressed it to his children.

Relief swept over both their faces.

"I'll go, I need the loo anyway." Steph had no idea what had just happened, but she'd ask Erin later. "Where's she likely to be?"

"The kitchen," all three of them replied at once.

Steph strolled out of the marquee, its inside already warm in the muggy May air. She glanced up at the sky. Rain was brewing, if she was any judge, but hopefully it would pass by tomorrow's party. Below her, the loch doffed its cap in her direction, and she gave it a smile. Whatever else was happening today, this loch was a welcome distraction.

Something was in the air. Steph had sensed it this morning. She'd definitely felt it on the drive to Skye. Erin had been tense the whole way there and back. Then she'd disappeared for a while and returned with a puffy face. Had she been crying? What was Steph missing? And what the hell had just gone on? Some part of this supposedly happy family dynamic didn't quite add up.

She let herself into the house, the air studded with the smell of baking and the sound of Patsy singing along to classic Kylie. Patsy was a star in the kitchen, so much so she was considering putting in an application for the Great British Bake-Off. Steph looked forward to tasting her cakes and bakes at the party. By the sound of it, she could also give Kylie a run for her money.

Before she sought Patsy out, though, Steph walked over to the giant double-height windows that looked out onto the loch. What was it like living in such picturesque surroundings? They should be the most relaxed family in the world—but they weren't. Was it just the party stress, or was it more than that? Steph could feel the lumps and bumps on the surface, but she had no idea of the source.

She walked over to a wall of photos, showing the happy family. Erin and Alex outside the house when it wasn't as grand and spectacular as it was now. The pair of them boating. On holiday somewhere with an ultra-sandy beach, Erin shielding her teenage frown with her hand. She was cute even as an awkward teen.

Steph pictured her mum's house, with all the photos of her throughout her childhood, even when she was pale and had tubes coming out of her nose. And that's when it hit her. There were no photos in this house of Erin and Alex as kids. Not *true* kids. All the photos of them as a family were all taken later on, when Erin and Alex were both in their teens. Where were the gap-toothed school shots? The wonky fringes? The chubby pre-teen stage that nobody wanted to be reminded of?

Erin said they'd moved here when she was 17. Had they just put up photos from that moment on? What happened to the rest? Did they lose them in a fire? It was the only explanation Steph could come up with that made sense. Maybe that's why they moved. Maybe that's why the Skye trip was tense today. Or perhaps Erin and Alex were so bad as kids, her parents burned all the early photos in a fit of pique. That made her smile. Patsy and Duncan certainly weren't anti-kids, as there were photos of the triplets from birth.

Footsteps made Steph look up. Patsy walked towards her in a sky-blue apron, flour splattered up her bare forearm. She smiled, just at the same time the main door opened, and Erin walked in. Her and her mum traded looks Steph couldn't quite decipher, then they both drew up beside her.

"Sorry, I was meant to come and get you," Steph said to Patsy. "But I got side-tracked by the loch, and then these photos."

The heat of both Patsy's and Erin's stares warmed the side of her face.

Steph ploughed on. "Where was the sandy beach photo taken, where you look like a surly teen?" She smiled even though she felt like she'd been caught doing something she shouldn't.

"That was taken on a beach not far from here, believe it or not."

Clare Lydon

"It looks like the Caribbean."

"I'll take you tomorrow, if we have time."

Patsy nodded. "You've got time. Tomorrow is party day, but it doesn't start until seven."

"I was also wondering where your earlier photos are?" Steph wasn't sure she should have said anything, but now she could only press on. "These are all later on. I was hoping to catch a glimpse of baby Erin." She gave her broadest smile, hoping to slice through the weird tension in the air.

"I rehung a lot when we got the windows done a few years ago, and we just never got around to putting the rest back up." Patsy gave a brittle smile. Like if she moved, it might fall off and shatter at their feet. "You know how it is. Plus, we're replacing them with photos of the triplets now." She glanced at Erin, then at Steph. "Who knows, you two might want kids someday, too." She gave Steph an exaggerated wink. "I'll save some wall space."

Steph cleared her throat and wasn't sure where to look.

The look Erin gave her mother could have started world wars.

Patsy cleared her throat, then returned her gaze to Steph. She wiped her hands on her apron. "Now, what did you want me for again?"

* * *

Steph took advantage of Erin's shower time to walk to the edge of the property and call her mum. It was where the best signal seemed to be. That, and she needed some air. Today's mood had only got weirder as the day went on.

It had all made Steph homesick for her own mum. Yes,

they had their moments, but her mum would never take down her childhood photos and forget to put them back up.

Or perhaps Steph was overreacting?

Her thoughts were interrupted as her mum answered her call.

"There's my wayward daughter," she said, as was her usual greeting. Steph was never sure if it was a compliment, or she was being chastised. "How are you? Are you back working in the bar now you're between jobs? I called you the other night but there was no answer, so I thought you might be."

She'd hadn't told her mum about this new spell of work. Had she been embarrassed? Perhaps. But now she was here, it was surprisingly normal. In fact, being a fake girlfriend was fairly similar to being the real thing. Navigating family dynamics, putting up with your partner's mood swings, and not having sex. It perfectly encapsulated her time with Andrea's family.

"Actually, I'm up in Scotland."

"Oooh," replied her mum. "Your spiritual homeland. What are you doing up there?"

"A job. For Michael's company." She paused. Did her mum need to know the truth?

"Michael? Didn't you say he was running an escort agency? I hope things haven't got that bad. I might not be made of money, but you can always come to me if you're short."

"It's fine, I'm not up here selling my body." A fleeting image of Erin's cleavage crossed her mind. Her tongue running up it. That had seemed like a possibility after last night. It didn't after today. "I'm doing a small acting job for the weekend, very niche. It's in the Highlands, which is why I said yes."

"The Highlands? How wonderful."

Steph's heart thudded that little bit faster. Did *it* know where it was? "It is. It's nice to be back. I know this is only my second time, but it always feels calming here. Like I'm home." She still remembered the phone call. Still recalled the absolute elation that she might be able to lead a normal life. It had proved to be true. Whatever else happened in her life, Steph was forever grateful to Scotland for her second chance.

"I can understand why. Plus, all that gorgeous scenery. You've got me jealous now. Here I am in Haywards Heath, and you're in the Highlands. Life always feels that little more manageable with so much space around you."

Not if the space was filled with weird energy. Steph turned back to the house which was lit up for their Friday night dinner.

"It's great to get a change of scene if nothing else. Michael is coming up on Monday and we're going to do a few days here. Retrace our trip from all those years ago."

"Say hi to my favourite nearly son." Her mum had a lot of time for Michael. Mainly because he was an outrageous flirt with her every time she saw him.

"I will," Steph replied. "Can I ask, did you ever think about taking down my childhood photos?"

There was a pause on the other end of the line. "That's a very strange question. Do you want me to? I might feel a bit bereft."

Steph shook her head. "No, I just wondered if there was a time limit on them, do you think?" Even as she was saying it, she could hear how crazy it sounded. "You know what, ignore me. I'm rambling."

"Is everything okay with you? You sound… I don't know, a little flat. Especially considering where you are."

Steph smiled. Her mum had a sixth sense, even when there were miles between them. If she had a child—which she wasn't ruling out, Patsy would be pleased to know—would she be able to read them in the same way? She hoped not, it was bloody annoying at times.

"I'm fine. This job is just a bit different." *I'm being the fake girlfriend of a woman I have a connection with, but I'm treading on eggshells with everything I say.* "It's long hours, and very intense."

"Make sure Michael's paying you a decent wage, then. Sounds like you're doing him a favour."

"He is, don't worry. I just wanted to ring to hear your voice, that's all." Seeing Patsy and Erin being so weird had made her think warm thoughts about her own mum. She'd always been there for her throughout her life, and that hadn't always been easy.

"You sound like you need a big hug, so consider this one down the phone."

A warm rush streaked through Steph. She could almost feel her mum's arms around her. It was enough for now.

"Listen, I better go. I'm on a break. Are you doing anything tonight?"

"I'm going round to Evelyn's. She's bought a pizza oven and we're making them in the garden!"

If her mum's nosey neighbour bought one it meant pizza ovens had gone mainstream. "Delicious. Remember the golden rule: no pineapple."

"Piff and paff." Her mum laughed.

"I'll come and see you when I'm back."

"Make sure you do. Have fun in Scotland!"

Steph wasn't sure what the next few days were going to hold, but she hoped fun might feature somewhere.

Chapter Eleven

The barbecue had been bearable mainly because of Erin's three nieces: Kay, Haley, and Elise. Erin couldn't imagine coping with one toddler full-time, never mind three. At one particular point this evening, two of the three had a meltdown because they didn't want butter on their corn on the cob. They'd then proceeded to wail with all the subtlety of a 1950s nuclear attack siren. Normally, Erin would be trying to get away from such a noise, but tonight, she had a different focus. She'd navigated through the barbed emotions as best she could, but by the end, it felt like she'd been crawling through mud on her stomach the whole night.

Eventually, Alex and Wendy took the children back to their lodge, leaving Erin and Steph to clear the outside table. Once done, her parents shooed them away, telling them to relax on their deck. Erin would lay bets that altruistic act was so her mum didn't have to deal with any more enquiries about their past from Steph. Although, since this afternoon, she'd let up on the questioning. Erin was sure she'd picked up on the vibe and come to her own conclusions. Should she tell Steph the story in full? She guessed it would be easier and save her any embarrassment over the next couple of days. Steph didn't know the truth, so how could she skirt around it?

Erin took the opportunity to grab a bottle of her dad's single malt collection—she went for a bottle of Jura, which was solid and reliable. She picked up two glasses, then left her parents to it. She found Steph on their deck, staring at the night sky, which was only marginally different to the day.

"I wonder if the kids are sleeping differently in the summer, being it's still so light," Steph said as Erin sat opposite her at the wooden table.

"I think they're used to it. They'll grow up knowing very short winter days and very long summer ones, and not much in between. It's the Highland way." She shot Steph a grin. "After the triplets' meltdown tonight, what do you think about having one like my mum suggested? Shall we check out some sperm donors?"

"I'll just grab my phone." Steph's face cracked with a smile. She glanced over towards the pool. "Does your family use the pool in the summer?"

Erin nodded. "Oh yes. I think the kids were in it today. We should go in. Tomorrow, after the party. Or Sunday."

"I don't have a swimsuit."

"You can borrow one of mine. Or go without." Erin grinned, then held up the bottle. "I didn't ask if you drink whisky, but would you like a glass?"

"When in Scotland, it'd be rude not to, right?"

"Unless you're my brother. He hates whisky."

Steph made a mock-shocked face. "Is that allowed?"

"He's appearing in court next week. Accused of being unpatriotic. His defence? He loves Irn Bru."

Steph threw her head back and laughed, as if giving herself more room to enjoy the joke.

Erin liked the way it looked and sounded.

"I've never had an Irn Bru. I was hoping to rectify that while I'm here."

"We'll get you one at the beach tomorrow." Erin poured the whisky, then held up her glass to Steph. "To us, and dealing with stressful days like today." She paused. "Thanks for being so affable with my parents. They can be a challenge when they want to be. Also, my nieces and their ear-curdling screams. You're playing this role very well, and I'm grateful."

Steph met her eyes. "It's not just a role. I like you and I like them. I want their party to go well, and I want it to go well for you. I know how being queer, while still accepted, can make you feel not quite part of your own family. Even with me, an only child of a single parent, my mum was still surprised and took a while to get her head around it. Your family seem fine with it, but I know it still marks you out as 'other'."

Erin nodded. It did, even in a family as accepting as her own. "There's a reason I hired you. To blend in a little more, and so my extended family don't ask about my love life with sympathetic looks on their faces. With my family, I know they worry about stuff that happened in our past. That it still holds me back." She paused. Her ears prickled, and her toes clenched. Erin took another swig of whisky and winced as the liquid burned its way down her body. Was she ready to go there? It was now or never.

"They might have a point."

Steph's gaze rested on her with curiosity. "Is this something about you and your mum? I felt some tension earlier."

Erin nodded. "That's the understatement of the year."

"Families have their secrets."

"But ours is an open secret. Everybody knows. Nobody talks about it. It drives Alex and me mad, but it's so hard to change the pattern." Even saying those words was hard. It wasn't something she did often. She still kept it all bottled up, sloshing around inside. Erin cleared her throat and sat up straight. Then she gathered all her strength and began to speak.

"I had a twin sister. Nadia. She died in a car crash when we'd both just turned 17. She learned to drive before me. She learned to do everything faster than me. She was the one who everyone expected something of. She was my best friend." A screw tightened in her chest, but she carried on. "She passed her driving test first, and I needed to be picked up from a friend's house. She was on her way to get me and she swerved to avoid a lamb. She skidded off the road and hit a tree."

Her right hand shook, and she held it with her left. It had been a long time since she told this story. It still made her want to hurl something across the room, even after all these years.

Steph put a hand to her mouth. "Oh my god." Her eyes went wide. "I take it that's why you moved when you were 17?"

Erin nodded. "We lived on Skye, but after Nadia died, our parents decided a fresh start was best for us all. So we moved here, and they renovated and built the lodges while being the local GPs. Anything to give them a project and keep them busy. Those who got to know us got the story when they needed to, but after Nadia died, there was an unspoken mandate that we had to get on with things. Yes, it was sad, but life carried on." Erin shook her head. "Our parents have got so stuck in that way of living they don't know how to change it. We should be talking to the triplets about Nadia, showing them what a great person she was, but we don't. Not without our parents' permission. They never give it."

Steph exhaled, then shook her head. "I'm so sorry. What a thing to carry with you. I can understand your parents' actions, but you can't run away from grief. It catches up with you eventually. And it's unfair to expect you and Alex to follow suit."

Erin shook her head. "We haven't." It took a while, but they'd done the work. "We've both done therapy and we talk to each other. We'd go mad otherwise. I try to speak to Mum and Dad about it, but they don't know how to even start a conversation, only how to shut it down and move on."

Steph took a sip of her drink while she tried to absorb Erin's words. Then she sucked in a breath. "This afternoon, when I was asking about the photographs. That's why there are no photos of you before then?"

Erin nodded. "Because they've got Nadia in, and it's too painful for them."

Steph flinched. "And there was me opening my big mouth. I'm sorry." She looked like she wanted the ground to swallow her up.

"It's not your fault. You didn't know. Plus, I actually think it's good for someone else to notice. Good for them to be challenged."

"Even so. That's just awful. For everyone."

Erin didn't need to be told that. It had shaped her whole life. "They're not bad parents. They're just full of hurt and they've never dealt with it. They've always been there for Alex and me in every other way." Why was she suddenly defending them? Family loyalty. Learned behaviour. All of it muddled up in one big soup.

"But there's still the unsaid words, the topic nobody goes near."

There was indeed. Seeing it from someone else's perspective made it sound more concrete. More shocking. Erin hadn't told most people in her life. Only close family and a handful of friends knew. It had always been that way. When she'd thought about this weekend, she'd been pretty clear she wasn't going to tell Steph. But that was before she got to know her. Before they'd shared the past few days. She hadn't fully appreciated that in bringing her home, there was no choice but to open up.

"That's another reason I wanted someone else here tomorrow. To take the spotlight off me. Maybe it's not true, but on big occasions, I always get the feeling that everyone's looking at me, wondering if Nadia would look the same, act the same. Sometimes I feel like my parents might have preferred Nadia to still be alive than me."

"Don't say that."

Steph reached across and brushed her fingertips over Erin's knuckles.

Erin shivered at the touch. Candyfloss danced in her mouth.

Hello, Nadia.

"I don't believe that for a second. Your parents love you, and they're proud of you. I can see that from the couple of days I've spent with you. But I get it must be a headfuck having a twin who's no longer here." Steph paused. "Were you very close?"

Erin bowed her head.

Steph's fingers came back, but this time, she wrapped them around Erin's hand.

A rush of emotion swelled in Erin. Simple things like that never happened to her, apart from when she was with Morag. In general, she dealt with life alone. She could almost believe Steph was real if she tried hard enough. What would Nadia have said about her hiring a girlfriend?

"She was my buddy from day one. Nobody else ever came close." Erin couldn't take her eyes from Steph's fingers. "But because we never talk about her, I feel like a part of me died that day, too. It's why I don't come home nearly as much as I should. The pressure of keeping silent is too much. I can never be sad, because I don't want to bring my parents down. They've had enough sadness in their life."

"But you're not responsible for their feelings or their life."

Erin freed her hand, leaned her head back and stared up to the sky. "It would be nice to believe that." When she brought her head back down, Steph's warm gaze was on her. But far from running from it, Erin wanted to luxuriate in it. That was a new, welcome feeling. Was it because the pressure was off? She wasn't trying to impress Steph. They were just two strangers, thrown together for a weekend.

"I'm so sorry to hear it all. I bet Nadia was a phenomenal woman. I know her sister is."

A smile tugged the edges of Erin's lips, then her heart. Steph's gaze seemed real, but Erin couldn't decipher the code. They hadn't hung out long enough. She'd love to ask, love to iron out any wrinkles. But this was a business arrangement. She was Richard Gere. Steph was definitely her pretty woman.

"Nadia was phenomenal. I mean, she was a pain in the arse too, don't get me wrong." Erin laughed. "But one of my biggest regrets is not knowing her as an adult. Not sharing a glass of whisky together. She should be here now. We should be fighting over this lodge and who gets to stay in it."

"Who would have won?"

Erin flicked her gaze to Steph once more. When their eyes locked, a tiny dart of electricity landed in her gut.

"Probably Nadia. She was way smarter."

Steph leaned back and shook her head. "Even in this idyllic place, there are secrets." She glanced back at Erin. "I knew a Nadia Brown at school."

Erin frowned. Nadia Brown? Who the hell was Nadia Brown? Then she remembered. The false name she'd asked Morag to supply just in case she and Steph were at loggerheads. But that didn't matter. If Steph thought she was called Erin Brown, and her sister was Nadia Brown, no harm done.

"Is she buried around here?"

Erin shook her head. "Her ashes are in the study-cum-junk room in the house. We were meant to scatter them as a family, but it never happened."

Steph sat forward in her chair. "After all this time?" Her voice was stamped with disbelief.

Again, it made Erin sit up and take note of how ludicrous it sounded. She'd got so used to the shape of the words on her tongue, she'd almost forgotten their meaning. "Wendy says the same. She's always on at Alex to just pick up the urn and take it to the loch Nadia loved the most. I'd rather she was there than in the junk room."

Steph let out a low whistle.

Erin could almost see it sailing through the air.

"If there's anything I can do over the weekend to make things easier, just say the word."

"Thanks." Erin's insides warmed. "You being here has already made a difference."

"Thanks for telling me, though. I know it can't have been easy."

"You're part of an exclusive club."

"I'm honoured to be so."

"Actually, the beach we're going to in the morning was Nadia's favourite. Mine, too. And Alex. If I die on the way there, be sure to scatter my ashes there, okay?"

Steph's face fell. "Don't even joke."

"Sorry. You get into the habit of bad taste jokes after the past two decades. I know Nadia would have laughed at that."

"I'm sorry I never met her."

Chapter Twelve

The next day, Steph and Erin were on the road by 8am, determined to make the most of the early morning sunshine. They drove down the steep drive, then to the main street, the loch glistening beside them. Steph had packed for changeable weather, but today was forecast to climb to 25 degrees, so she'd dressed in cut-off jeans and a T-shirt. Meanwhile, Erin's toned legs were clad in black denim. Steph took them in as Erin drove, as well as the muscles in her forearms that flexed as she drove. Painting clearly kept her toned and in shape.

After last night's revelations, Erin's smile this morning had been far more genuine. As if now she'd unburdened herself, she could relax. If she carried that around with her in day-to-day life, it was a wonder she was able to function at all. Perhaps that was why Erin hadn't had a serious relationship in a long time. If you couldn't be yourself, it was difficult letting anybody else in. For Erin, coming out wasn't about her sexuality. It was about survivor guilt.

They drove out of the village and along the loch, the hills to their right covered in bright yellow gorse. Within five minutes, they hit a long stretch of road with lochs on both sides and no cars anywhere to be seen.

Steph sucked in a breath. "I'll never get over the vastness of the Highlands. How small we all seem in comparison."

Erin smiled. "We are small, but we can all make our mark if we want to."

"Even your sister." Steph glanced right, unsure if she'd overstepped.

But Erin produced a wry smile. "Especially her. It's amazing what you can pack into 17 years." She sighed. "I couldn't get to sleep last night thinking about her, but I'm glad I told you. You didn't know her, so you don't have any preconceived ideas. Nadia was special, but sometimes I feel like I get lost in her memories."

"Do you not think you should say this to your parents?"

Erin gave a sad shake of her head. "We've tried, both Alex and I. But they're very good at avoiding what they don't want to deal with."

They drove on for a while longer in silence. The scenery was more than enough to keep Steph occupied. When they passed some castle ruins, Erin broke sharply after a car backed out of a layby with no warning. She swore loudly as the car skidded to a halt.

Did Erin think about Nadia every time she drove up here? How long had it taken her to get back behind a wheel after the accident?

A few miles further down the road, they turned off and wound their way down a smaller track barely wide enough for a single car. Steph clasped her seat tight as Erin drove over blind crests and around blind corners. She did it all with expert ease.

"You get used to it," she told Steph.

Eventually the ocean came into view, a blue and sunlit-gold oasis straight ahead. The car vibrated as they drove over a steel cattle grid. Steph spotted sheep in the surrounding hills, but no cows in view. To their left, an array of static caravans and tents made the most of the sea view. They drove past a small wooden hut, advertising coffee, breakfast and gifts. To their right, rocky green hills spilled down to the sea. Erin turned right to the car park, then parked up, one of only two cars.

Steph breathed in the salty air as they slammed the doors. The sand underfoot kicked up as they strolled onto the grass verge, back onto the main path and towards the wooden hut. A woman with dark red hair sat on the porch in denim dungarees reading her Kindle. She looked up when she heard their footsteps, and her round face warped into a smile when she saw Erin. She sprang up and pulled her into a long hug.

"Bloody hell, you are not who I expected to see this morning." The woman held Erin at arm's length. "I haven't seen you in ages! How long's it been?"

Erin shook her head. "Two years. I didn't come back last Christmas and didn't get over here the summer before. How are you?"

The woman shrugged, then nodded towards the aqua ocean behind her. "Life could be worse. Still serving coffee to tourists. Still seeing the gorgeous Sharon." She turned to Steph, giving her a discreet once-over. "I'm Nancy."

The way Nancy just hugged Erin, Steph suspected she was more than just a friend.

Steph's stomach rolled as their gazes connected. She pulled herself up to her full height. She needed to impress this woman. Nancy ignited Steph's protective gene.

Was it mixed with a speck of jealousy, too? No. Steph was just looking out for Erin. She'd endured a rough ride, after all.

"Steph," she said, offering a hand which Nancy shook with gusto.

"Steph's come up with me from Edinburgh for Mum and Dad's anniversary. We've just started seeing each other." Erin gave Steph an unsure smile as if she wasn't sure about that sentence one bit, then stared out to sea, avoiding everybody's gaze.

"That's great news!" Nancy's smile was infectious. "Did you want some food or just a drink?"

After consulting with Steph, Erin ordered two bacon rolls and two coffees. "I'll get Mum to start on the rolls." She flicked her head back to the hut. "I do the coffee in there with my flashy machine."

Nancy disappeared into a weather-beaten white-stone cottage, set a short distance to the left of the hut, and beside a strapping wooden lodge at least three times the size of the one she and Erin were currently sharing.

"That's Nancy's lodge," Erin explained. "She used to live in Edinburgh. We had a brief thing ages ago, but then she moved back to open this." She pointed to the world's smallest cafe in the wooden hut.

Now she was stood beside it, Steph could see four picnic tables round to the side.

"Her mum rustles up the food in the cottage, and Nancy does the coffees. She lives right by the sea and makes more here than she ever did in the city. Plus, she's going out with the woman who delivers her milk, Sharon. It was love over a stack of four-pinters."

Steph was pleased to see her gaydar still worked, even in such a remote spot as this with dodgy reception.

Nancy returned and set to work in the hut, shouting out things that nobody could hear thanks to the din of the coffee machine. After a couple of minutes, she appeared with two takeaway cups. She set them on the wooden ledge at the front of her hut, then pressed the lids down carefully.

"They're environmentally friendly, just in case you were wondering." She tapped the lids again. "Sugar's there. If you need more milk, just shout." She eyed Erin as she leaned against the porch pole. "You're still in Edinburgh?"

Erin nodded. "Not leaving anytime soon." She glanced around. "Even with the lure of this."

Nancy laughed. "If you ever change your mind, we always need work doing around here." She glanced at Steph. "My mum runs the caravan park." She tilted her head towards Erin. "I hope you're putting her to good use in Edinburgh, too. Erin's very good with her hands." It was only after the words were out of her mouth that Nancy turned a shade of red Steph hadn't even known existed until then.

"I didn't know you cared," Erin replied.

Nancy shook her head. "You know what I mean."

An older woman came out of the house, saving Nancy's blushes. She handed over the rolls, then disappeared just as quickly.

"We're going to eat these on the beach. Save you from saying anything else." Erin gave Nancy a grin, then a hug, before she waved them off.

They walked across the cattle grid, Steph holding the coffee away from her body lest she spill any. Then it was down a sandy path, over a small dune, and they were spat out on to a crescent-shaped beach small enough to pretend it was their own, which it seemed like this morning.

Steph's gaze swung left to the smooth shoreline and the caravans sat atop the small hill; then to the green hill that climbed right. But it was ahead that held her attention, the glossy sand a prelude to the Atlantic Ocean that stretched as far as her eye could see. The beach was everything Erin had told her and more. It was a dream beach; one you normally only saw in movies or on photos of idyllic Caribbean islands. But this was Scotland. They shed their flip-flops and sat on them. At 9.30am, the sun was bright but there was still a slight chill in the air.

Steph took a bite of her bacon roll, grease staining the white paper bag it was wrapped in. Her stomach growled. She hadn't been hungry until then, but now, she was ravenous. Was there a more perfect setting to eat a bacon roll than on a beach like this? Steph had been to plenty of fancy brunch places in London, but none could top this for romance. A coffee, a hot bacon roll, and she was here with her fake girlfriend, who felt more real by the minute.

She swallowed down a snort at how implausible the whole situation was.

"What was that noise for?"

Steph slowed her chewing. Should she lie or tell the truth? She glanced at Erin, then went with the latter. There were enough lies in Erin's life. She didn't want to add to them.

"I was just thinking that this breakfast is very romantic. Simple but delicious, with the perfect setting. Far more romantic than any of my past partners ever managed, or me." She bumped her shoulder against Erin's. "And here I am enjoying it with my fake girlfriend."

Erin returned her smile. "I know what you mean." She sipped her coffee, then stared out at the ocean. "I never expected us to get along so well. For you to be such a good listener. Or someone I might end up liking." Erin glanced at Steph, then blinked. "As a person, I mean. I know this is a job. Don't worry, I'm not suggesting anything else."

Steph's heartbeat thudded in her ears.

Did Erin protest too quickly? Steph's gaze settled on her beauty spot, then on her lips. She forced herself to look away. Something had changed between them. When they'd met, there'd been an ocean between them. Now, the waves were in touching distance, right in front of them. Steph wanted to dip a toe and test the water, but she couldn't go there, today of all days. This was what Erin had hired her for. Support and reassurance, as Michael had drilled home. Steph was going to do both.

"If it helps, I like you, too," she replied.

Erin stopped chewing, and her gaze dropped to Steph's lips.

A jolt of desire landed right in Steph's centre. So much so, she wondered if she'd jumped when it happened. It felt like it had shaken the beach. But when she looked around, the sand was flat, the water calm.

Steph took another bite of her roll and bit down her feelings. Anything to get rid of the kaleidoscope of emotions inside her. Why couldn't she just do her job? She pushed back her shoulders and sat up straighter. She wasn't going to fall for Erin just because she was cute, and they'd shared such an intense few days.

Although, when she thought about it, that was precisely the reason she *could* fall for Erin.

"It's ironic. I haven't had that many girlfriends, but I've never brought any real ones here. Only my fake one."

That lightened the mood, and Steph was grateful for it. She laughed. "Are we both fatally flawed when it comes to romance?"

Erin snorted. "Me, definitely." She ate the last bite of her roll, then screwed up the white paper bag in her hand. "Maybe because the pressure's off? I'm not out to impress you and be someone I'm not. At least, not after last night. I'm being myself, warts and all. It's a bit easier, isn't it?"

Steph nodded. She was right, it was. "For what it's worth, I'm enjoying being with the real you. So maybe next time you go on a real date, consider showing it off. You might be surprised what happens."

"Maybe I will." She turned her head and held Steph's gaze. "This was Nadia's favourite beach. Probably another reason I don't chance bringing girlfriends here. I don't want to taint it."

Steph didn't take her focus from Erin.

"I need to start reclaiming it, don't I?" Erin stared at her. "Not always letting it be Nadia's thing. I can have things, too."

"You can have whatever you want if you put your mind to it."

* * *

A delicious tension hovered in the car on the drive back. Steph was trying to work out how to handle it.

Erin put the radio on and concentrated on driving, which left Steph alone with her thoughts.

She'd thought this would be a simple job. Arrive Wednesday evening, leave Monday afternoon, a shake of the hand and get on with her life. But being dropped into this situation was just too personal. You'd have to have a heart of steel not to feel something, to get involved while pretending to be Erin's girlfriend. This job meant she was front and centre, in the firing line of the family dynamic. It was her job not to duck, and she was determined to follow through.

Her thoughts were interrupted as a lamb ran out into the road.

Erin slammed her foot on the brake and braced hard.

Steph pressed both her feet to the floor, too. She squeezed her eyes shut and snapped her head back, waiting for the impact.

It never happened.

Instead, when the car stopped and she dared to look, the lamb was nowhere to be seen. Rather, a fat cartoon-style sheep now stood in front of the car, staring at them. Was that the lamb's mum or dad? Whoever it was, the sheep was doing a great job of giving her and Erin a storming slice of side-eye.

Steph exhaled. "Fucking hellfire! Are you okay?" A lamb, of all things. She was glad she knew the full story now. She wasn't sure she'd be able to drive these roads if it were her.

Erin banged her palm on the steering wheel, then let out a controlled yelp. Eventually, after a few deep breaths, she turned to Steph. "I'm fine."

The sheep wandered to the other side of the road, its eyes still on them.

"The sheep is not amused."

Erin shook her head, then gave a tiny smile. "Neither am I." She sighed. "One other thing I haven't told you in the spirit of full disclosure."

Steph glanced her way. What now?

"Tomorrow is the anniversary of Nadia's crash. Twenty years. It was freakish weather that day, which didn't help. One minute it was fine, which it was when Nadia set off. The next it was torrential rain, which the police said would have added to it. I tried to make my parents move their anniversary party, but they were insistent. Which means there might be added tension tomorrow. However, I made a promise to myself I wasn't going to spoil their party." She paused. "Just so you know."

Steph swallowed down a lump that had formed in her throat. It'd been almost 20 years since her life-saving procedure. A question mark hovered in her mind. She couldn't go there. Not when she had a job to do.

Her stomach turned.

"Did you say Nadia died right away?" She tried to make her comment light, but she knew the words were anything but.

"Pretty much." Erin turned. "Why do you ask?"

Steph balled her fist by her side. She was being ridiculous. "Just curious." She steadied her breathing. Today wasn't about her.

Also, *damn*. If it was the anniversary of Nadia's crash, the family tension was about to ramp up that little bit more. This weekend had more drama than most of Steph's former acting jobs. Steph contorted her mouth into a myriad of poses, then turned to Erin. What she went through every time she was home was unbelievable. Life took chunks out of everyone, but Erin more than most. Steph complained when her mum invited her neighbour around when she went to visit. She made a mental note never to complain about Evelyn again.

"Okay. Thanks for telling me." Steph stared at Erin, the side of her jaw flexing. Steph's focus was back on the job, 100 per cent. Her instinct was to reach out, but was that more than she should do? She wasn't a real girlfriend. But hadn't Erin said they were friends? Plus, the line had been crossed last night.

Steph wrestled with herself for a moment, then did what felt right.

"Don't get too involved," Michael had said.

Easier said than done as she'd got to know Erin. However this weekend played out, even if she never saw Erin again, she'd never forget her. Erin was already under Steph's skin.

She reached out and squeezed Erin's thigh.

Erin stalled, then looked down.

Steph was sure her arm was vibrating. Could Erin feel it?

"Whatever happens, I'm here for you. You're not doing this alone, okay?"

Erin stared ahead, then turned to Steph.

Steph's heart spread across her chest like hot butter. The fingers of her other hand gripped the side of her seat.

Erin stared straight at her, then licked her lips. "I'll remember that."

Chapter Thirteen

Erin stood at the lodge window, overlooking the loch. She wanted to run down the hill, dive in and forget all the people that were coming tonight. But she couldn't. She was the only surviving daughter, and she had to play the part. Even if going to the beach today had stirred up her emotional sludge. Some good, some suspect. Where Steph was concerned, the emotions weren't very helpful. Which was the opposite of Steph herself. She could still remember how her insides had heated to thermal when Steph squeezed her thigh earlier. She wasn't doing this alone. Erin clung to that thought as she heard a cough behind her.

She turned, and there was Steph. If Erin had been trying to play it cool, to pretend there was nothing there, she was about to fail dismally. If this was a performance, Steph was definitely the leading lady. Her hot-pink dress — Nadia would have approved — had a halter neck design that showcased her glorious shoulders and back to a tee. It hugged her tall, hour-glass figure perfectly, its hem sitting mid-thigh so her long legs got a look-in, too. If you'd asked Erin what her perfect date would look like, this would pretty much be it. She took a deep breath and tried not to wail that this was just for show.

But it was hard when she longed to walk over and lay a kiss on Steph's strong, capable shoulders.

"You look incredible." The words tripped off Erin's tongue with ease. She had to tell her, because it was the truth. She'd tried to hide the fact she was attracted to Steph, but tonight, she could afford to revel in it. Tonight, she was going to play the perfect daughter for her parents, but tomorrow, she was going to bring up Nadia. Tackle the issue head-on. Steph had been instrumental in that. Seeing her reaction had made Erin see that what they were doing was wrong.

But that was tomorrow. Tonight, she got to go to the ball with her fake princess. The one walking across the room with a look on her face Erin couldn't quite work out.

"You don't look so bad yourself."

As Steph got closer, her gaze raked Erin's body from head to cleavage, and stopped there. Steph's half-smile shifted from friendly into something she couldn't name.

Erin felt every single millisecond of it. It rattled through her body like a freight train, and she curled her feet in her black heels to keep her on the ground.

Maybe she was lying. Maybe she could name it.

It might have been a while, but she'd been on the receiving end of this vibe before. Could it be that Steph felt something for her, too? That she wanted to take their fake relationship to the un-fake level? Sure, it wasn't ever going to be a grand love affair, but maybe a kiss would leave them both with a smile on their faces this weekend.

What Erin knew for sure was she couldn't be the one to make the first move. She was the client, the one with the power, and she never wanted to come over as a sleaze.

Her rational brain told her to be sensible. To keep this professional.

But her body was reacting the only way it knew how. She licked her lips and imagined what Steph might look like with that dress pooled around her ankles. How she might feel with Steph's eyes focused on her, Steph's impossibly glossy lips sliding across her own. A flutter of anticipation swept through Erin. She wanted to know what was coming next, and yet, this close-to-the-edge feeling fed her. It made her feel more alive than she had in forever.

"About tonight."

Steph's voice was somehow different. Like rich velvet, dense and luxurious. She could talk to Erin about anything if she talked like that.

"What about it?"

Steph stepped forward. "I was thinking, maybe we should talk about the kissing portion of our agreement. Because that might happen tonight, right? I lean down to kiss you on the lips in a casual manner to confirm things with onlookers."

Steph smelt so good. Like citrus and bergamot. She smelt good enough to eat, and now she wanted to talk about kissing? Was she trying to kill Erin before they'd even started the evening?

"What are you suggesting?"

"That we have a trial run now. Just to get us both used to it. Check out our reactions. Make sure you don't run for the hills when our lips collide."

Erin's blood ran hot. That was the most ludicrous thing she'd heard in a long time. She scrunched her forehead, then nodded, trying to keep her cool. "We better make sure of that."

Steph licked her lips again. "It's the professional thing to do."

Was it just Erin, or had the lights dimmed, too, along with the volume of Steph's voice? She flicked her gaze out the window, just to check there was no immediate family hovering. The coast was clear. For some reason, she didn't want an audience for this first time. She wanted it to be just them. Practising their hearts out.

Erin stepped within kissing range of Steph's illegal shoulders. Her breath became light, her palms started to sweat. How was this going to work? How did professional kisses begin? Erin was just about to ask who should take the lead, when Steph put her hands loosely on Erin's waist, then looked her right in the eye as if this was something they did every single day.

"When we did this in drama school, we planned what was going to happen. Where we were going to put our hands. Was the kiss going to be real or fake? Should we kiss anywhere else but the lips first? How long should it last?"

Erin's gaze followed Steph's lips, only vaguely hearing the words. She did register 'anywhere else but the lips' however. Then almost fainted.

"I'm assuming you'd prefer a closed-mouth kiss?"

Ohmyfuckinggod. She half expected Steph to present her with a kiss menu, the options ranging from lip-graze, to French, to full-on Olympic gold. Erin gulped, stared at Steph's soft chin, then gave a small shrug. "I don't know." She really didn't. Her mind had just burned down. "I trust you, you're the professional. You take the lead."

Steph's perfect lips quirked into a smile. "Okay." She paused. "For instance, I might lay a light peck on your beauty spot first." She leaned down and did just that.

Erin flinched, and apparently jumped a foot in the air.

Steph pulled back and raised an eyebrow. "Bad?" Her face spelt worried. How could someone be so drop-dead gorgeous, but doubt themselves?

Erin wasn't sure how she was still standing. Her skin where Steph's lips had just been was on fire. She shook her head.

"All good."

Steph gave a firm nod, then gripped Erin's waist and pulled her towards her, holding her gaze.

"No fake kiss, that's too risky. I'll aim for five to ten seconds, but I don't have a stopwatch, so don't judge me." Steph flexed her neck, then brought her mouth within inches of Erin's. Her hot breath was almost too much to take. Her pupils fixed on Erin. "Ready?"

No, but also, yes. She stayed silent, then gave Steph a languid nod, as if her head had come loose from her neck. Had her nose gone as red as it felt?

If it had, Steph didn't seem to notice. She simply leaned forward and pressed her lips to Erin's.

Just like that, Erin's fantasy from just a few minutes ago came true.

This didn't happen to her.

As Steph's lips slipped across hers, Erin's head emptied of everything that had been clogging it for years. In her mind's eye, when she stared ahead, all she saw was Steph walking towards her, a vision in pink. The only thing that mattered was this moment. The spark of lust in her gut. The fuzz of static in her brain. Steph's lips were soft but insistent, and her kisses felt like hot, sticky sunshine injected straight into Erin's veins. Their lips melted together at breakneck speed. Steph was tangled up in her head, she was in Erin's weeds, her hip bones pressed into her as if nothing else mattered.

Right then, it didn't.

Erin's fingers travelled up Steph's arms and she traced the line of her collarbone with her thumb.

When Steph slipped the tip of her tongue into Erin's willing mouth, she wanted to close the shutters, strip naked and call off tonight. Her parents could party without them. They'd see them tomorrow. Tonight was suddenly all about Steph and her exquisite kisses.

Concentrating on anything else later was going to be nigh-on impossible.

Steph groaned into her mouth as Erin's fingertips rested on her neck. A whoosh fizzed up Erin's body as she sucked in Steph's groan. Her pulse hammered, her head was light, she swayed on her feet. It had been some time since Erin had been kissed. Some time since she'd had a kiss *like this*. Then a thought flicked across her brain as Steph's fingers dug into her waist.

Had she ever had a kiss like this?

If this was a practice, the real thing might just kill her.

How long had they been kissing? She was pretty sure they were past the ten-second timer.

She got her answer a few moments later as Steph swiped her tongue along Erin's bottom lip, kissed her once more, then pulled back.

Erin felt woozy. Drunk on Steph's kisses. Her gaze trailed up to Steph's eyes, then she stood back and cleared her throat. But what was she going to say? What could she say?

That their practice kiss had lit a fire and she never wanted it to end?

That was not professional. But Erin had a feeling that professional had shut for the day. She'd lay bets that was not how practice kissing normally played out.

Had Steph felt it, too? Their insane connection? She couldn't ask. She'd made a commitment to herself. But that was before Steph planted the smacker of all smackers on her. Now she had to go to her parents' party and meet all her family, after a fake kiss that was better than every damn one of her real ones all stacked together.

Steph licked her lips, which really didn't help. Then she cleared her throat again.

Why did Erin feel like a teenager again? Maybe because the girl she had a crush on had just snogged her behind the metaphorical bike sheds, and she wanted to run around the room and scream.

"I think that went okay?" Steph's voice cracked as she spoke, then she raised a single thumb and swept it across Erin's cheek.

Erin blinked rapidly. She had to focus. Had to remember who she was and where she was. That wasn't easy with Steph's brown stare burrowing into her.

She wanted to let it in, and for it to be her and Steph, in this room, forever more.

Erin took a lungful of hot air, then nodded. "A good warm-up for later." But she wasn't allowing herself to think that far ahead, or she might have a meltdown.

Steph dropped her hands from Erin's waist, stared at them, then stepped back.

Erin wanted to grab them and press them to her breasts. She wanted to pin Steph down and lick her shoulders.

But they had a party to go to. They had to pretend to be together. That, at least, would not be hard.

"Let's go face the relatives shall we, girlfriend?" Erin kept her hands by her side.

Steph raised a single styled eyebrow, then held out an arm. "Let's go."

* * *

The fairy lights lit the marquee well, neat rows of magic perfectly hung. At 7.15pm, the space was half full, the bar had a small queue, and the buffet was being prodded by a steady line of guests. The muggy evening meant the doors on both sides of the posh tent were open to the elements.

Erin walked in with her hand wrapped around Steph's, her insides molten from *that* kiss. How was she going to cope if they had to do the same in public? She couldn't worry about that now. The practice kiss—the stage kiss—had gone well. Steph's professional training had shone through. It wasn't going to be hard to fake it.

Was that the only reason, though? What about the look in her eye just before it happened? The delicious, slick tension in the room? Erin couldn't think about that now. She had people to charm, parents to celebrate. She grabbed a glass of champagne from one of the many trays being circulated by the catering staff. When Steph did the same, Erin wrestled her gaze from the way Steph's slim fingers caressed the glass. To their right, Alex and Wendy introduced the triplets to cooing relatives, while simultaneously trying to stop them slapping anyone or pulling over the cake stand. It was a delicate operation.

Mum had outdone herself with the three-tier Genoese sponge cake, topped with lemon icing and intricate flower work. It wouldn't look out of place on a wedding table, which this was, of sorts. Forty years of marriage. Erin had to hand it to her parents for reaching that milestone. It was impressive, especially with everything they'd been through. She'd settle for meeting someone she wanted to marry and having a few good years together. She glanced left at Steph, who gave their entwined fingers a squeeze. Steph looked at her in a way she hadn't done before. Like she cared. Acting or not, it *felt* real. Plus, the imprint of Steph's delectable lips still warmed her own. She wasn't likely to forget them in a hurry. She wanted to run into the main house, set up the projector screen and watch their kiss back, over and over.

"There you are." Aunt Helena grabbed her arm, eyes wide. "I have to say, even though I love that you've met someone, I can't help feeling somewhat abandoned in our spinster club." She made a face. "How are *things*?"

Erin tried to ignore the frown that accompanied that question. As if her aunt was hoping for doom. If she stuck around longer than this weekend, it was coming.

"Early days, but so far, so good." It *was* good. Everything about Steph was beyond good. Apart from the fact Erin had hired her to play a part. She kept forgetting that important fact when it didn't suit her mood. Just as it hadn't over the past half hour with that kiss. The kiss to end all kisses.

She shook herself, then blinked. She had to put it to the back of her mind. Not easy, when the most gorgeous woman in the room was stood beside her.

As if sensing this was the time to interrogate Erin about

her love life, her gran took that moment to rock up and say hi. Her dad's mum was the only grandparent she had left, and she never tired of telling her that. She wasn't a traditional grandma, either. She was what her mum called "stagey". Erin always thought it took one to know one.

"Hello my darling one, is that a girlfriend I see on your arm?" Her gran shook Steph's hand, then pulled Erin in for a hug. She smelled like sandalwood, just like always. Her gran's perfume hadn't moved on since 1983. "She's very pretty, so I approve," her gran whispered. "Haven't I said it's my dying wish to see you settled, just like Alex?"

"You're not dying, Gran."

She reached out an arm. "We're all dying, dear. Make sure this one doesn't slip through your fingers, okay?"

Thanks for the vote of confidence.

"I have to say, though, you're glowing." Gran leaned over and tapped Steph's arm. "Whatever you're doing my dear, keep doing it. It's clearly working wonders for my granddaughter."

Erin closed her eyes and her gran quizzed Steph on her job and her prospects. Erin hoped the buffet opened soon: Gran and Aunt Helena wouldn't hang around when it did. Sure enough, ten minutes later the cling film was off and so were they. One thing was certain, though: Erin's family standing had shot through the roof. It made her grow taller, which was only magnified when Steph slipped her fingers back around hers, then put her lips to Erin's ear. "Was that okay? Did I pass the test?"

"You were perfect."

Steph's breath was hot on her ear. Erin's insides went to jelly.

"One other thing."

Erin lifted her gaze to Steph. A roll of desire unfurled in her body.

"Let me know when you want me to lay a proper kiss on you. Like we practised."

Erin sucked in a breath, fighting the urge to take Steph in her arms and lay one on her right there and then.

"Hello lovebirds, or should I say, talk of the tent?" Alex had Elise hanging off his hip, smearing what looked like soggy biscuit into his suit lapel. He didn't seem to care. He held up his hand, all fingers and thumbs spread apart. "Five relatives — count them, five — have asked me who Steph is, so I think we can say you've got tongues wagging."

Steph put a gentle hand on the base of Erin's spine. "I'll leave you two to gossip about me while I go to the loo." She kissed Erin's cheek, and made her way to the posh Portaloos.

Erin watched her go, sure her cheek was glowing. Oh boy, she'd thought things were changing on the beach that morning. But since that kiss and the way Steph looked tonight, a line had definitely been crossed. A line Erin was currently laying on, an alluring smile on her face.

A few minutes later, Morag and her boyfriend Tim bowled across the marquee towards her. When she reached Erin, she gave her a hug, then looked around.

"This place! Honestly, I forgot how incredible it is. Could it *be* any more perfect? Your family are just next level. This marquee, it's like I'm in an episode of *Monarch of the Glen*. I was just disappointed there was no bagpiper to pipe me in, or is that coming later?" She didn't wait for an answer. "Where's your girlfriend?"

Erin's eyes widened. Morag was the only one in this tent who knew the truth apart from her and Steph. She also had one of the biggest mouths and no tact. She glanced at Alex, then gave Morag a pointed look, trying to communicate she had to be careful.

Morag sent one right back, either telling Erin that she knew, or that she was going cross-eyed. Erin couldn't be sure.

"She's in the loo, should be back soon."

"And how's it going? Has she mortally offended your gran yet?"

"They're the talk of the tent," Alex interjected, just as Elise smacked him in the face. He winced, then introduced himself to Tim, who made a big show of bowing when he was introduced to Elise. Judging by how Erin's niece shrieked, she clearly thought Tim was hilarious.

"What's going on? You look," Morag waved a hand in front of Erin. "I don't know. Part-freaked, part-something else that I can't quite put my finger on." She paused, then narrowed her eyes. She leaned in, putting her lips where Steph's had just been.

Erin wanted to shoo her away, as if her lips being there might erase the impact of Steph's. They didn't, but she much preferred Steph's.

"Has something happened? You don't have to say anything, just give me a yes or a no," Morag whispered.

Erin shot a glance Alex's way, but he was still wrapped up in conversation with Tim.

Erin flashed through her possible answers. If she said yes, Morag wouldn't be able to hold it together. Plus, nothing had really happened, had it? They'd shared some life facts. Practised kissing. Nothing of note. But if she said no, would the lie radiate through her skin for everyone to see, like a lighthouse flashing on a foggy day? Whatever, she had to make a decision soon, otherwise Morag would fill in the blanks for her. It was something she had a tendency to do. Wasn't that how Erin had ended up in this mess in the first place? Although, right now she wasn't considering Steph much of a mess. If that label belonged to anyone, it was Erin.

"Nothing's happened," Erin told Morag with as much authority as she could muster. "But she is… Nicer than I expected. Supportive." She leaned in closer to Morag's ear. "It almost makes it feel like we're a couple, which is a nice change." She hadn't meant to say that much to Morag, but once she realised her friend was the only one who knew the truth, she had to say something.

Morag's eyes lit up at her words. "You really like her."

She did like her. However, she had to try to put a lid on it tonight, which would be easier said than done. Particularly if there was another kiss on the horizon. Erin raised her gaze just as Steph approached. Yes, definitely easier said than done. If anything, she looked even more gorgeous as she sashayed across the room. How had it come to pass that this glorious woman had stepped into her life and given her something else to think about? That was all down to Morag. She should be thankful, but right now, Erin wanted Morag to disappear.

All eyes were on Steph as she drew up next to Erin.

"Talk of the devil." Erin tried to play it cool, but it wasn't made easier by Steph taking her hand and kissing her on the lips.

Morag's eyes went wide.

"You remember Morag," Erin said to Steph, squeezing her best friend's arm to tell her to behave. Their story was Morag and Steph had met for a minute in passing, nothing else. They were going to play the story out whether they needed to or not.

"Of course. It was short but sweet, but everything Erin's told me since has been nothing but perfect." Steph shook Morag's hand.

"In that case, it's definitely all lies," Morag replied.

Erin stared at the two of them as they did the left, right feint of where they lived, where they worked. In another life, if this was real, this would be an important meeting. Everybody knew that girlfriends and best friends had to get on for the relationship to be successful. She had a momentary wave of sadness that it wasn't. But her sour thoughts were soon interrupted by her parents getting up on stage and tapping the microphone. The whole party swivelled their heads to face them.

Her parents looked like the sort of parents you find in a Hollywood movie: smooth skin, tailored clothes, manufactured smiles. They thanked everyone for coming, and her dad took the party on a trip down memory lane, with tales of how they met, their marriage, and then it was time to talk about their children.

"We couldn't be prouder of our kids, Alex and Erin. Alex has gifted us with three beautiful grandchildren and has carried on the family tradition of medicine, while Erin is a successful entrepreneur in the big city of Edinburgh. I would love it if you would raise a glass to them both, because without them, our lives would not have been as complete."

The whole party raised their glasses, and Erin stood rooted to the spot, waiting for the next sentence to drop. For her dad to say something about Nadia. To at least acknowledge her existence. She was her twin sister. Their daughter. But he said nothing. Beside him, her mum gave the whole party her practised, shiny smile. The one she saved especially for public appearances.

Erin threw a look across to Alex.

He was already giving her a 'what the fuck?' stare, as was Wendy.

"Now please, eat, drink and be merry. Enjoy the party!" Her parents waved as the party applauded.

Erin gulped, then had to get some air, some space. The tent was too stifling. It was a metaphor for her whole family life. Next thing, her parents would be getting snapped in the photo booth with some candyfloss, like that was completely normal.

She dropped Steph's hand, then weaved through the crowd, accepting well wishes as she went. She took lungfuls of warm air as she walked down the slope and past the pool, then gave a huge sigh as she got to the hammocks. She closed her eyes and shook her head. Nadia had been their daughter for 17 years. Why did they just airbrush her out of their history? It wasn't like everyone in the tent didn't know, but it had always been this way.

"Are you okay?"

The words made Erin jump to her feet. "Jesus!" When she turned, Steph's concerned stare was on her. "You're so quiet you're like a fucking Prius."

"Sorry, I didn't mean to scare you. It's just, you hotfooted it out of there pretty quickly."

"I'm fine." She wasn't. But that was their stock family response. She gripped the sides of the hammock and slowly lowered herself. She wasn't going to fall tonight. It was imperative she didn't. She had a woman to impress. Plus, the last thing she needed tonight was to face-plant on the concrete.

Steph stayed standing. "I take it this is about your sister. Them not mentioning her."

Erin chewed her bottom lip. She could deny it, but what was the point? It *was* about Nadia. It was always about Nadia.

She nodded. "I just don't get it. She was their daughter for 17 years, yet they want to erase her completely. She should be a part of this celebration. Instead, she's the elephant in the room." Erin snorted. "And honestly, Nadia would hate that remark. She would never want to be an elephant."

Steph smiled. "I think we'd have got on, as I'd say the same."

Erin tried a half-smile. It worked. Even though Steph had never met Nadia, she still said the right thing. Apart from Alex, nobody in her family ever said *anything*. All of which made her think maybe it wasn't that hard to say the right thing. She would just love her parents to say *something*. She threw up her hands, and nearly fell backwards.

"Shit." She grabbed the edge of the hammock and steadied herself. The air licked her face. It was suddenly muggy as hell, as if it might pour down at any minute. She glanced up at the clouds. She hoped she was wrong. But that was the least of her problems.

An image of Nadia running beside the local loch came into her head. It was so vivid, it almost knocked her backwards. Candyfloss flavour filled her mouth. Erin had spent her days reading, while Nadia had always been on the move. Always going places. She'd died going places. It had always seemed apt.

Erin put a hand to her chest, pushed her feet into the ground and swayed. Her beloved, clever, gorgeous twin. Of all people, she deserved to be remembered by her family. Erin shook her head as tears threatened. Fuck, she couldn't lose it now. Not with the party in full swing, everyone expecting her to be there, and her fake date beside her. She took a deep breath and struggled to keep control.

Within seconds, Steph sat beside her looking like a hammock pro. Not even a wobble. Then her arms were tight around Erin.

Steph was *there* for her.

It was still so strange.

Erin froze at the contact, but then melted. She had no idea what this was and why Steph was doing it, but at that second, it was what she needed.

"Your feelings are valid, so don't try to push them down," Steph said. "You need to speak to your parents, and I think you need to do it this weekend." She paused. "Not *right* now, but perhaps tomorrow? Because this needs to be dealt with for everyone's sake. But tonight, we should probably head back inside."

Her words seeped into Erin's brain. Steph was right. They did need to talk about this. She burrowed into Steph's embrace and allowed herself a moment of contentment in the arms of someone else. As if she was living someone else's life. It definitely wasn't her own.

"Imagine if I ran in there now, all guns blazing." She smiled, despite herself.

"You'd get noticed." Steph's words rumbled through her. She wanted to gather them up and hold them close. This special moment. Just for them.

"I never told you about the candyfloss, did I?" Erin began.

"There you are!" Morag said from behind.

At least, it *had* been just for them.

Erin untangled herself from Steph, whose hands steadied her as she scrambled up. Erin fell off the hammock at least three times every summer. It was her speciality trick. She would have laid bets it happened tonight. Not with Steph by her side. Her cheeks burned as she turned to face Morag. She didn't meet her eye. Morag already knew she'd lied to her.

Nothing was going on, and yet, something was.

"We were just coming back in." Erin threw a shy smile Steph's way, then threaded an arm through Morag's and walked towards the tent. "I needed some air after... that speech."

"I thought you might. But I came to get you because the DJ's spinning tunes now, and I've requested Chesney Hawkes, 'The One and Only' especially for you."

Erin grinned. It was good to be with an old friend, someone who knew her. But it was good to be with Steph, too. She felt backed up, heard. With that behind her, she could cope with whatever lay ahead.

Chapter Fourteen

As they walked back into the party, Erin took Steph's hand.

Steph glanced down, then gave Erin a firm nod. "Ready to have a good time?" Whatever happened, they were going to do this together.

"There you are!" Erin's mum pulled up in front of them.

Erin's mouth twitched and she balled the hand that wasn't holding Steph's into a fist.

"Someone said you'd rushed out after the speeches. Everything okay?" Patsy's gaze slipped from Erin, to Steph, then back.

"Yes, just wanted to check it wasn't raining." Erin's face hardly moved as she spoke.

"Someone else wondered the same, but it'll be fine." Patsy's focus had already skipped to the next person she might talk to. "We always have good weather on our anniversary weekend, don't we?" Her smile faltered for a second and something flashed across her perfectly blushed cheeks.

Erin's fingers gripped Steph's that little bit harder. "Mostly." Her voice came out as a whisper.

Steph knew she was thinking about Nadia. She wanted to shake Patsy, but that wouldn't be the done thing.

Patsy reached over, pressed her lips to Erin's cheek, then wafted away to greet another guest dressed in a Germolene-pink sundress.

On stage, the DJ cranked his microphone to life, and announced he was about to play a floor filler to get things underway. "Let's have you on the floor for the *Time Warp* please!"

Morag whooped, clapped her hands and ran off to find Tim.

Erin glanced at Steph. "Fancy a jump to the left?"

Steph grinned. "I thought you'd never ask."

It turned out, Erin could *really* dance. At least she could do the *Time Warp*, and that was a key test in any fledging relationship, fake or not. Her anger and frustration on hold, the energy flowed out of her as she jumped to the left, then stepped to the right like her life depended on it. Perhaps, for those five minutes, it did. Steph recalled her ex, Andrea, hadn't ever danced it before. She hadn't even seen the film, whereas Steph had seen the musical twice and the film too many times to mention. She should have known then that their relationship wouldn't work.

She was far better suited to someone like Erin.

Or perhaps, even, *Erin*.

Despite being miles from home and thrown into a situation that could explode at any minute, when Erin's crystal-blue gaze landed on her, there was nowhere else Steph would rather be. How could things change so much in a few days? She still remembered telling Michael she wasn't sure she could do this. She still wasn't sure it was meant to be this easy. This natural. Now, there were no thoughts about how much longer she had to work this job. Only thoughts about how quickly the time had dashed by. Thoughts that she didn't want tonight to end, because that would lead to tomorrow, and then Monday, when she had to leave. As for that kiss…

When the song ended, they segued into Abba, then Neil Diamond, and then Glenn Campbell. But when Rod Stewart came on, the foursome left the floor. Morag grabbed Steph's hand and hauled her to the bar "to help with drinks". But Steph knew what this was. Michael had warned her. Was this Erin's friend wanting to make sure she was doing right by her? Even though she knew the truth.

"How are things going?" Morag signalled to the bartender while never taking her eyes from Steph.

Quite the skill.

"Erin seems on edge, but you seem to have it covered." Morag tilted her head. "Is she coping being here? Being home often overwhelms her."

"She's doing okay, but I'd say things might come to a head soon. But she's filled me in, so I'm going to be there for her. I *want* to be there for her. She deserves to be happy."

Morag's eyes softened. "She does. She's my best fucking friend, and she does." She gripped Steph's arm. "Whatever you do, support is good. But don't fuck with her. She might seem tough, but she's fragile. Especially when it comes to her family. *Particularly* when it comes to love."

Steph ground her teeth together, then gave Morag a nod. Michael had been right. It was the intentions talk. A flashback of their earlier kiss sizzled in her mind. She knew it would happen again.

"You have my word. Erin's wellbeing is top of my list."

* * *

The rest of the night passed without incident. Steph had been introduced around and passed as Erin's girlfriend. All she had to do was look lovingly at Erin, which wasn't difficult. She still couldn't believe she got paid to be beside her. No wonder Michael had abandoned acting. This job had more twists and turns, and could go off course at any moment. It reminded her of when she first started acting professionally after drama school. The newness of it. The uncertainty of it. When she'd first arrived, she'd been certain she'd stay professional. Not get sucked in. But that was before she met Erin. Before she stared into her eyes. Before Erin opened up. How could she not be invested after that?

"And now, at the happy couple's request, we're going to have some slow dances to finish off the night in style. Here's a set of three, with the song they first danced to at their wedding. Could you welcome back Patsy and Duncan to the floor, and please, once the first verse is done, they'd love you to join them."

Whoops from the crowd, as in the distance, a clap of thunder boomed across the glen.

The tent hushed, then everyone laughed. A couple of staff hastily shut the doors.

"Even nature is welcoming you both," the DJ added.

Erin's parents took to the floor as Frankie Valli's 'Can't Take My Eyes Off Of You' filled the air. They glided and twirled, and the crowd whistled. When the chorus hit, they urged their friends and family to join them. Alex grabbed Wendy. Morag grabbed Tim. Not for the first time today, nerves crept up Steph's spine.

If they danced now, would that lead to more kissing, this time in public? She couldn't worry about that. She had a job to do. Kissing Erin again might be part of it, but right now, dancing with her was an imperative. Her client wanted to feel normal in her family, just like everyone else. Well, everyone else was on the dance floor in pairs. It was time Erin danced among them.

Steph held out a hand. "May I have this dance?" She raised a single eyebrow and gave Erin a bow.

Erin's cheeks turned candyfloss pink as she placed a hand in Steph's. "I'd be delighted."

Their second time on the dance floor was markedly different to the first. That time had been all about letting off steam, flinging limbs. This time was about showing a united front. Making sure everyone knew Erin could be loved. That Erin doubted that made Steph's heart contract. Erin was supremely loveable, and it was about time someone did it. As the interim person until the right one came along, it was Steph's job to show her how it might feel. She was a love fluffer.

First, she took Erin in her arms, her left hand resting lightly on the small of her back. She clasped Erin's right hand in hers, and pressed it against her collarbone.

Erin stiffened in her embrace.

Steph eyed her. "Just relax," she whispered.

Erin gave her a stiff nod.

They moved gently around the floor in this way for a few seconds, settling into each other's rhythms and the curves of the other's body. Everyone here thought they were a couple, that they'd felt each other before. They hadn't. Endorphins flooded Steph's system.

"Thank you for inviting me here. I'm having a good time."

Erin twitched, before raising her head and looking around. "Really? Even in my dysfunctional family with everyone in the tent monitoring our every move? Uncle David is over there, and he's even pointing at us. Subtlety was never his strong point."

"It's because we make such a devastatingly handsome couple," Steph told her with a grin. "Is he the one in the burgundy waistcoat and the handlebar moustache, looks like he rode here on a Penny Farthing?" Steph had spied him earlier. He was hard to miss.

Erin smiled. "How did you know? For Uncle David, it's always 1932. If you think he dresses vintage, you should see his house. But I'm glad you're enjoying yourself." She paused, giving Steph an odd look. "You mean it, though? It's not all just part of the act, something you say to all your fake girlfriends?"

"You're the first, remember? When it comes to this, I'm a virgin. You're popping my fake cherry." Steph winced. "That didn't sound awkward at all, did it?"

To their left, Alex and Wendy floated by, both shooting them sly winks. To their right, Erin's parents beamed.

On the marquee roof, above the swirl of music, she could make out hard splats of rain falling. A whoosh of air opened the marquee flap doors and pushed over a couple of chairs. Some nearby guests zipped the door tight, and they were back inside their cocoon.

Steph held Erin, bodies pressed together, and everything else that had ever happened in her life before melted into the background. This was what Erin had hired her for. This moment above all others, the one to imprint on the party's collective memory. But Steph still wasn't prepared for Erin to snake out a hand and press it to her cheek. "You think we can put our kissing into practice now?" Her words were breathy. "Just to drive it home we're truly together?"

A massive boom of thunder outside caused a huge cheer, and then the rain hammered down on the roof. All around, people peered upwards.

Steph looked around, Erin's request reverberating through her body. "We can do whatever you want." She stroked a thumb down Erin's soft cheek, tracing the ridge of her cheekbone. The knuckle of her hand caressed the underside of her chin. "If we were doing this as a fake kiss, I'd put my thumb across your lips like this." She placed her thumb on Erin's lips. "And then I'd kiss you like this." She bent and kissed her own thumb. Then she removed it, and smiled.

Erin frowned. "I think we should stick to what we practised." She snagged Steph's gaze. "I liked that better."

Steph cleared her throat, and her insides blazed. "Of course." Then she leaned down, placed a delicate kiss on Erin's beauty spot, kissed a path to her lips, and then did what her client asked. More to the point, just what Steph wanted, too.

She closed her eyes and kissed Erin. Kissed her like she meant it. Kissed her like this might be the one and only time it happened, and she was going to make this the best finest kiss Erin ever had. World-beating. Simply the best.

Erin responded by curling a hand around Steph's waist, holding her as if she never wanted to let her go.

That's how it felt to Steph. She might be deluded. But Erin never needed to know.

They spun and kissed. Twirled and kissed. It felt like the world might fall down around them, but this was the snog of a lifetime. Maybe all they'd needed was a stage, after all.

Steph was sure nobody was timing this kiss.

She sank further in, her fingertips sliding up Erin's cheeks and into her jet-black hair. It was so soft. Everything about Erin was soft. She deserved better from everyone in this tent, and Steph was going to make sure she didn't let her down, too. This kiss, this moment, had to be perfect. It felt perfect to her. Her heart told her so.

Moments later, just as Steph was about to notch their smooch up a level, something landed on her. Something wet. She was wet enough already. Damn it, what the fuck was that?

She broke the kiss, and looked up just in time to see a drop of water. Then another. Until suddenly, before Steph could comprehend what was going on, a steady drip of water began to come in. It seemed like the gutter systems Duncan had been so proud of weren't quite working as planned.

Steph shook her head, her mind and body still reeling from that *epic* kiss. What colossally shit timing for the marquee to spring a leak. The way Erin was staring at her like she wanted to eat Steph suggested she felt the same way, too.

But Steph had to take charge. This was part of her job today, right? She moved Erin and everyone nearby away just in time. When Steph turned back, the drip had turned into a steady flow. She had to get something underneath it before it really burst. If she'd guessed right, the whole nearby billowy ceiling might be filled with water and just about to burst.

She eyed Erin. The temptation to use the chaos of the leak to slip away and kiss some more was strong, but it wasn't going to happen.

Steph looked down. Her dress was already splashed. Adrenaline spiked through her. What had she been thinking about this being her most unpredictable job yet? It was just about to take another turn. "Is there a bucket anywhere nearby? Something the water can flow into if it doesn't flow over the edge?"

Erin thought, then nodded, dashing off.

In a flash, Alex appeared, taking off his jacket and rolling up his sleeves. "What can I do to help?"

Steph glanced around. What a difference two minutes could make. She'd far prefer to be still attached to Erin's lips. "Help me put a circle of chairs around where I think the water is. That way, if it bursts, nobody's going to be dancing under it."

Alex nodded and they worked together, pushing the dancers away from the bottom left corner of the tent and sealing it off with chairs. Everyone else was oblivious, still wrapped up in the slow dances. With luck, they could contain this and get it sorted.

Erin arrived back with two bar staff carrying a massive ice bath.

Steph could have kissed her. She already had. She desperately wanted to do it again, but it had to take a back seat for now. "Can you place it near the door where hopefully the water will go when we nudge this bit of the ceiling? We also need something else to put under the drip just in case this backfires."

The two men did as they were told, then rushed back with

a smaller ice bath and placed it under the leak. They gave the ceiling a frown, then scurried away.

Steph glanced at the door. "Is it still raining?"

"I'll check." Alex ran towards the door, unzipped it and peered out. He moved the ice bath, then came back in and shook his head.

Steph walked over to the water. The ceiling was still bowing. With luck, she could nudge it along, and the water would fall into the ice bath by the door.

Without luck, she could nudge it and she'd get soaked. Whichever happened, it still meant a load of guests wouldn't get drenched. It might even endear her to Erin that bit more.

Before she could talk herself out of it, Steph took off her shoes and stood on a chair, hoping her jelly knees would hold her. Had she mentioned the terrible timing of this? Then Alex handed her another chair, which she upended. Alex got up on a chair next to her and did the same. They both used the chairs they were holding to nudge the bowing part of the ceiling. The water shifted, making Steph's heart slow, but in moments it fell into the ice bath by the door. Steph exhaled. The water splashed the tables near the door, but that was all.

Erin clapped.

Alex gave her a thumbs-up and held his chair aloft.

A few dancers looked on, probably thinking Steph and Alex had drunk a bit too much and were dancing on their chairs.

Steph grinned. They'd done it. They'd saved the party and managed not to get soaked. Perhaps now, she could get back to kissing Erin.

She jumped down and stood under where the leak had been. A steady trickle persisted. Was there more? She dragged a chair nearer, got up again, and instructed Alex to give her a chair. The trickle was coming from a small hole in the roof. *Shit.* If she couldn't shift it, the ceiling might tear. She stabbed the white material with the chair leg, but only succeeded in getting the leg stuck. With a ripping noise, the hole expanded and the pocket of water flowed out, hitting her square in the face.

Oh. My. Fucking. God.

She let out a shriek and almost fell off the chair. The water was colder and wetter than she'd anticipated. She spat it out and squeezed her eyes tight shut, as Alex took the chair from her hands. So much for being the stylish hero. Why hadn't she left well alone? It probably wouldn't have got worse. Steph couldn't answer the question. She'd have to settle for being the soggy hero instead.

When she focused back on the room, Erin was at her side. She helped her down and gave her napkins. More party-goers stared. Erin's parents were still oblivious, thankfully.

"You so nearly did that smoothly." Erin stifled a grin.

Steph gave a wan smile. "I know." She dabbed her face and hair, but knew it was a thankless task. Her dress stuck to her body like cling film.

She caught Erin's eyes travelling upwards, and instantly pictured Erin peeling the wet dress from her body. Steph's breathing stilled, and their gazes locked. She gulped, then crossed her arm over her chest just in case her nipples were showing.

Erin cleared her throat, as if resetting. "Thanks for saving the day. If it helps any, you're going to be forever the hero in my family's eyes. Talked about for years to come as 'that girlfriend of yours who saved the party' from going down like the Titanic'." Erin smiled at Steph, then her gaze dropped from Steph's face to her neck, then further down.

The blood rushed to Steph's cheeks. She must look a state. "I'm going to get changed, then come back as if nothing ever happened. Don't go anywhere."

Erin nodded. "I'll be right here."

Chapter Fifteen

It was gone midnight. Erin sat on the side of the pool, her bare feet in the water. Erin had shucked her dress, too, and put on shorts and a T-shirt just like Steph. Unlike Steph, Erin still had full hair and make-up, so she probably looked a little dressed down. But they were in the Scottish Highlands, and she didn't care. She had nobody to impress. Apart from her fake girlfriend, the one causing palpitations in her chest. Steph smelt shower-fresh, and her feet were perfect: long, slim toes, elegant ankles. Those ankles were attached to long, smooth legs too. Legs Erin could well imagine straddled around her neck.

She coughed, then put a hand to her chest. She was still mad at the leak for spoiling their dance floor kiss. Steph had looked stunning in her dress, but even more so when it was stuck to her body. Erin had tried not to stare, but the thought of peeling it off Steph had never been far from her thoughts. She moved her hands under her thighs, palms down on the poolside stonework. Safer for everyone, lest her fingers stray onto one of Steph's inviting thighs. It'd nearly happened a few times tonight. They'd fallen into being tactile with alarming ease. But it all ended on Monday.

She wasn't going to think about that.

Erin rolled her neck, the late-night air surprisingly warm

on her skin, even after the downpour. She'd been determined to make good on her pool promise tonight.

When Erin's eyes caught Steph's, she stilled. This feeling inside was so new, so confusing. It was led by *that* kiss, but also by all the emotion queueing up behind it. Yes, Steph looked good, but this was way more than that. It was about their connection. Steph's kindness. The way they looked at each other. How Erin's breath kept sticking in her throat. But she couldn't bring it up. This wasn't that sort of weekend. Neither was it that sort of relationship.

But Steph was braver. "That leak came at an inopportune time," she said.

Damn, she was going there.

Erin's body shifted that bit closer. She was just about to reply when another body landed next to her.

Dammit, Alex.

"You mind if I join you for a quick one, ladies. Wendy's given me permission."

It was a statement rather than a question. He really did pick his moments.

When he pulled a bottle of Jura from behind his back, along with three plastic tumblers from the party, she forgave him a little bit. When he produced a bag of rainbow candyfloss, too, she grinned wider.

Erin opened the bag, took a handful and sucked. She always forgot it was pure sugar. She winced like she always did. Nadia never had. She could never get enough of funfairs or candyfloss. But mainly, candyfloss. Beside her, Steph tucked in, drawing out strands of spun sugar with her long fingers and licking from the tips slowly.

Steph cast her gaze to Erin as she did.

Erin really wished Alex wasn't here now. Her clit hardened. She ignored it.

"I need to finish my candyfloss story, don't I?"

Steph nodded, her mouth full.

"It was Nadia's favourite. Just like you, she loved candyfloss and funfairs. It's a little weird you share the same sugar kink, but nice." Erin took a breath, remembering her sister's joy every time she got to eat candyfloss. Her face had always lit up. Erin couldn't quite put into words what it meant that she'd found Nadia's candyfloss twin, but it was special. It made her heart surge in her chest, her cheeks pink with pleasure. Like she was pretty sure they were doing now. "The machine is my parents' one concession to her memory."

Steph stopped chewing, eyes wide. "Fuck. I didn't know." She looked down at the candyfloss, guilt written across her face.

Erin shook her head. "How could you? If it helps, I love that you have that in common. You sharing that with my sister is kinda special." Steph being here and loving the same thing kept Nadia's memory alive that little bit more. That meant more than anything.

Steph grimaced, her eyes questioning. "It is?"

Erin nodded, then locked her gaze with Steph's. "More than you know." Steph was her sugar-spun angel, sent to shake up her world.

Alex poured the drinks without asking if they wanted one, then handed them out. He swept a hand through his thick, dark hair. Erin could see from his bloodshot eyes he was a bit drunk. He was still in his suit trousers, but they were rolled up and his feet were bare. His white shirt was untucked, his tie and jacket long since discarded.

"Is now a good time to point out you don't like whisky?" Erin had never seen him drink it in her entire life.

"People change." Alex gave her a *you don't know everything about me* look.

Erin let it slide.

"Good party? A little wetter than you expected?" Alex asked.

Steph smiled. "A little."

"Have you told her?" He nudged Erin, nodding towards Steph.

"About?"

"Nadia. All of it."

Erin nodded.

Alex tipped his head back and surveyed the night sky with a sigh. "I never get bored of summer nights, do you?"

Erin shook her head. "Never."

Alex held up his glass. "Here's to you, Nadia!" He took a slug, then winced. "God, this stuff is awful." He drank the rest. "You know the other thing that's awful? Our parents refusing to acknowledge they have another child."

Erin's insides tightened. She drank some whisky, then squeezed Alex's thigh.

He flinched. "I mean, what does it take? I've got three kids, and if one of them died—"

"—Don't say that."

"But if they did, I wouldn't just pretend they never existed." He sat forward, then shook his head. "I just don't understand it. Wendy thinks we should say something tomorrow. That it needs to happen for everyone's sake."

Wendy always had, but Erin and Alex had never had the courage.

"So does Steph." Erin wasn't sure when Steph's opinion had become important, but somewhere along the line, it had.

That made Alex sit up a little straighter. "Right. We say something tomorrow?" His words had more steel than before. The party speech had been the final straw. "Because I can't do this anymore. They need to deal with the fact that we had a sister, and they had another daughter. She was real and I miss her every single day of my life."

Erin put down her drink and took her brother in her arms. She felt Steph get up.

"You don't have to go." Erin turned to look at her.

"Are you sure?"

Steph looked anything but.

"Positive. I want you to stay."

Alex blew out his cheeks. "Sorry to bring the mood down, ladies. It's just, tonight was a bit much."

Steph settled back in place next to Erin. An unexpected warmth stole through her.

Erin fished a tissue from the pocket of her shorts and blew her nose. "Let's do it tomorrow at breakfast. There's never going to be a right time. We've let them have their party. Tomorrow we confront them." She glanced at her brother. "You in?"

He nodded. "I'm in. It's time to get this family back together. With all their children."

Erin hugged him, and it felt good. It took her back to all the times they'd done it as kids. She missed Nadia's arms around them, too, but she always would. She'd waited too long to fight for her sister's place in the family. It wasn't lost on her that it was a stranger who'd come along and made them take action.

They finished their drinks, then Alex left, giving them a salute. "Until tomorrow. D-Day." He paused. "And sorry if I arrived at an inappropriate time and poured my emotions all over you. But you've got the rest of your lives to stare into each other's eyes like you were on the dance floor, right?" He gave them a whimsical grin. "Young love, before kids come along and ruin your life. I remember it well." He left, leaving his words draped all over them.

Erin waited until her brother was out of earshot before turning to Steph. "Little does he know. We've only got two days left." She hated that thought.

Steph reached out and laid a hand on Erin's thigh.

A frisson skipped down Erin's body, landing right in her core. She clenched her buttocks and tried to think of anything but Steph naked.

All she remembered were Steph's nipples, winking at her through her wet dress.

"We better make the most of those two days, then, hadn't we?"

Steph's gaze connected with her own.

Erin held on to the side of the pool that little bit tighter. If she didn't, she feared she might fall into Steph's liquid stare.

"For what it's worth, you think your family are dysfunctional, and you're right, there are definitely some things they could work on." Steph stroked her thumb across Erin's inner thigh.

She gripped tighter.

"But at least your family are together. You have a good

153

base. They love you, they want to see you, and they welcome your partner into their lives unconditionally. Remember I told you about my ex, Andrea? Her parents were *so* rude when I met them. They refused to acknowledge or even speak to me. Her mum even turned her back when I walked into a room. They put me off meeting parents for life." She nodded towards the marquee, where the staff were still packing up. "Whereas your family have restored that faith."

"I'm glad they've done something right."

Steph's hand was still on her leg. Erin hardly dared to breathe. She didn't want to lose the connection, and yet, it was all she could focus on. She fought to get her thoughts in order. It was an uphill battle. She wanted to kiss Steph's skin, to press herself into her. She wanted to know everything about her. All about her dreams and ambitions. Most of all, though, she wanted to kiss her again. More than anything else she'd ever wanted in her entire life.

"But I'm sorry you've got dragged into the family drama. For some reason I thought I might be able to keep it from you. Which was stupid of me."

"There's definitely been more drama in the past few days than in some of the plays I've been involved in."

Erin laughed. She could feel the warmth underpinning Steph's words.

"But you know what? Nobody could script tonight. You and I practising our kiss. Dancing. Then getting drenched. That's a movie in the making." She squeezed Erin's thigh with her fingertips.

Erin felt it everywhere. Oh god, she was in way over her head, wasn't she?

"Thanks for changing the energy," she whispered.

"I didn't do much."

"You did more than you could ever imagine. You've given me strength and hope. Plus, you've made me feel attractive." Erin paused. Steph had made her brave, too.

"I hate to break it to you, but you *are* attractive. Inside and out."

Erin searched her mind to recall how to breathe. She remembered just in time.

"This started out as a job, but it doesn't feel that way anymore. My friend who runs the agency would kill me, but this doesn't feel fake. It feels real." Steph moved her finger between the two of them. "You looked amazing tonight. That dress was everything; you looked like a movie star." She lifted Erin's fingers and kissed her knuckle.

Stars fizzed in Erin's eyes and a rumble of desire exploded inside her. It wasn't just her. Steph wanted her, too.

She wasn't quite sure what to do with this information.

She stood up and looked over at the house. The lights were off. The guests were gone. They were completely alone. Erin wasn't quite sure what came over her, but she knew exactly what she was going to do next. Something that was so out of character, if she were watching this from afar, she'd have laughed her head off. But this whole weekend was out of character, wasn't it? She'd hired a girlfriend. She was going to confront her parents. But before all of that, she was going to swim naked.

"There's something I've always wanted to do and never have. As this is a weekend of firsts, how about you do it with me?"

Before she could talk herself out of it, Erin pulled her T-shirt over her head. Then she slipped down the straps of her peach-coloured bra, hesitated for a moment, then unclipped it. Far from feeling exposed standing in just her knickers, Erin felt emboldened. Tomorrow she might regret it, but today, she was a refreshing version of herself. One who saw what she wanted and went after it. What she wanted right now was to skinny dip, and for Steph to join her. Erin took a deep breath, then eased her knickers to the floor.

Steph's mouth fell slightly ajar. "Holy shit. I'm guessing we're not using swimsuits."

Erin raised a single eyebrow, gave Steph a brief grin, then jumped into the pool. When she surfaced, Steph still stared. "You coming in?"

Steph hesitated, then scrambled to her feet. She stripped off, turning her back to Erin.

She was shy.

That made Erin feel better.

When she was naked, every hair on Erin's body stood to attention. A desire alarm sounded in her brain. She drank in Steph's sculpted muscles, her smooth skin, her long legs. She took note of the scar on her chest. Her gaze stalled when she reached the middle of Steph, with her perfect dark triangle. Erin's breath hitched.

Then Steph lowered herself into the water and swam over to meet her.

* * *

"I already knew you looked incredible covered in water from earlier." Her mind flashed back to a soaked Steph. To her nipples in that dress. "But I prefer you naked." Erin gave Steph a wide grin. It didn't convey how she was feeling. Nerves jangled all over her body. She'd made the move, and Steph had followed. Now Erin's resolve wobbled just like the water all around them.

"Nadia and I used to skinny dip all the time in the lochs on Skye. I stopped doing it after she died." Erin closed her eyes. She was babbling to fill the space. Why had she brought up Nadia? She might be on her mind, but it wasn't sexy.

Steph moved closer to her. Dusky moonlight danced in her hair. "You haven't done it since?"

Erin shook her head. "No."

"Then I'm glad I'm here with you."

"I am, too." Erin tingled all over. "Even if it did mean taking your clothes off, which wasn't in your contract. I promise I'll give you a good tip."

Their gazes locked.

An undeniable thirst streaked through her. It was thirst for Steph, and nobody else.

"No tip required."

Erin tried not to look down.

"But now we're naked, we have two options. We could float, dry off, and pretend we're not attracted to each other."

Erin's lips quirked up at the edges. This was no time to pretend. "What's the second option?"

"We don't float, don't get dry, and don't pretend."

Steph's bravery was such a turn-on. It was also inspiring.

Erin reached out and pulled Steph to her, then draped her arms around her neck. Their naked bodies touched, and it was almost too much for Erin. It had been so long since she'd been naked with anyone. *Too long.* Why had she denied herself all this time? She knew why. Because she didn't want to get involved with anyone in case they disappeared. The pain of Nadia had been too much. It was always there, flickering away in the background of her life, on standby. But Steph was right in front of her now, offering her a chance to reach for who she truly was.

Would Erin still remember how to do it? She wouldn't know until she tried.

"I vote for option two."

The water rippled its applause as their bodies pressed together.

"We're in agreement." Steph's gaze landed on Erin's lips, and within seconds, she closed the gap between them.

Erin gasped as they connected once more. The intensity of the kiss shouldn't have shocked her, but it did. It reaffirmed what she'd thought earlier.

This wasn't usual. Steph wasn't usual. *They* weren't usual. With usual dates, you built up to a first kiss, to no clothes. But this wasn't a first date. Steph was on a time-limited offer. Love her or lose her. The clock was ticking. Erin chose love.

If Morag could see her now, she'd applaud. Morag had said that Erin needed to let go, to let someone in. And yes, this someone might be fleeting, and after Monday, they might never see each other again, but maybe that was the reason Erin was prepared to open up. Steph might not be her Mrs Right, but she was her Mrs Right Now. And in this moment, that was all that mattered.

Steph's tongue parted her lips, then slid into her mouth.

Erin groaned at the sensation. If this was what her tongue felt like, how were her fingers going to feel elsewhere?

As if reading her mind, Steph slid her hand through the water and cupped Erin between her legs.

Erin had almost forgotten she wasn't wearing anything. She was very aware now. She opened her eyes, her breathing spiked and heavy. Part of her wanted to tease this out, to work up to how Steph might feel inside her. But they'd been teasing each other all night, and they didn't have long. She'd started this by getting naked in the first place. She'd pressed fast-forward on this encounter.

She wasn't even vaguely sorry.

Steph's intense, half-lidded stare met hers, asking questions Erin was desperate to answer. She held Erin's gaze as her fingers skated over Erin's core.

Erin sucked in a jagged breath.

Then Steph leaned in, and as her tongue traced the seam of Erin's lips, she slid a finger inside her.

Erin's mind emptied until there was nothing but blue sky and sunshine.

"What are you doing to me?" she whispered, as her whole body shook. Now the moment had arrived, she wondered why she'd tried to deny it. She'd been attracted to Steph since they met. Now, here they were, lips locked, eyes wide shut, Steph's fingers curling into Erin with exquisite precision.

"I hope I'm doing exactly what you want me to."

Erin crushed her lips to Steph's and kissed her as if this might be the last kiss of her life. Kissed her with a fire she didn't even know existed before now. Then she spread her legs and pressed down on Steph's hand. "Fuck me like you mean it," she whispered in her ear. Then she laid a line of wet kisses along Steph's glorious shoulders. She was lighter than she'd been in years.

In return, Steph kissed her again, then slid another finger inside.

Erin wrapped her legs around Steph's waist, and thrust forward, a cracked groan escaping into the night air. She'd missed this connection with another person. This physical intimacy that brought a whole other level to any relationship. Yes, this was a one-night stand, but it was with someone she'd got to know, someone she trusted. Someone who understood Erin enough to know what this meant.

But she couldn't know the whole truth. Because as Steph began to fuck her, she slowly brought her back to life. Deep inside Erin, a light switched on. One that had been turned off for years. Just like the water Steph had dislodged earlier, she'd achieved the same with Erin's fears. She'd dislodged them, and now Erin had room for other things. Like pleasure. Erin surrendered herself to the moment.

She could do this. Sex didn't have to mean commitment and love — it could just be about Erin learning to trust again. To feel again. If this was all that was, she'd accept it. She couldn't think of anyone in the whole world she'd rather do this with than Steph. If necessary, tonight could be about Erin getting fucked until she cried out and threw her head back, revelling in the moment.

Steph willingly obliged.

As Erin toppled over the edge, she gripped Steph's shoulders and let herself fall. She hadn't fallen in years. Now she did. Because Steph was there to catch her.

They were quiet for a few minutes afterwards, Erin lost in her thoughts, her arms and legs still wrapped around Steph. Eventually, she untangled her legs, then gave Steph a shy grin.

"That was amazing. *Really amazing.*" She kissed her again. Steph would never know just how much it had meant.

Steph squinted, as if trying to work her out. "It was my pleasure. I've never had sex in a swimming pool before. You're the first."

"I'm glad."

Steph eyed her. "Although, I don't think my friend who runs the agency is going to be happy. The first thing he said to me before I came here was not to have sex with you. I told him I wasn't that sort of girl. Clearly, as a fake girlfriend, I am a different woman."

"I like that woman, if it's any consolation."

"I do, too."

"Plus, your boss can't be angry. I don't normally do this either, but tonight after looking at you all night in that dress, I wanted this to happen. I promise to give you a glowing review. He doesn't need to know, does he?"

"He'll know. We've known each other far too long." She shook her head and kissed Erin. "But let's not talk about Michael now." Steph kissed her lips again. "I'd rather talk about how sexy you are, and how I'd like to take this back to the lodge. Somewhere less wet where I can kiss your cleavage properly."

"I'm not sure I'm likely to get less wet." Erin's clit still throbbed. "That's your fault."

"Sorry, not sorry." Steph grinned.

Erin kissed her again, long and slow. When she pulled back, she was still dazed.

They stared at each other, and Erin shivered. She already knew they'd have sex again tonight. Perhaps tomorrow, too. And that when it came to saying goodbye to Steph, she was going to have some trouble doing so. But she couldn't dwell on that. Right now, she had to get out of the pool, take Steph back to the lodge and do unspeakable things to her shoulders, and then to the rest of her delicious body.

Chapter Sixteen

The next morning, Steph woke up disorientated. Also, despite the small number of hours she'd actually had her eyes closed, it was the best she'd slept in ages. They were still in the same position they'd fallen asleep in: Steph on her back, Erin's thigh on top of hers. Erin's arm hooked lightly on her waist. It wasn't the position of a one-night stand, that much Steph knew.

But how much of a cliché was she? She was an actor, for god's sake. She took on roles, played the character, then stepped out of it when the job was over. Only, this time around, the role had seeped into her being. Erin was not only under her skin, she was on top of it, in Steph's pores, in her blood stream. When Steph took a breath, it was Erin she inhaled. That shift had taken place before last night. But now, it was pressed into every part of her body. They'd spent the night exploring each other, and now Steph couldn't fathom walking away from this tomorrow. Why did she have to make her life so complicated?

Maybe Michael would have some wisdom.

She slipped out of the sheets, careful not to wake Erin, who looked so peaceful. Her eyelids twitched as Steph stared at her. Steph hoped she'd given Erin sweet dreams. She deserved them. Because today was going to be difficult for everyone. She grabbed her jeans and green top, then tiptoed out into the lounge, to where the sofa was still just that. No sofabed needed last night. She sat on it with a silent thump and made the call.

"You keep phoning me at really odd times this weekend."

Steph's pulse picked up speed. "I can't talk long," she whispered.

There was a pause before Michael replied. "Okay, odd times and you're whispering. Did something happen?"

Steph nodded. "Yeah." She stared out at the loch. Was it her imagination, or was it smiling at her?

Michael drew in a breath. "I guessed it might from what you said the other night. I take it you slept with her?"

"I'm sorry. I know this is your business and I was trying to be professional. But it was just too much. I know I'm meant to be a fake girlfriend, but this doesn't feel fake. When I'm around her, I have a feeling I can't quite explain." Those words were like a bucket of ice over her head. It had never been fake, had it? She'd found this role easy, because she liked Erin as if she *were* her girlfriend.

"Sometimes, you can try all you like, but you can't help what happens."

Steph waited for more, but it never came. "You're not going to berate me? Tell me I did the wrong thing?" A part of her wanted him to. To tell her she'd never work for him again. That she was a terrible employee. She deserved something.

"I can if you like, but it wouldn't change what happened or how you feel, would it?" He paused. "I told you not to sleep with her, but sometimes, the heart wants what the heart wants."

Her Scottish heart had decided on a Scottish woman. It had flicked through the romance catalogue and settled on its ideal mate.

"What I will say is, you had one job," Michael added, then laughed. "Where are you? Couldn't you go somewhere where you didn't have to whisper?"

"I'm in the lounge, I didn't want to sneak out after we had sex. I just wondered if you had any words of advice on how to handle this? I've still got a big day ahead of me."

"Just keep going. You've got so into the part—perhaps a little too much with the method acting—but whatever happens, you have to see the job through, okay?" He paused. "Still on for being picked up at lunchtime tomorrow?"

Steph nodded. "Yes. Although I'll be sad to leave."

"Emotions are heightened right now. You're all sexed up, and you want more. But don't do anything hasty. See this job through, then see how you feel this week, okay?"

* * *

Steph stripped off her clothes, then slid her tongue across her freshly brushed, minty teeth as she crept back into Erin's bed. She had enough to deal with today without having morning breath.

Erin rolled over and into her. Her beauty spot winked up at Steph.

Without thinking, she leaned down and kissed it.

Damn.

So much for playing it cool.

A smile worked its way onto Erin's face before she eased open her eyelids.

"I could get used to being kissed awake." Sleep stained her voice.

Steph gave her a grin, even as her brain went into overdrive. Was it just a figure of speech, or did Erin really want that?

Then she told herself to shut up. It was what you said the morning after. Steph had said it plenty of times. Some she'd meant, some she hadn't.

"But I know you crept out a while ago." Erin opened her eyes fully.

Steph tried not to fall straight in.

"Were you thinking of running away? Only, you wouldn't get far without a car."

Steph laughed, then shook her head. "Not running away. That would be very rude, considering how much bodily fluid we shared last night."

Erin let out a shockwave of laughter. "You have a way with words. If acting doesn't work out, you should consider being a poet."

Steph grinned, then burrowed her head into the pillow. There was a lot for Erin's family to do today. A lot to process. But right now, Steph had five minutes to stare at Erin. To replay last night with a goofy grin on her face.

Erin rolled onto her side, and her gaze dropped to Steph's chest. She reached out a finger and traced a path from Steph's mouth to the top of her neck. She stopped exactly where Steph knew she would.

"What's this scar from?" Erin's gaze flicked up to meet Steph's. Erin had asked briefly last night, but Steph had managed to deflect her with more pressing matters. She'd already vowed she wasn't going to get into the other reason she wanted to come to Scotland. She was determined to stick to one of her plans this weekend. Steph had crumpled spectacularly on the no-sex part.

"You know I told Wendy that first night that I had a health issue when I was a kid? I had a heart condition and had an operation to fix it, and that's the scar."

Erin frowned. "Does it hurt?"

Steph shook her head.

"Does the scar bother you?"

"At first, maybe." When she was 17, a long scar down the front of her body had seemed like the end of the world. She'd wondered how anybody would ever find her attractive again. But that had soon faded, along with the scar. "But now it's part of me, it's *my* scar. It's been there for two decades of my life. Without it, I might have died. So no, it doesn't bother me."

"Can I touch it?"

Erin's finger hadn't moved.

A glow had formed underneath it. Steph's heart thumped in her chest. "Of course. It's part of me, and you touched most of that last night." But she still held her breath as Erin's fingertip moved over the ridge of her scar. Steph tried not to shudder but failed. Most of her ex-lovers had asked about the scar, but not many had touched it with such tenderness and care. She was sure that nobody had done so after just one night together. But Erin wasn't like the others. Steph already knew that. Which is what was giving her so many issues right now.

"I've never met a woman with a scar down her chest before. It's kinda cool. Like you're a warrior who survived."

A smile hooked onto Steph's face. "My mum used to call me her little warrior."

Erin met her gaze. "She was right. It was clearly a big operation, and you're still here, fighting the good fight." She moved towards Steph and kissed her on the lips.

Steph saw stars.

"Talking the good talk." Another kiss.

Steph's lips tingled.

"Sleeping with hot women." Erin flexed a single eyebrow, then pressed her lips to Steph's once more, this time with purpose.

Steph was immediately transported back to last night. Back to Erin sliding into her, holding her gaze, taking her to the edge and never letting up. She surrendered to the feeling and let herself drop. She didn't want to hold back this morning. She didn't want to give the wrong impression. Because Erin had made a lasting one on her. Her lips tasted like a standing ovation on opening night. A Brighton sunrise. A flat with an en-suite and a dressing room. They tasted like Steph's version of perfection.

When they pulled back, Steph was breathless.

Erin said nothing, just stared.

The air around them was thick with their unsaid thoughts.

She took a deep breath and tried to ignore Erin's hand on her naked thigh, her skin hot under its touch. She didn't want to start what they couldn't finish. Alex was arriving to pick Erin up in just over an hour. She needed to get her head in the game. For now, Steph was still on the clock and she had to act accordingly. Professionally.

Even if all she wanted to do was lock the lodge's front door and fuck Erin all day long.

"Big morning today. Shall I make you a cuppa before Alex gets here?"

Erin's face paled, then she nodded. "I've been trying not to think about it, but yes, that would be lovely." She smiled. "Sexy *and* caring. You're the best fake girlfriend ever."

Chapter Seventeen

Erin approached the main house. She could hear the clang of the marquee poles coming down on the other side, the shouts of the staff doing the job. The party was over, and now it was back to real life. She glanced at her brother. He looked tired, but that was his and Wendy's permanent state. Last night's whisky probably hadn't helped either. Erin was pleased she hadn't overdone it on the booze. A hangover was the last thing she needed today. She looked tired, too, but at least the excuse was worth it. She sucked in a breath and pushed those thoughts aside. Now was not the time.

"Ready?"

Alex ran a hand over his dark stubble. "No." But he pushed open the door anyway.

Their mum was already at the big wooden table, the Sunday papers laid out on one end, the breakfast table set up with fruits, cereals, juice, yoghurt. It looked for all the world like a normal Sunday. It was anything but. Erin swallowed down something that tasted like fear, then pulled her shoulders back. She didn't want to think about this morning like going into war, but she could be forgiven for thinking it was.

"Good morning you two!" Their mum looked up, then

walked over. She gave them both a kiss, then ushered them to the table. "No Steph, Wendy, or the kids?"

"Not this morning, Mum," Erin said. "We've got something we want to talk to you about. Is Dad here, too?"

"He's just bringing fresh tea." She frowned. "You both look very serious." She put a hand to her chest and gulped. "Is everything okay? Is one of you sick?"

Both Erin and Alex shook their heads.

"We're fine." Erin flicked her head towards the table. "Can we just sit?" Their dad came out of the kitchen carrying a tea pot, milk, and mugs on a tray. "All of us."

Their parents sat on one side of the rectangular wooden table, Erin and Alex along the end. Erin went to speak but her throat dried up. She'd practised a million speeches in her head, but now the time was here, her mind was blank. She glanced at Alex and hoped he understood he needed to get the ball rolling. Luckily, he did.

"Mum, Dad, we want you to know that we both love you very much, and we know you love us, too. But after last night, we can't carry on in this family the way we have been."

Dad blinked, then sat up straight. "Can't carry on? What the hell are you talking about?"

Erin cleared her throat. "It's more what we're not talking about." She paused for maximum impact. "We need to talk about Nadia."

It had the desired effect. Her parents immediately looked at the floor, then slowly back up and at each other.

Outside the massive windows, three men in hard hats walked by carrying the marquee's metal frame. They waved to them.

Ever polite, all four waved back.

Erin forged on. "Last night, you said thank you to both of us, but you didn't mention Nadia." She waved a hand and swept her gaze around the room. "Look around this house. All the photos of our family are from after the time Nadia died. You've airbrushed her out of your lives, but also out of ours. We don't want that, either of us."

"She's still a part of this family even if she's not here." Alex ran his hands slowly through his hair. He looked like he wanted to tear it out.

Their parents simply stared.

"She wasn't just your child. She was our sister. Can you understand that? Bringing her up is a *good* thing." Alex shook as he spoke. "We already buried her once, and that was the worst day of my life. I don't want to carry on burying her over and over. I want to remember her and celebrate her. Because she was worth celebrating. She was a fabulous sister and daughter, and she deserves more. We all deserve more."

He reached out, gripped Erin's hand under the table and squeezed it tight. His eyes were bloodshot and he was barely holding it together. Was the heavy lifting going to fall to her? She gulped down more air as it all seemed to have left her body. She'd done so well up to this point. But now, with her parents still saying nothing, she wasn't sure where to go.

She pictured Steph's concerned face this morning over tea, telling her to be strong whatever happened. She needed to invoke that spirit now.

"Say something, please." Erin wasn't sure what she'd expected them to do, but to have no reaction was weird. She glanced at Alex. He raised both his eyebrows, then turned back to their parents.

The silence overwhelmed her. It was so markedly different to last night, when the whole place had been full of laughter and love. That hadn't gone away. But this needed to be said.

"I don't know what you want us to say." Her dad almost choked on his words.

"For god's sake, Dad. Tell us you feel something. We never speak about her! It's not normal." Alex took a breath then balled both his fists. His face turned red. "If one of my children died, I wouldn't act like they'd never lived."

"We don't act like that!" Mum hissed. She twisted one of the pearls on her necklace.

"You do!" Erin hadn't meant to shout, but she couldn't put up with lies.

More staff walked by with more metal frame. More waving. More waving back.

It almost made Erin laugh. Almost.

"We had a candyfloss machine at the party last night. That was for Nadia." Her mum almost pouted when she spoke.

"Fantastic. What do you want, a fucking medal?" Alex spat the words. "Does anybody else know the reason why you have it? Did you tell anyone? You think you can just get a candyfloss machine every party and that's it, your job's done?"

Erin rubbed his back and stepped back in. "I know it's not from a place of malice. I know you're hurting. But you have to deal with it. You're both doctors. You know how to heal physical pain. But you've never dealt with your emotions."

"What happened when you had a patient who bereaved?" Alex added. "I'm sure you did. When they come to me, I offer counselling services, I'm kind and understanding.

What did you do? Advise them to never speak about it again, to act as if the dead person never existed?"

At those words, their mum drew a deep breath, then got up and walked over to the window. She stared out at the loch and hugged herself.

Erin, Alex, and their dad watched her, for the want of something to focus on. Eventually, she turned.

"We're not perfect." Her arms were crossed over the top of her lemon-yellow jumper. "I'm sorry we're not perfect parents."

Erin shook her head. "I'm not asking you to be, and neither is Alex. None of us are perfect. Hell, I haven't had a relationship since Nadia died because I've been scared of getting too close to someone and them dying on me." Saying those words to her parents wasn't the norm. She felt like she'd been sliced open. They didn't talk about Nadia; indeed they didn't talk much about anything at all. Admitting that was like admitting a failing. An open mental wound. One that no amount of plasters would fix.

Her mum drew in a sharp breath. "But you've got Steph now."

Her mum's throwaway line was like a brick to her skull.

Erin was so dazed she almost fell sideways. She didn't have Steph. Steph was a charade. A gorgeous, sexy charade, but a charade nonetheless.

She shook her head. "That's early days. But the point is, I find it hard to have a relationship with anybody, but especially with you. Alex finds it hard, too. Can't you see that?"

"We did what we thought was best at the time. Getting away. Starting again." Dad's words were quiet, but firm.

At the window, her mum wrung her hands together.

"You always were more sensitive. But I think you have to get on with things. You can't let one little event define your life."

Alex stood up abruptly. His chair scraped along the floor sharply with a high-pitched squeal.

The noise made her dad jump.

"She wasn't a *little* event, Mum. She was your daughter and our sister. Her dying blew up our lives. All we're asking is for you to remember her and allow us to remember her." He took a deep breath and turned to their dad. "You should have mentioned her in your speech last night." He sat, then put his hand over his eyes and began to sob.

Erin sat very still. She'd known this would be hard, but this was so much worse than she'd imagined. She wanted to fling her chair back, too, and run out of the house. Bury it all again. But they needed to feel this. To be confronted. It was the only way to move forward. When she looked over at her dad, he was crying, too. She'd never seen him cry in her whole life. Not even at Nadia's funeral. She wasn't quite sure what to do. She pressed her hands down on her thighs, then glanced out the window at the perfect setting.

Then she ran her gaze over her not-so-perfect family. But no family was perfect, was it? Steph had told her that. She didn't have any siblings and only one parent. Families came in all shapes and sizes. Erin didn't want a perfect family. She wanted an honest one.

Her mum walked over and sat next to her dad. She reached out and held his hand.

He didn't look up.

"I know you did the best you could. I know it was hard. But we want you to put the photos up." Erin held her mum's gaze.

"To talk about her. We think you could both benefit from some therapy. We'll come too if it helps. We want us to be closer as a family. We can't do that without Nadia in it, too."

Alex rubbed his palms up and down his face, then got up and blew his nose. "I back everything that Erin just said. I want the girls to know about their Auntie Nadia. I wish they could have met her, but this is the best we can do. I want to give my daughters the real version of her. Make her as alive as we possibly can."

Their mum looked at them, then bowed her head before she spoke.

"We lost one child, and we've failed the ones we've got left."

Erin sighed. "You've got to stop being so passive aggressive, Mum. It's not helpful. You haven't failed us; we've always felt loved. But you failed Nadia. We all have. But we can put it right, starting today." She took a deep breath. "We want to drive to Skye this afternoon. Scatter Nadia's ashes where she was happiest, at her favourite spot. The nature reserve and loch. She's been cooped up in that pink pot for too long. She doesn't need to be here anymore. She'll always be in our hearts."

Erin's heart couldn't possibly beat any harder. She was surprised the ground wasn't shaking under her feet. She'd got the words out. She'd practised it earlier with Steph, and it had worked. Having someone by her side had really made the difference this weekend. She'd always be thankful to her.

Was she really going tomorrow?

Erin shook her head. She couldn't think about that now.

Dad looked up and wiped his eyes as he spoke. "You want to go today?" He looked older all of a sudden. More frail. But Erin was sure doing this would take a weight off his shoulders.

Alex nodded. "As good a time as any. We're all here as a family, and the sooner we start acknowledging Nadia was part of it, the better."

Their mum raised her head, then took a deep breath. "We can do it today if you want. It seems apt on the anniversary." She took their dad's hand in hers. "We want to try. But this isn't easy for us."

"It's not easy for any of us." Erin wanted to be clear.

Dad took another deep breath. "Will it just be us four, or will Steph, Wendy and the girls come, too?"

"All of us." Alex's tone was firm. "We're all part of this family, Steph included. I get a good feeling about her. One that says she might stick around."

Erin's heart hit the floor. Her family had such faith in her relationship. She'd have that conversation another time. Instead, she smiled like it might be true. She packed away all her real feelings and slapped on the fake ones.

"Is that a deal? We'll take Nadia back to Skye, and say a final farewell?"

It took a few seconds, but eventually both her parents nodded. "We will."

Chapter Eighteen

Steph was fresh out of the shower and still in her dressing gown on the sofa when Erin got back from the morning showdown. She put her phone on the wooden side table and studied Erin's face, but couldn't read her expression. The late morning sun poured into the room, the light catching on the log burner's stainless-steel flue.

Erin didn't say anything. She simply walked in, sat next to Steph, then put her head on her shoulder.

Despite Steph's promise to Michael earlier to keep things professional, she put her lips to Erin's hair and kissed her. In the circumstances, it was the only human thing to do. Erin needed consoling, and that was part of the job.

They sat like that for a few moments before Steph spoke. "How did it go?"

Erin sighed, then moved slightly away. Eventually, she met Steph's stare.

"It was awful, but it's done. I don't think it was how they expected their Sunday morning to go." She stroked her hands through her cropped hair.

"Do you feel lighter?"

Erin frowned. "I think I will. Right now, it's still a bit too raw. But at least getting it out there was a good thing.

We asked them to put the photos back up, and to start acknowledging her. It's a lot for them to take in, I know that. But we're starting today by driving to Skye to scatter her ashes."

"Wow. Big stuff." Steph chewed on the stew of feelings inside. They were so close, their gazes so intense, Steph looked away in case she said something she couldn't take back.

"And you're a big part of it." Erin's gaze dropped to the exposed skin below Steph's neck, then back up to her lips.

The hairs on Steph's arms stood up at the appraisal. Erin's scrutiny was something she could well get used to.

She wanted it to happen again and again.

Keep it professional, Steph.

"But tell me something to take my mind off it for a bit. I need to not obsess over the next couple of hours before we go." Erin paused. "You being naked under that dressing gown is one way to distract me."

Steph pulled the dressing gown tighter, then leaned over and pressed her lips to Erin's. A flush of desire sailed through her. Erin's effect on her was still far too fresh in her system. She pulled back, glanced at Erin's fingers, then her lips. She was well aware of what they'd done to her. What she'd like them to do again. Steph licked her lips, then gave Erin a grin.

"Okay, things to take your mind off it. I called my boss earlier and confessed we had sex."

Erin's gaze raked her face. She raised an eyebrow. "Did he tell you off?"

"I expected him to, but he didn't. Which was weird." Steph was still pondering why. "He should have. But when I'm with you, this feels too real. Not like a job. Completely unprofessional." She gulped. *Shit.* She hadn't meant to pour out her heart.

Erin's face froze.

Had she said too much? Did Erin not feel the same? Maybe she didn't, and Steph had got this all wrong. It wouldn't be the first time. She waited for a response for what seemed like an eternity.

Then Erin smiled.

Relief seeped from every one of Steph's pores.

"I keep having to remind myself this isn't real too. Because it feels like it is." Erin pressed her hands over the top of her chest. "It feels real in here. I know we've only known each other five days, but it feels like way longer. Mainly because we've been in each other's pockets ever since we met."

"We've squeezed three months of dates into five days." It wasn't such an exaggeration.

Erin's face creased with a smile.

Steph could watch her smile for hours. It was like a hundred fresh sunrises baked together. It was like answering the door in your dressing gown on a Saturday morning to find a surprise package. The one that made your heart skip a beat.

"We have. We've shared so much. You've seen into the very heart of my family which I wouldn't wish on my worst enemy." Erin pressed her cheek into Steph's shoulder.

"Nobody's family's perfect, and yours has a lot to offer. You just need to sort this crucial part, and then things will fall into place. In your family and in your life. You might even find yourself in a relationship." Steph's words thumped in her brain. Was it going to be a relationship with her? No matter what she thought she might want right now, that was too far-fetched. Their lives weren't in the same places, literally and metaphorically. No matter how much she'd like them to be.

Erin stared at Steph for a long moment. "I know this is a job for you. But I can't let you walk away without saying something." She exhaled. "Meeting you, it's like this was meant to be. I've got a feeling here." She pressed her palm to her chest. "Do you have it, too?"

"A hundred times over." That wasn't even an exaggeration. Steph had woken up with a handful of women in her lifetime. She'd never woken up with a heartbeat like this. A *feeling* like this. Like Erin could be the woman.

Like Erin could be The One.

Her chest heaved. That was ridiculous. She didn't believe in The One.

Did she?

"You could have been anyone turning up to be my fake girlfriend. We could have been really different people. But we're not."

Steph shook her head. "No, we're not." She could hardly breathe waiting for the next words to fall from Erin's lips.

"Plus, my family have fallen for you, hook, line and sinker. Alex told Mum and Dad you were coming to scatter the ashes too as you're part of the family." Erin screwed up her face. "It feels dishonest, but I can't tell them otherwise. There's too much else going on today."

Steph picked up Erin's hand in hers. "If you don't want me to come, I don't have to. I can be sick, excuse myself. I know coming with you might be overstepping the mark."

Erin shook her head. "That's the thing, though. It doesn't feel like that. I want you there. I feel supported with you there.

It's been nice having you in my corner." She paused. "Even if I'm paying you."

Steph's stomach lurched. "I hate that you're paying me."

"A deal's a deal." Erin pursed her lips. "You're getting paid, like it or not."

Steph sighed. "Okay, but let me be there for you today. This isn't about me doing a good job. This is about me meeting someone, then spending an incredible five days with them, and having an amazing time last night." Steph's breath was laboured.

Don't say it. Don't say it.

"I know I shouldn't say this, but I don't want to walk away from this. I'm not sure I can."

Fuck. You couldn't just hold it together for another day?

"You don't?" Erin's eyes were shiny.

Steph's brain buzzed with the weight of her words. She shook her head, then carved out a smile. "And don't ask me how it can work, because I've no idea. I'm playing Chlamydia in a sexual health tour for the next two months, which is fucking hilarious when I think about it." She gave an ironic laugh. "But the thought of walking away and never seeing you again after tomorrow feels… impossible."

"For me, too." Erin picked up Steph's hand and kissed it.

Steph's focus faltered. She stared at her hand. Then at Erin's lips. This thing between them was like a trance. Her hands brushed up to Erin's shoulders, the dip of her throat, the bottom of her jaw. When she finally looked up, Erin's gaze was soft and steady. Then Steph did the only thing she could do. She leaned forward, her breath heavy, and kissed Erin with everything she had.

When she came up for air, she stared into her eyes. Did they hold the key to everything she wanted? Steph didn't know the answer for sure, but she was prepared to gamble.

"I can't let you go. But I can't work out a way to stay, either."

Erin sat up, kissed Steph again, then pulled back a fraction.

Her lips were still tantalisingly close. Too close for comfort. Close enough to make Steph's body rage with want. She ground her teeth together to stop from shaking.

"Sorry, I shouldn't have dropped this on you now. You've got so much else to deal with today." She squeezed the top of her nose with her thumb and forefinger. "I promised Michael I'd get through today without opening my big mouth. Without collapsing. I failed."

Erin shook her head, her gaze warm on Steph's skin. "You're not collapsing. You're being honest. It's good to know you feel the same. But we might have to come back to it later." She leaned in, never taking her eyes from Steph. "I like sitting down because we're the same height. It means I can kiss you without being on tiptoes."

"You have the power. You can do whatever you want."

Erin's eyes widened. Before Steph could stop her, Erin climbed onto her lap, straddled her, then leaned her head so their noses touched. "We've got just under two hours before we need to leave. I need to have a shower, but we've got time to take my mind off things. To relax. You want that, right?"

She'd promised Michael she'd do a good job. See it through. She wasn't going to renege. "It's my number one priority."

"Good." Erin leaned back, ran a hand down Steph's exposed

chest, then slowly pulled the string on Steph's white towelling gown. She nudged it open on both sides.

Steph's head spun as Erin's gaze locked on hers. She went to move, but Erin shook her head, then put her fingertips on Steph's stomach.

"I don't want you to move. I want you to stay still." She licked her lips. "Just close your eyes and think of England." Her pupils darkened. "Let Scotland do the work."

Erin wrapped her fingers around Steph's wrist and her racing pulse, then slid off her lap and sank to her knees.

Steph's body rattled once more as her mind reclined to a lounging position. Erin had an intense look on her face, a certainty of what was about to happen. Shafts of sunlight played in her hair and cheeks as she moved downwards. Steph couldn't take her eyes from Erin. Her skin shone bright. Her tongue skated along her top lip. Erin settled between Steph's knees, and pushed her legs apart gently.

Steph punched the back of her head into the sofa, every muscle in her tense. She shook as Erin glanced up, the look on her face so tender, it almost undid Steph before anything had even happened. Without words, it told Steph she was safe. She was about to be loved. That Erin had her. That this was only the start of their journey.

"No moving. You have to do as I say. I'm the boss, remember?"

Steph closed her eyes and nodded. What was Erin trying to do to her? She was making herself unforgettable. A memory Steph would never want to shake. A showreel that would play over and over long after their agreement was done. Steph already couldn't remember a time in her life more thrilling than this moment. With Erin on her knees, Steph's legs spread, pressure pushing her knees apart. Still air smoothing itself into her pores. A time stamp on her heart.

But then that moment was left behind, replaced by something even more thrilling. Erin's hot breath began to whisper into her very core.

"I was thinking about doing this to you in the shower the day we got here."

Steph opened her eyes. The world had changed shape, but it felt like this was how it was meant to be. It was Erin-shaped. It was perfection.

"You were?" Hot damn, could you die of anticipation? It felt like it might happen any moment now.

Erin ran her tongue over her bottom lip. "Uh-huh." She pushed Steph's legs a fraction more apart. "I didn't tell you. I thought I'd wait to show you."

Everything glowed. The world grew hotter. Shades of red swept across Steph's eyeline. Outside, she heard the sound of children screaming.

"If any of my nieces knock on the door now, I swear I'll scream." Erin grinned deliciously.

Steph trembled, then pulsed some more. "The door's locked. The blinds are set to privacy. Do your worst."

Erin took her at her word, and swept her hot tongue up and through Steph's slick core.

A thousand different images blazed through Steph's mind in quick succession. Erin smiling at the beach. Kissing her in the marquee. Erin driving, knuckles white. Now, Erin was in total charge. She was Steph's desire croupier. She slid her lips, rolled her tongue, shuffled her fingers until Steph had no idea which way was up, and which was down. Did the world have sides anymore? Steph didn't think so. Erin had shaved the edges, softened the lens. The world was now malleable and hazy. Steph could roll around here for days, with Erin calling the shots.

Erin's hands clamped down on Steph's quads. Her hair tickled the soft skin of Steph's inner thighs. Steph never felt so vulnerable, yet so sure this was what she wanted and where she wanted to be. Others had knelt before her, but she'd never welcomed any of them in like she had Erin. Erin had the magical touch, the sure shimmer, the unmistakable X factor. Why hadn't any of Steph's past relationships worked out? Because nobody had got her so swiftly, so wholly.

Erin did. She knew what Steph wanted before Steph did. Now that Erin had taken over Steph's body and mind, all Steph could do was come along for the ride. All she had to do was give in. Surrender to Erin's surety of touch. So she did.

Erin swooped and circled Steph as if she were made just for her.

Steph's insides swayed. Heightened ripples of pleasure skidded through her. Pin pricks of glee broke out all over her body. She wanted to stand up, to yell out, to punch the air. But she couldn't. Because every atom of her being was consumed keeping up with Erin as she slowly but surely brought Steph to the edge of glory. Her fingers thrust. Her tongue pirouetted. Her breath fogged Steph's brain.

Everything went fuzzy. Erin's tongue pressed and her fingers lodged right where Steph wanted them. Right where she could take no more. As her mind buckled like a train track in a Californian heatwave, Steph cracked an agonised grin and a tsunami of pleasure short-circuited her soul. She gripped the sides of her long-forgotten dressing gown to steady herself as she fell. It was a long way down. Steph's muscles creaked, her nerves shook, her mind stretched for days. Then she let out an almighty guttural groan as the rat-a-tat of her mind-bending orgasm flowed through her like a raging river, one that left Steph completely spent.

But Erin didn't let up. She let the river flow, let Steph wriggle and groan. But she stayed where she was. Then, when Steph opened an eye, Erin's mouth was back on her, casting spells, creating futures. Her tongue did that crazy manoeuvre once more, the one that caused Steph to buck her hips and smack Erin in the nose with her pubic bone.

"Oof!" Erin paused momentarily, but the river didn't.

Steph gazed down and mouthed a silent "sorry".

Erin shook her head, winked, then picked up where she left off.

Steph slammed her head back, and prepared for the white-water rapids. Whatever happened, she was going to get wetter. She raised her hips as Erin turned the screw.

Steph tightened, turned, held on, and then she succumbed, hanging on for dear life as the second wave crashed over her, then the third. She'd never felt so turned on in her life, so in the moment. A kaleidoscope of colour danced on the inside of her eyelids, and she tried not to get overwhelmed. It was almost impossible.

Erin had undone her completely.

Moments later, Steph opened her eyes. Her hands were buried in Erin's short hair. She freed them and stroked Erin's cheek, then exhaled.

Steph tugged her up, then kissed her lips. They were still warm. She wasn't sure how she was going to compose herself for the rest of the day. But she'd acted before, and she could do it again. She hadn't acted one bit for the past 24 hours. This was as real as it got.

From the size of Erin's pupils, it was pretty real for her, too.

"I'm not quite sure what to say after that. Only that I hope I managed to take your mind off things?" Steph said.

Erin laid a light kiss on her lips.

Steph's whole body lit up again.

"Very much so," Erin replied. "You were the perfect foil."

"Then I'm glad to be of service." Steph kissed her lips. How were they going to do this? How were they going to make this work? She didn't have a clue, but it was now her number one priority. She and Erin had started something big, and Steph didn't want it to finish. It would be a crime if they didn't continue. Every bone in her body agreed. But she had to put it on the backburner until this job was over.

She refocused. This was work.

She'd never enjoyed her job so much in her life.

"You should get ready. Have a shower so you don't smell of sex."

Erin's smile was loose. "Can I tempt you in with me?"

Steph shook her head. "We're on a time limit. Later, I promise."

"I'll hold you to that."

Chapter Nineteen

Erin sucked on her top lip and stared out of the car window. The scenery was just as breathtaking as always, but whenever she drove onto Skye, she always tensed up. This was where Nadia died, so it made sense. But it was also where they lived happily for so long. Where they grew up. They had to make their peace with it as a family.

Nobody spoke much on the way. Alex had volunteered to drive, and her mum was in the passenger seat. Erin took the middle seat in the back, with her dad on one side, and Steph on the other. After some discussion, Wendy had decided to stay home with the kids, as she thought the drive would be too much for them. So they'd left Wendy by the pool with some friends to help, and it was just the five of them.

When they approached the turn-off where Nadia had died, Erin reached out and held her dad's hand, and he squeezed right back. That felt like a breakthrough. After years of silence, they were finally communicating. Yes, today was going to be hard, but it was necessary. In the front, her mum clutched Nadia's ashes in her lap. She hadn't said a word the whole journey.

Eventually, they pulled up at Nadia's favourite nature reserve and loch. Alex eased the Range Rover into the car park, then killed the engine. He turned, and gave them a nod. "Ready?" It was a rhetorical question.

Erin got out, and the wind whipped around her. She'd worn shorts as she'd been hot after the morning's activities. Also, the lodge had been sun-drenched. Her hair had been hot to the touch as she made Steph come once, twice, three times. She gulped at the thought. Sex to take her mind off things had been brilliant, and Steph was the ultimate. But now, Erin had to focus on the present. On one of the most difficult days the family had endured since Nadia's death. She wished she'd had the foresight to pack trousers. To wear a jumper. She shook her head. With what was about to happen, cold knees and bare arms were the least of her worries.

"Shall we walk over to the edge of the loch?"

Nods all around.

Steph walked up beside her and took her hand. That almost broke Erin. How she'd craved this over the years. It wasn't fake, either. Yes, they'd only known each other for a crazy-short amount of time, but the intention and intensity were solid, carved in stone. When would Erin ever introduce someone to her family so quickly? Never. When would she invite them to scatter her dead sister's ashes? Again, never. What she and Steph had shared was special, even without the sex. But when you added that into the mix, what they had couldn't be ignored. Erin had known it when they first kissed. She'd known it with Steph inside her. But more than anything, she knew it right now. If anything, this moment was the most intimate they'd had so far. She'd let Steph into her life and her body. Now Erin was opening herself up whole. She glanced at Steph's gorgeous face, drank in her encouraging smile, and squeezed her hand tight.

Steph had her back. They'd talked about a possible future. That was more than enough for now.

When they got close to the water, Erin slowed, then turned to her family. Every muscle in her body tensed, but in the back of her mind, there was a lightness on the horizon. There was only one way to get there. She took a deep breath. "Thanks for coming today, Mum, Dad."

Her mum still clutched the pink china pot that held Nadia's ashes.

"We've wanted to do this for ages, but it would have been pointless without you. Thanks to Wendy for staying with the kids and allowing Alex to come." Erin gave her brother a smile; she knew Wendy had wanted to come, too. "And thanks to Steph for being my support this weekend."

More than she'd ever know.

Keep it together.

Erin turned to her parents. "Today is the 20th anniversary of our lives changing forever. We've all been alive longer without Nadia than with her, which is so weird, because she's with me every day."

A rook swooped down and past them, its deep-blue metallic wings audible as they flapped. A breeze tickled her nose, and the skin on her knees glowed cold. Up above, grey clouds gathered, as if in consultation. The sun hummed in the background, its yellow rays muted.

"She's with us, too." Her mum's body shook as she spoke.

Her mum was finally being real about her other daughter. Admitting she existed. Admitting she had feelings.

Erin's heart punched a hole in her chest.

"You don't know what it means to hear you say that."

"We're sorry we let you down." Now her dad joined in, too.

Erin blinked, just to make sure she wasn't dreaming. When she glanced at Steph, her face was set to intense, and her hair slid across her face. She scooped it away with her index finger.

Her dad turned to Alex. "We've talked about it since this morning, and we're sorry we let you both down."

"And Nadia." Alex's fists were balled at his sides.

Her dad nodded. "Yes, and Nadia. But we're going to try to do better from now on. We're going to put the photos back up, and we're going to honour her memory properly."

Erin's throat went dry. She'd dreamed of this moment for so long. Now it was here. Was everything really going to change from today forward? She hardly dared to believe it. If she reached out a hand, would it touch real objects or would they be made of dust?

"That's all we can ask," Alex replied.

They all stared at each other for a few moments, unsure of what to do next.

But Erin knew this had all happened since Steph arrived in their lives. She shot a warm smile Steph's way.

Steph beamed right back.

Erin wanted to hug her. She couldn't imagine how awkward this was for Steph, but she was coping admirably. Erin was so glad she was here. Steph was her good luck charm. Erin took a deep breath. She nodded to her mum. "Do you want to do the honours?"

Her mum's brows knitted together. She shook her head. "You two should. She'd want to be closer to her siblings."

Erin shook her head in response. "I'd really like you to do it." It was important. Her parents had been distancing themselves from Nadia for years. They needed to own this moment.

Her mum stared, then nodded. "Okay. If it's what you both want."

"It is," Alex replied, then stepped closer to Erin and took her hand.

Erin squeezed it hard, then took a breath. There was nobody else around, just the five of them, nature, and their thoughts. But she was sure Nadia was here too. In ashes, and in spirit. She tilted her head to the sky, then back down to the loch. "Nadia, if you're listening, we've brought you back to your favourite spot. Remember the time we came here and drank terrible rosé when we were 16?" Erin glanced at her parents. "Don't worry, we shared a bottle between five of us and it put us off rosé for life."

Her mum gave a glimmer of a smile.

"I always imagined my life would be spent growing old with you. We were born together, and we grew up together. You're my big sister by four minutes, and I miss you every single day. But I want to leave you here, by the loch that you loved. I'll come back to visit. We all will. And I promise, you'll always be in our hearts."

"She will." Dad coughed. "We love you, Nadia."

That did Erin in. She'd held it together this long. Now, hot grief sped through her body, and tears rose in her throat. She let them fall. Now she was glad her parents were spreading the ashes. She'd probably drop the pot the state she was in. An arm encircled her shoulders and pulled her close. The arm she didn't want to leave.

Steph.

Erin leaned in and let herself be held. She'd kept herself upright all these years. It was nice to lean on someone else for a change.

Alex dropped her hand and cleared his throat. "You want me to help, Mum?"

Through her tears, Erin saw her mum nod. Alex stepped up and lifted the lid off the pot. Together, Alex and Mum walked a few steps, then tipped the pot upside down. Right at that moment, a gust of wind caught the ashes they were trying to tip into the water, and swung them back the other way.

Instead of sailing into the water, they landed all over Alex and her mum.

Erin's mouth dropped open. She didn't know whether to laugh or cry.

"Shit!" Alex jumped from foot to foot like he'd just trodden in something unsavoury. His face contorted as he brushed down his front, just as another gust of wind rolled through. This time, the ashes Alex was in the process of brushing off flew across and hit Erin.

Seriously?

Erin began frantically brushing herself down. She slapped her bare knees, swept her arms, billowed her T-shirt like it was a sail. Some of the ashes whipped upwards and hit her cheeks. She squeezed her eyes tight shut and flicked her face. If Nadia was watching, she'd be killing herself laughing. Erin internally rolled her eyes. Then she brushed herself down once again, took a few deep breaths, and straightened up.

Steph and her dad stared at the three of them, not quite sure what to do.

It was only when Erin began to laugh softly, then harder

still, that everyone else joined in. Soon, their cackles could be heard around the glen. Erin wiped her gritty eyes — she didn't like to think it might be Nadia — then snorted once more. "Fucking hell, Nadia, is that your idea of a joke? Sending wind right when Mum tipped the pot over?" She wiped a few more of her sister's ashes from her bare arm, then shook her head. "She always was the joker in the pack."

"That's true." Her dad shook his head, then took a deep breath. "We love you, Nadia Jane Stewart!" he bellowed. With that, her dad stepped forward and hugged Erin tight, wrapping his arms right around her.

When was the last time that had happened? Sure, he always gave her a peck on the cheek when he saw her, and was always pleased to see her. But a full-on bear hug? She couldn't remember. Plus, it was all the more sweet considering they had Nadia all over them. From being on the periphery of their lives, she was now front and centre. She wanted to be included in this hug, and she wasn't taking no for an answer. Erin had never been more glad. Her dad looked up and pulled Alex into the hug, then her mum.

Feelings that Erin had buried for years bubbled up, and there was a ringing in her ears.

Her mum stepped back and beckoned Steph to the circle. "You too, Steph. You had a say in this, and you're part of the family now."

Could this day get any more surreal? When Erin looked at her parents and her brother, they all had hot tears running down their cheeks, just like her. But she didn't care, and by the look of it, neither did they. It felt right. It felt liberating. It felt perfect, just like this moment.

Erin glanced over at Steph. Was she going to accept her mum's invitation? She had a strange look on her face. Erin gave her a look that said 'Come on!', then waved her hand towards her.

Steph's eyes darted left, then right, then she shook her head. She stared at Erin, then looked away.

Erin's stomach churned. She frowned. Why wasn't Steph coming over? Had this been too much to put on a relative stranger, after all, despite what had happened between them this weekend? Maybe so.

But Erin's dad was having none of it. He broke from their hug, took Steph by the hand and dragged her in.

Erin sensed the tension in Steph's body when she put her arm around her. It hadn't been there when they arrived. At least, she didn't think it had. Today was a whirlwind, a blur. So many highs, so many maybes, so many promises for the future. She already wanted to hang today in her hall of fame. The breakthrough with her parents *and* with Steph? This was a day to cherish.

After a few moments, they came up for air, their smiles so big, they almost fell from their faces.

A warmth stole through Erin in a rush, and a taste flooded her mouth. Candyfloss, hot from the village fair. She shook with the gravity of it all.

"She's here," Erin declared. "Nadia's here."

They all turned her way.

Erin wrapped her arms around herself and shook her head. "She's happy we finally laid her to rest."

Chapter Twenty

Steph spent the whole drive back nodding politely, avoiding eye contact with Erin, and trying not to pass out with panic. It was the biggest acting job of her career so far.

Her memory clawed at the edges of her mind as she tried to piece back the information her mum had given her years ago. A family from the Scottish Highlands. A terrible tragedy that meant Steph's life might continue. A girl with the surname of Stewart. Those three facts were real. Plus, the timeline was close enough if Nadia hadn't died right away. The only thing Steph couldn't fathom was that Erin's surname was Brown. Which meant that the slow, creeping feeling covering her skin must be false. Maybe she misheard. She didn't have all the facts.

True or not, her Scottish heart sat like a blackbird in her chest. When it fluttered, Steph clung to the car door. If it spread its wings, she might not be able to breathe.

By the time Alex swung the car up the steep, black drive and into the flat parking outside the house, Steph's nails had left deep red marks on her fingertips. She regulated her breathing, then swallowed down her sense of doom. It might be nothing. It might be okay.

Then again, it might be the worse news ever.

But she couldn't jump the gun.

Erin's parents decamped to the house, their steps lighter. Today had been a revolution for their family. For everyone, apart from Steph. Alex joined Wendy by the pool, picking up one of their cute daughters and twirling her around. What was their surname? Were the triplets Browns or Stewarts? Steph's mind warped. It made no sense at all. This morning her world had been clear. Now, it was listing and reeling. She didn't want to ask the question, but it was the only thing on her lips.

They opened the door to the lodge. Erin threw the keys on the counter, waited for Steph to follow her in, then walked over to her.

When she clocked her face, she stopped. Her eyes narrowed as they focused on Steph.

"Can we sit down?" The lump in Steph's throat pulsed. It had a sour taste.

Erin nodded, then led the way to the sofa.

Steph tried to airbrush images from earlier from her mind.

"What's wrong? You've been quiet the whole drive back. I know that was all a bit much, but you said you were happy to come."

Steph nodded. "I was. But it's just something your dad said at the end that's stuck in my mind." She paused. "When he said your sister's full name. Nadia Jane Stewart. How come she's got a different last name to you?"

"I don't follow," Erin began, then stopped. She smiled, then winced. "Oh, fuck. Yes. Erin Brown."

Steph stared. The next moments were crucial. It was like she was having her heart transplant all over again.

"Is that not your name?" Her heart kicked in her chest. It no longer felt like her heart.

Erin winced a little more. "No. I gave you a fake surname, just in case things went pear-shaped. It's a tactic my friends use on dating sites."

Steph closed her eyes as nausea overwhelmed her. She glanced up at the log burner. The loch out the window. The laminate floor beneath her feet.

Everything else was exactly the same as it had been this morning.

Yet *nothing* was as it had been this morning.

She clutched her chest, got up and began pacing.

Oh fuck oh fuck oh fuck.

How could this happen? How was it possible? How was she going to tell her?

Out of the corner of her vision, Erin stood up. "What's wrong?" Her voice was studded with concern, but it was a little late for that.

Steph sucked in a deep breath. She had to call her mum and check the facts. But a woman with the surname of Stewart who died 20 years ago in Scotland? How many of them could there be? She took a deep breath, steadied herself, then looked up. Into Erin's eyes. The woman she'd woken up with this morning. The woman she'd spoken of a future with.

The woman whose world she was about to shatter.

She began to shake.

"I just need to get this straight in my head. Your name is Erin Stewart?" Steph balled her fists at her side. She willed Erin to say no.

But Erin nodded, as Steph knew she would.

"Yes." She stared at her. "And you're freaking me out now."

Steph swallowed down bile. "Not half as much as you're freaking me out." She blew out a long breath, then walked over to the kitchen counter and gripped it. *Think, Steph.* She needed to call her mum. She glanced up at Erin, her face creased with concern.

"I don't understand, what's going on?"

"I just need to make a call. And I need to get some air. You go be with your family, it's important."

Erin stared, bit her lip, then stared some more. "You're important, too."

Dread crawled across Steph's scalp. She wanted to scream. "I'll come and find you when I get the answers I need."

With that, she grabbed her phone, stared at Erin, then strode out of the lodge.

This day was turning into a scrambled nightmare.

* * *

There was so much adrenalin rushing around her system as she strode down the hill. The loch was still there, but Steph barely noticed it. Now, all she was aware of was her gifted heart beating at breakneck speed, her shaking hand, and the shivers running up and down her spine. This couldn't be happening.

She made the call, and her mum answered in a few rings.

"Hello daughter dear. I wondered if I'd hear from you. How's it going?"

Steph tensed. Even her mum's voice couldn't soothe her.

"It was going fine up until a while ago." She paused, then exhaled. "I've got a question to ask you."

"You're worrying me, but fire away."

Steph sat on the stone wall behind her. "My heart transplant donor. Do you remember her name? Her full name? You only ever told me her surname was Stewart. Do you remember her first name?"

Her mum paused for a few seconds. "I do, because it was quite unusual. Very pretty name. Nadia."

Steph had known it instinctively. Her heart had known. But hearing it confirmed was another thing altogether. She sank to the ground, drenched in sadness, as if her chest cavity was full of rainwater. Her heart thudded like it never had before.

Nadia's heart.

Not hers.

If she'd known Erin's surname from the start, she'd never have come. Certainly never have slept with her. But that was all ifs and buts, because she had, and now, here she was. Her skin ached with the injustice of it all. Her teeth rocked in her mouth. Her fingers scraped across the rough cement beneath their tips.

"Why do you ask? Has something happened? Is your heart okay?"

What to tell her mum? That she'd slept with the twin sister of her heart transplant donor? It was too far-fetched for her brain to even form that sentence. But it was true. However, Steph needed to digest the news first before she told anybody else. She glanced backwards to the house, where the whole family were. They'd talked about having a special dinner tonight to celebrate Nadia and their breakthrough.

She couldn't stay now. What on earth would they all think?

There was nothing inherently wrong with what had happened.

She hadn't committed a crime.

And yet, somehow she felt like she'd been fooling them all by being here. She'd trespassed on part of her past.

There was everything wrong with it.

She'd stolen one twin's heart. Then tried to steal the other.

She felt sick to her stomach.

"Steph? Say something you're worrying me."

She cleared her throat, heat swirling around her body. "Sorry, I was just thinking. Everything's fine. It's just... there was a plaque dedicated to a Nadia Stewart today, by a loch we drove by." It was the best she could come up with on the spot. "I wondered if it was the girl that gave me life. Turns out, it was."

"Oh, love," her mum replied. "Gosh, that must have been emotional."

She had no idea.

"You'll have to let me know where it was and if I ever go to the Highlands, I can pay my respects. I often think of that poor family who lost their daughter."

Steph's brain blared with the impossibility of it all.

She rang off, with promises to call her mum when she got back. Then she sat, trying to regulate her breathing. Her short fingernails left red marks on her palms. She dropped her head and ran through her options.

First, she could run, and never look back. Tempting, but not very practical.

Second, she could stay and pretend nothing was wrong. Her stomach fizzed. Her mouth went dry. She couldn't stay.

That left her with option three. The worst option of all.

She turned, walked towards the house, then stopped. What

the hell was she going to say? Should she lie? She couldn't. Maybe if she hadn't slept with Erin, she could. But once Steph told her the truth, she'd probably want her to leave anyway. It was all too weird for her to stay.

How was she going to tell Erin that she had her sister's heart? That the heart that had sped up as she came last night, again and again, belonged to her twin?

That thought made Steph dry retch. She leaned over, coughed, then spat.

Nothing about this was planned, yet it looked ominous.

She stood up. Inhaled, then refocused.

She had to go back, pack, tell Erin, and leave. To make that happen, she just had to put one foot in front of the other.

Easier said than done, when her feet were suddenly made of lead.

Chapter Twenty-One

Erin hadn't settled by the pool. Everyone else was more relaxed than she'd seen her family in years. Alex had regaled Wendy with the scene of the ashes, and Wendy hadn't stopped laughing. However, Erin's mind was on Steph. What had changed since this morning, since she was on her knees in front of her just before they left? Erin would love to know. Was she having doubts about trying to make them work? Had Erin pushed her too far? She was desperate to know. She'd left her alone for an hour, but maybe now Steph would want to talk. Erin slipped away without her family noticing.

When she let herself into the lodge, the last thing she expected to see was Steph in the lounge, zipping up her case. She wasn't due to leave until tomorrow lunchtime, when her friend Michael was picking her up so they could go on their tour of the Highlands. Erin already had plans to surprise Steph and meet her somewhere. She was sure she could talk Michael into helping her. But right now, that didn't look likely.

None of this made any sense.

"What's going on?"

Steph looked up. Her eyes were red and puffy. Now Erin was *really* confused. Was taking her to scatter the ashes too much? Was this about them, or did Steph have a death in her past she'd yet to deal with? Erin had been so wrapped up in Nadia, she hadn't stopped to consider that. There was only one way to find out.

"Why are you all packed?"

"Because this has all been a mistake and I have to go." Steph stood up, then walked over to her. She wrung her hands together, then took a step back. "I'm sorry."

Erin blinked. Panic spread across her skin. Okay, now *nothing* made any sense at all.

"I don't understand what's changed in the last couple of hours? We were talking about seeing where this could go this morning." She stared at Steph, then tried a half-hearted smile.

Steph didn't break.

They'd spent more of the past 24 hours having sex than not. They'd shared big things. Monumental moments. Erin had no idea what was going on.

Steph took a deep breath, and met Erin's gaze.

"What I'm about to say isn't easy, so give me a moment." She ran a hand through her still glossy hair.

Erin wanted to do the same, but she kept her hands by her side.

"I didn't tell you the full story of my childhood. I gave you the light, abbreviated version because we'd just met and it takes a while before I let anybody in fully. Plus, I was here on a job and this job is about you and your family." Pain was etched on her face. "However, that changed after we scattered Nadia's ashes. Because I realised something." She paused, her eyes searching Erin's face. "You saw my scar. You know I had a major operation when I was 17. I had a condition called hypertrophic cardiomyopathy. I needed a heart transplant.

I was on the waiting list for six months, and then I got one. The surgery saved my life."

Erin gulped. "I assumed it was either a transplant or a bypass." She frowned. "That's great, though, right? You're living a good life, a normal life. Why should I be concerned with that?"

"The thing I didn't tell you is that my heart donor was from Scotland. And my heart transplant happened 20 years ago." She paused for a very long moment. "Your sister donated her organs 20 years ago." Steph stared at her.

The words hung in the air like a bad smell. Erin tried to shut the door on them, to avoid them. She tried to spray them with aerosol, but it didn't work. Nadia donated her organs. Steph had a heart transplant. What was she saying?

That's when the penny dropped, and her breath started to falter.

Steph had a heart transplant 20 years ago.

No.

It couldn't be true.

She eventually broke the waterlogged silence.

"Are you saying what I think you're saying?" Sweat broke out on her back. Her ears tingled. She blinked and reassessed everything she knew about Steph.

She stared at Steph's chest. As if she could see her sister's heart beating under her skin.

She'd felt Steph's heart beat last night.

Gripped Steph's wrist. Felt her walls pulsing around her fingers.

That pulse had all been supplied by Nadia's heart.

Her brain tilted on its axis.

Candyfloss flavours filled her mouth.

Really not helpful.

Steph took a breath, then nodded. "I'm saying that my heart donor was a Scottish woman named Nadia Stewart. My mum only ever told me her surname, so I didn't put two and two together because I thought your surname was Brown. I never knew my donor's first name until half an hour ago when my mum confirmed it. My mum never wanted me to know Nadia's history or seek her family out, so she never gave me the full details. She wanted me to look forward, not back." She shook her head. "That's backfired spectacularly, hasn't it?" She blew out her cheeks. "When you told me Nadia died in a car crash, I thought it was instant. The name didn't match up. The timing didn't match up, as my transplant anniversary is in two weeks."

Erin stepped back from Steph. Every sense she had reeled. "She was on life support for a while." She shook her head. "That time is all blurred in my head." But today was very sharply in focus. "Fuck. I slept with a woman who has my twin sister's heart inside her body? That is… I don't know what that is."

"A headfuck?"

"You could say that." And then, she could say so much more. She'd put her hand on Steph's chest last night. Traced the scar this morning.

Nadia's heart was beating underneath.

A shiver ran through her.

It was wrong. *So very wrong.* But then why had it felt so right?

"Which is why I've packed my case. I can't pretend nothing's happened. I can't be here now. Not with this. Especially not after today. Your whole family just did something huge. Something that centres around you and Nadia. I can't ruin that." Steph's face crumpled.

Erin wanted to reach out and touch her, but to what end? What could she say? Nothing right now. She couldn't compute any of this.

Her heart burned in her chest.

Was Nadia's heart burning in Steph's chest? She was at once repulsed, but also fascinated. She shook her head to get rid of her thoughts. It didn't work. She couldn't stop staring.

"How the hell could this happen? The one woman I connect with in ages has my sister's heart? Is it a kind of incest?" Erin flinched at her final word.

Steph's eyes clouded over. "Don't say that. It's not incest. I'm not your sister. She just donated her heart to me." She still frowned.

Erin shook her head. "I know, I know. But you've got her heart. And that's… too weird." She shuddered. She simply couldn't work out what to feel, how she should feel. It was too strange.

"Which is why I booked into The Lochside Hotel. The one where Michael's staying tonight." Steph blew out a long breath. "He's arriving this evening, so I'll go there." Her shoulders were heavy. "I'm still not sure why you used a fake name."

"I already told you. It made sense at the time." Erin shook her head. "If I'd have said my name was Erin Stewart, you wouldn't have taken the job?"

"No." Steph's answer was firm.

"Then we'd never have met." Erin eyed her, then dropped her gaze.

"Maybe you'd rather that had happened?"

They stood in silence. Was that true? Erin didn't think so. But then, she had no idea what she thought in this moment. Nadia helped Steph live a full life. More than that, she'd helped Steph *live*, full stop. Some good had come from her death. Her twin had given Steph what had cruelly been snatched away from her. That should make Erin happy. Instead, it only made her want to scream the house down.

Because it was Nadia's heart that pumped the blood around Steph's body.

Steph wouldn't have come had she known.

Erin wasn't sure she'd have gone anywhere near Steph if she'd known from the start either.

But that was immaterial. She had gone near her. She had slept with her. And now feelings were involved. Overflowing, bucketloads of them.

It was too much for Erin to work out. All she knew for sure was that she needed to be alone. Steph was right. She had to go.

"I'm going to make this easy for you." Steph turned and grabbed her suitcase. "I'm really sorry it's ended like this."

Erin stood back and watched Steph leave as if she was someone she'd just met. Not someone she'd spent the weekend with. Someone who'd made a difference in her life.

Someone she'd categorically fallen for.

Chapter Twenty-Two

Michael arrived at just gone 8pm. Steph had no doubt he had grand plans of having dinner, a quick drink, then a good night's sleep before meeting her tomorrow. She had news for him that his plan wasn't going to work.

She knocked on his door after he messaged her his room number and to tell her he got there safely. The look on his face when he opened the door spelt surprise.

"What are you doing here?" No matter it was unexpected, he stepped forward and gave her a hug anyway. Then he held her at arm's length as he scanned her face. "Lovely as it is to see you, I can't help but think this is a bad thing as far as you finishing your job goes."

She didn't let him continue. "Can I come in and raid your minibar?"

He stepped back and waved her in. "I don't have a minibar."

His room was bigger than hers, with a Nespresso machine, king-size bed and a sofa. He also had a loch view, whereas her room faced a stone wall. That was the difference when you booked in advance, as opposed to the same day.

She turned to him. "Then can we go and buy one?"

He got hold of her shoulders and sat her down. The sofa was chequered in a pattern seen on kilts everywhere, which perfectly suited the setting. The Lodge had been far too modern in styling. You needed tartan in the Highlands. Just the thought of their lodge sent Steph's mind scampering back to this morning. Sitting on the cream sofa, with Erin between her legs, bringing her to a glorious climax.

She blinked.

She had to put that to the back of her mind.

They were simply a case of wrong place, wrong time. Never meant to be. It's not like they knew each other that well anyway. This time last week, they hadn't even met.

She could totally get over Erin and get on with her life. She had to pretend the last week never happened, and move on.

That didn't stop Michael needing an answer as to why she was in his hotel room when she should still be working. He wasn't going to wait all night.

"What's going on? You should be up the hill playing happy families. This morning you told me you had feelings for her."

Steph sank back into the cushions and closed her eyes. She was pleased Michael was here. She'd been driving herself mad with torment all afternoon.

"A lot can happen in a few short hours."

Michael blew out his cheeks, then frowned. "This morning she was incredible and last night was incredible."

"It was." Steph paused. "But that was before I found out that the heart I had transplanted into my body 20 years ago belonged to her dead twin sister." Steph focused on Michael to see how long it took his face to register her words. He struggled for a few seconds, but then his features clouded over. There it was.

He blinked, then shook his head rapidly. "Your heart belongs to who?"

"To nobody but me now as my doctors told me at the time. But originally, it belonged to Erin's twin sister, Nadia. Who was killed in a car crash 20 years ago. Whose heart is now in my body."

"So you slept with your heart's twin sister." He paused, then wrinkled his face. "That's too weird."

"Which is why I'm here and not there."

"Did you tell her?"

"Of course I told her! I couldn't stick around after I found out. The family just scattered her ashes this morning, and they're just mending things. I couldn't bring my weirdness into the picture."

He shook his head. "I can see why you need a drink."

"You have no idea." She stood up and paced to the window, then turned back to him. "But I keep thinking, did I do the right thing? I care for her. We've had an amazing few days. But I felt like I couldn't do anything else."

"It's not a usual situation."

Steph snorted. "Understatement of the year." She paused. "I never would have taken the job if I knew her surname was Stewart, because I knew that was the name of my donor. Only the surname, not the first name." She paused. "You took the booking. Did you know she'd used a false name?"

Michael winced and tried not to look anywhere but Steph. It didn't work.

"Of course, her credit card had her real name. She asked if she could be called Brown, and I said yes just as I've said yes to a ton of people who've asked for the same thing since

I set up this business. It's never been a problem before. If people are hiring fake friends or partners, they often use a fake name."

"It backfired this time."

"I can see that." He got up and walked over to her. "I knew your heart donor was from Scotland, but for you to end up in the bed of her twin sister?" He shook his head. "What are the chances? Did you know your donor was a twin?"

"No."

He shivered. "It's a bit freaky."

Steph put a hand to her face. "It is, but then, it isn't. It's just a weird coincidence. But if you'd seen Erin's face today when she found out. She said she'd committed a kind of incest."

Michael put an arm around her shoulders and pulled her close.

Steph let him. It was nice to be held. It would be better if Michael could let her know everything was going to be okay. Even if he was lying.

"That's not the best reaction." Michael spoke to the top of Steph's head.

She shook her head, then lifted it to meet his gaze. "She was shocked and confused. So was I. But no, it wasn't the best first reaction from someone you've just spent the best part of 24 hours in bed with."

"She probably just needs time to get her head around it," Michael replied.

Steph nodded. "Maybe." She walked over and sat on the sofa again, then waited for Michael to do the same. "Or maybe this is it, and I just need to forget this weekend ever happened?" Easier said than done. Erin wasn't just under Steph's skin.

She was woven into the Highland landscape and now, Steph's landscape, too.

"That has to be up to her. She hired you to start with. Then the lines blurred, which always makes things more tricky." He held up a hand. "Don't worry, I'm not going to give you a lecture on that. I might have done it myself once or twice." Something passed over his features that Steph couldn't quite read. Then Michael forced a half-smile and carried on. "This isn't a normal situation, so normal rules don't apply. But think it through. Is this something you really want to take further? Or should it just be left where it is? In the category marked 'Highland Fling'?

Steph stared at her friend. She knew he meant well. But she and Erin had been more than a fling. She felt it deep in her bones. Could they pursue it to see where it might go? Only if they both wanted to. The way Erin had looked at her when she walked out the door, Steph had no idea if that still applied.

Chapter Twenty-Three

Erin couldn't recall a day like it in living memory. One that had started so well, been jam-packed with emotion, and then ended with such a spectacular fail. A fail so huge, she was still digesting it. Her parents had cleared up the remnants of this afternoon's barbecue and gone for a shower. Her brother and his wife had taken her nieces to get ready for bed, and the neighbours had said goodbye. Now should be the time to be lying with Steph in this hammock, limbs entwined, picking up where they left off this morning. She still remembered the night of the party when Steph had held her in this very place.

Instead, she lay alone, staring at the still-bright sky, wondering where it all went wrong. How could her giving a fake name lead to such a series of events? It was bad. Really bad. Stomach-churning, no-plan-B, end-of-the-fucking-world bad. Erin was still trying to process it.

Could she get to grips with Steph having Nadia's heart? Did a part of her resent Steph for having it in the first place, and not her sister? That was ridiculous and unfair, she knew, and yet, it had crossed her mind. She guessed that made her human. Flawed. It wasn't something she was proud of.

When the accident had first happened, and her parents

had made the decision to donate Nadia's organs, they'd all been traumatised. In the end, Nadia helped a few people to live with her donations. That had been of little solace at the time, but who those people were had flicked across Erin's mind occasionally. Had she ever passed them in the street? Sat in a bar nearby? But her curiosity had never gone further than that. She'd been happy with the recipients being a far-off concept.

Until she met one of them and slept with her.

Erin shuddered and the red hammock swayed. She gripped the sides and waited until it stilled.

If only her thoughts would do the same. It was as if someone had taken everything that she knew to be true, stuffed it into a blender, added kale for good measure, and whizzed it up. A truth smoothie, if you will.

It tasted sour. And green.

None of this was Steph's fault, of course. And yet, Erin felt like it was. Like Steph had been hiding something from her.

She closed her eyes, then immediately felt like she was going to fall. She opened them. Her knuckles tightened around the material's edge. When she really thought about it, it was mainly Morag's fault. Damn her friend for setting this up, giving her hope.

Was this weekend telling her she wasn't destined for a relationship? Even when she paid for a partner, Erin somehow found a way to fuck it up. Morag had sent her a barrage of texts today asking how it had gone last night with Steph. The answer was, it had gone fine. Fabulously, even. If Erin could carve out the hours of midnight to midday and replay them over and over, she would, in a heartbeat.

A heartbeat.

It was a phrase she'd used many times in her life, and yet never stopped to consider the true meaning. Her heartbeat had always been her own, never anybody else's.

Steph's heartbeat had once been Nadia's.

What had Steph called it? A mindfuck? She was right.

If Erin tried to continue this thing with Steph, would she forever be resentful that Steph had her sister's heart? Or would seeing Steph thrive go some way to mending Erin's own?

She screwed up her eyes and let out a huff of frustration. It was still too new. Too raw. Too real. Why couldn't she have slept with someone else? In the whole of the UK, she had to choose Steph?

Footsteps approaching made Erin sit up. Too quickly.

Whatever you did in a hammock, you had to do it slowly. Nadia had known that. She'd never fallen out once.

Erin, on the other hand…

As she turned her head to see her mum walking around the pool, Erin's eyes widened. She was unsteady. It was a metaphor for her life. She grabbed for the sides of the hammock, but she hit thin air. As Erin turned back, she wobbled one way, then the other. Then, like even the hammock despised her today, the material span inside out and Erin's world spun.

One minute she was sitting up, the next she was flipping through the air like one of her dad's pancakes.

She saw sky, loch, grass and then thump! Erin landed on the concrete underneath, her knees and elbows taking the brunt of the fall.

"Fuck!" Erin winced as pain seeped into her bones, quickly followed by embarrassment. First hammock fall of the year. At least the physical pain took her mind off everything else.

Erin took a deep breath, raised her head, gingerly got onto her haunches, then stood. She glanced down. No blood, just scratches. She'd survive. Just like Steph. What had Steph's mum called her? Her little warrior. An image of Steph's radiant smile filled her vision. Erin shook her head. It didn't matter now.

Within moments, her mum was by her side, concern and amusement mingling on her face.

"I came to see if you were okay, and if Steph was feeling any better." She patted Erin's arm. "Sorry to shock you."

Her mum saying Steph's name was a sucker punch to the gut. Erin reeled, winded.

"Good to get the first fall out of the way." Erin rubbed her elbows. "Steph's still asleep." She wasn't ready to tell her mum the truth just yet. She'd told her family Steph had a migraine. They'd all been sympathetic. Why wouldn't they be?

"If she needs anything to eat, just help yourself from the fridge. We've still got tons left from the party."

Erin nodded. "Thanks, I will."

Her mum walked towards the bench overlooking the loch, her mint-green cardigan buttoned halfway. She patted the space beside her. "Come sit with me."

Erin did as she was told, her bones still aching.

They sat in silence for a few moments.

"Your dad and I were speaking earlier. We might get a bench with a plaque and leave it where we scattered the ashes. As a memorial for Nadia." She looked straight ahead as she spoke. "What do you think?"

Erin's heart broke. For herself, her family, Nadia, and for Steph. It was all so tangled up and it was nobody's fault.

"Sounds like a wonderful idea." She turned to her mum and gave her a pained smile.

Her mum returned it.

"I'm sorry about everything with your sister. We handled it all wrong, we know that. If we could go back and do it all again, we would. But what we can do is look forward and make the right choices. Everything you said hit home. For both of us."

Yep, this day kept on surprising her. "It's not just me you should tell. It's Alex, too. It affected us both."

Her mum nodded. "We know." She took a deep breath. "We're going to sort through the photos this week and get some reframed and blown up." She paused, rubbing the fingers of her right hand with her left. "Also, your dad and I are going to see if we can talk to someone. See if it might help."

Erin shook her head and stared. She could hardly believe her ears.

At last.

Her mum took her head shake the wrong way. "You don't approve?"

Erin turned. "On the contrary, it sounds like a great step."

"Maybe you and Alex might like to come along eventually, too?" Her mum's glance was hesitant.

"We said we would. It's a fresh start for the whole family."

A new start that didn't include any complications that could throw them off course.

Like Steph.

A rush of warmth and doom spiralled up her body.

Erin exhaled a long breath, then stuffed it back down.

"I'm really proud of how you and Dad responded today."
She smiled at her mum. "I know it can't have been easy. It
wasn't for me."

Her mum stared at the loch. "We've touched on it over the
years, but the more accepting you get with how things are, the
more difficult it is to change. We got stuck in a rut, and it wasn't
because we wanted to forget Nadia. We could never forget her.
I hope you know that."

Erin nodded. She did. Even though her parents never
spoke about her twin, she'd never once considered that they
didn't love her or remember her. She just knew it was too hard
to deal with. "I never forgot her for a single second. I want to
be able to share her with the people who knew her best. That's
you, Dad, and Alex." She paused, forming the next question
with care. She went to speak, then stopped. She could do this.
No matter how much her heart broke. No matter if today had
already been a clusterfuck of emotions. She wanted to know.
She *needed* to know.

"I wanted to ask, was it hard to donate Nadia's organs
after she died? Making the decision after watching her on life
support can't have been easy."

Her mum's breathing slowed, and her eyes shut briefly.
"Everything happened so slowly, and yet, so fast. The accident,
Nadia's chances of survival plummeting by the day. When we
knew we'd lost her, the thought of someone cutting her up
wasn't one I wanted to think about. My initial reaction was
no. I couldn't face it. I wanted to at least be able to bury my
daughter whole."

Wow. Erin tensed every muscle she had. Then she took her
mum's hand in hers and squeezed. They'd never spoken like

this. Not once in 20 years. She wished they'd done it earlier. She wished she'd done a lot of things earlier.

"I can understand that." And she did.

"I'm glad you can." Her mum shook her head. "Despite knowing all the people she could help, I didn't want to. But it would have been the wrong decision, and I'm glad that you and your father persuaded me otherwise."

Erin sat up when she heard that. "We did?" The days after the accident and Nadia's death were a black hole in Erin's memory. She'd blocked them out, and they'd never come back to her. She'd been a part of the decision? She'd assumed that had been down to her parents alone.

Her mum nodded, then stroked her chin before she continued. "You were very insistent. Alex wasn't there, he was staying with friends, remember? I just wanted my little girl back to bury her, but you wouldn't hear of it. You told me it's what Nadia would have wanted." She smiled at Erin, the edges jagged. "In the end, she saved three lives by donating her heart, eyes, and liver. I hope those three people are thriving out in the world and living their lives to the full."

Hard heat blazed through Erin. She shook with the strength of her emotions, but she had to keep a lid on them. She didn't want her mum to find out the truth. Not now, maybe not ever. Her face flushed and she jumped up from the bench, then stuck her hands in the pockets of her denim shorts. The ones Steph had admired on Friday. It seemed like another lifetime after everything that had happened in between. She pushed back her shoulders so the blades nearly touched, then steadied her breath. After a few moments, she turned to her mum.

"Would you ever want to meet them or track them down to see how they were doing?"

Her mum frowned, came to stand beside her, then shook her head. "We sent a note at the time telling the recipients the name of the donor and where she was from, but that's all. It was done via the trust, and we never knew who they were. The trust advised us not to give her full name, but we wanted to. We felt it was important." She twisted her wedding ring. "They didn't advise getting to know them, but they advised to send a note, so we did."

Erin's palms sweated as she kneaded them. "But what if you *could* find out?"

Her mum stared at her, considering the question. "I'm not sure I would. I'm glad Nadia was able to help them, but I'd still prefer she was here. I'm still fucking furious she died."

Erin blinked. Her mum hardly ever swore.

"My feelings would be so mixed. Maybe after I've had a few months of therapy, who knows if that might change?" She exhaled. "Still, it's not something we have to worry about. The chances of it happening are pretty slim."

A crackling noise filled Erin's ears.

Suddenly, everything that had happened came crashing down on her. It was way, *way* too much.

Nadia had been the impulsive, daring one. Erin was stoic, she got on with things. She was rational, not emotional. However, the past few days had unlocked something deep within her. Something that needed to get out. Or rather, Steph had. What was it? Permission to be her whole self, maybe? To be loved?

Erin glanced down the hillside. She could see the hotel Steph was staying at. Knowing she was within touching distance and yet out of reach broke Erin's resolve and her heart.

Before she knew what was happening, tears streamed down her face.

This was not what Erin did. Apart from this whole bloody weekend. Perhaps this was a new beginning for everyone.

Her mum turned, her face horrified. She went to put her arm around Erin, but Erin shook her head.

"Don't." She was too jumpy, too fragile. She was more like her mum than she liked to think.

Erin walked a few steps and stared at the loch, then turned back to her mum, arms folded across her chest. Her face was wet with tears, and they were still coming. Five minutes ago, she wasn't sure she'd ever tell her mum. Now, she felt like she had no choice.

"What's wrong? Is it something we did? Something I said?"

Erin shook her head with firm resolve. "No, it's something *I* did." She wiped the back of her hand across her face. She needed a tissue but she didn't have one. She forged on with snotty resolve.

"The thing is, Steph doesn't have a migraine. She left. She was never my girlfriend. I hired her for the weekend." The words smashed onto the concrete at her feet. Erin winced at their ferocity.

Her mum blinked and stared, as if Erin had just spoken in a foreign language. "I don't understand—"

Erin nodded, on a roll. "That makes two of us. She was meant to be here until tomorrow and then I was going to make up a story that we broke up."

Her mum tilted her head. "You hired her? Why would

you do that?" She inhaled. "Is this a joke? It must be. She didn't seem like you'd just met. I spoke to her. I saw the way she looked at you. There was something there, or did my eyes deceive me?"

It was one of the many things Erin had packed away since Steph left. She wasn't ready to unzip that case of emotions just yet.

She knew the answer without looking.

"We connected, yes. Sod's law that the first woman I fall for in ages lives in London. And is also someone I hired."

Her mum walked towards her pulling her cardigan tighter. "I don't understand. Why would you pay someone to be your girlfriend?"

Erin threw up her hands. "Because I'm always the odd one out. Because everyone always asks me if I'm seeing anyone, and I wanted to be able to say 'yes, here she is'! Also because I wanted to make you proud of me. I was never good enough for you after Nadia died. Everything about me reminded you of her."

Right. She was going there.

Her mum took a step back, then put a hand over her mouth.

"Don't look so shocked like this is news." Erin was on a roll. "I reminded you of the daughter you lost. I still do. How could I not? As for me, I stopped trying to find someone because I couldn't bear the thought that they, too, might leave me, and I didn't want to disappoint you." Wow. She hadn't truly believed that until it came out of her mouth. But everything she was saying was true. Clearly, scattering the ashes was just the tip of the iceberg.

"But that's not even the reason Steph has gone. She was meant to stay until tomorrow, brazen out this whole charade until then. I paid her for five days."

Her mum still stared.

Erin was at a crossroads. Should she continue on, or slow the car down? She looked left, looked right, then floored the accelerator.

"But today, at the loch, when Steph heard Nadia's full name, she freaked out. Because 20 years ago, Steph had a heart transplant. The donor was from Scotland. The donor was Nadia. Steph didn't know until then. So well done me. Last night and this morning I finally managed to have sex with someone I cared about. Someone I developed feelings for. Then it turns out that woman has my dead sister's heart."

Nausea bubbled up again.

"What? Steph has Nadia's heart? But how did she end up here? Did she seek us out?" Her mum was trying to fathom it. Erin knew she'd be there some time.

"No, it's just a terrible coincidence."

Her mum shook her head. "She can't have Nadia's heart. She seems so… alive." She clamped her hand over her mouth as she uttered the final word. Then she turned sharply and marched back towards the house.

"Mum!" When Erin turned, her dad was standing by the pool, his face creased.

"What did your mum say?"

Erin stuck her hands in her pockets, then took another deep breath. It looked like she was coming completely clean this weekend. "Steph is my fake girlfriend, and I found out today that she has Nadia's heart."

When she looked left, Alex was there, too. From the look on his face, he'd clearly heard what she said. Was this what it was like to face a firing squad? It certainly felt like it.

Tears slipped down her cheeks as Erin crumpled to the ground. She sat cross-legged, her head in her hands. How had it all got so fucked up? Maybe it was better when they kept everything in. Now, they were a total mess.

Chapter Twenty-Four

"I've been thinking." Michael steered his hired BMW smoothly along the single-car road, still far too fast for Steph's liking.

"I wondered what that noise was." They'd already had words about his driving, but it hadn't made a difference.

"Very droll. You could sell your story. Make a tidy £250 for spilling your guts to one of those trashy magazines."

Steph glanced right and rolled her eyes. Even if he was a boy racer, she was glad he was there. His inane ramblings at least made her smile. But he could never understand what she was going through. Michael didn't do relationships. He preferred to stick to sex, and no more.

"Great plan."

"Glad you think so." He gave her a broad grin. "You know what they say: there's no such thing as a bad experience, just an experience."

"Finding out you've slept with a woman and you have her dead twin's heart is pretty bad."

He nodded, banging his hand on the steering wheel. "A bit left-field, I'll give you that."

Steph gripped the map of the Highlands tight. She'd enjoyed navigating today as they drove from Durness to

John O'Groats. It had given her something else to focus on. They'd stopped for lunch at a village called Tongue. Steph had been so preoccupied she hadn't even thought to make a joke about that. Instead, she'd eaten mussels in a daze overlooking yet another picture-perfect loch. But even such amazing scenery hadn't taken her mind off her Erin-shaped troubles. She kept picturing Erin's face as she'd left two days ago. A mix of disgust and confusion. She wished she could get the image out of her head.

She'd spent a fitful night wondering how Erin was coping. Steph's side of the bargain wasn't exactly peachy, but at least she could get up and walk away. Meanwhile, Erin had to stay and explain why Steph was no longer there. She didn't envy her that. Had she told the truth about hiring Steph, as well as the stark facts about her heart transplant? The Stewart family had been through so much already this past week. Getting this news was something that could tip them over the edge.

She glanced at her phone, at the last message Erin had sent. It was from the previous Wednesday night, when she'd first arrived in Edinburgh. They hadn't known each other at all. How far they'd come. Steph had got to know Erin, got to know her family, and she'd liked what she'd seen. Their five days had been intense, and she wanted more. But that wasn't going to happen, was it? The thing that had kept her alive and meant she was able to be Erin's fake girlfriend, was also what was going to drive them apart.

Steph's heart was something neither could get over.

Her eyes sailed over a list of place names she'd never heard of before. Murkle. Skinnet. Buldoo. Her brain would discard them soon enough. Could she do the same with Erin?

"I've got to forget her, haven't I?"

Michael waved his thanks to a black Range Rover that had pulled in to let them pass. He didn't answer for a long moment. "If that's what you want." He glanced her way as they took a bend a bit too quickly. He slammed on the brake, and the car skidded around the corner, where a spectacular view down to a loch opened up, with rolling hills either side and glassy still waters shimmying below. It was breathtaking. A little like Michael's driving.

"For fuck's sake, we're not in a grand prix." Steph pressed an imaginary foot pedal and clenched her teeth. Worrying about Erin was all well and good, but she needed to be alive to do it. "Please try not to get us killed."

"It would erase your problems, though, wouldn't it?" He gave her a sad smile. "But I don't think you want to," he added. "Forget her, I mean. I've known you a long time, and I know the signs."

Steph stared out the window at the sun high in the sky; it was that kind of blue you only ever saw in cartoons. It was the perfect day in the perfect location. But Steph was heartbroken.

She sat up, then pulled the seat belt away from her body. It had cut into her. She flexed her shoulder, then placed the seat belt once more.

"Of course I don't want to. I miss her."

In less than a week, she and Erin had become a team. They had a common purpose of making Erin appear sorted in love. Somewhere along the way, the lines had blurred, and now Steph's purpose in life was to see Erin smile. To hear her laugh. To hold her hand and kiss her lips. To make Erin believe in love again. Erin was a smiling shot of dopamine, and Steph a willing addict.

But she might have to walk away. Never get another hit of Erin ever again. Just the thought of that was like walking into a brick wall.

Steph gulped, then stared at her fingers. She still wasn't quite sure exactly when she'd fallen for Erin, but she clearly had. Was it when they'd danced? When they'd skinny dipped? Or maybe even before that, when Erin had let her into her life and told her about her sister. Taken her to her special beach. When she'd opened up.

It seemed all kinds of wrong for Steph to be in the Highlands and not be with Erin. This was *their* place, both together and as individuals. It was where they'd started their relationship. But it was also where Erin was born, and where Nadia had died, and given Steph the chance of a new life. The Highlands would always be a part of her, but now it went deeper. Without Erin in her life, it would also always be tainted. Steph would never come here again without thinking about this past week. About Erin, her family, and how their lives would always be intertwined.

Michael pulled into a passing place, even though there was no other car coming. He cut the engine, then nodded towards the view. "Shall we drink it in? You look like you could use some fresh air."

He opened the car door, and Steph followed. His phone rang. It had been ringing ever since he'd arrived. It turned out, Michael's business was very much in demand. He shook his head. "I'll call them back." He threw the phone on the front seat.

Michael was right to stop. The Highlands were so picturesque at every turn, it was easy to keep going, to take the next view for granted. She walked to the edge of the green-hued hill and breathed the impossibly fresh air. This was where her heart was from.

It was also where her heart had been won.

Michael stood beside her, his dark hair wafting in the slight breeze.

"If you miss her, chances are she's missing you, too."

Steph nodded. She knew he was right. But she still couldn't get Erin's look of disgust out of her head.

"My suggestion is that you try to relax. We've got three more days of driving around the Highlands, and I would like some smiles from you in among your hangdog expressions. I know this is hard, I know you've fallen for this woman, but you don't know how it's going to shake out. Everything is still very raw right now. She's probably in a fix trying to work out her emotions, too. It's a lot to take in, plus she's got her family to deal with. But you never know, you might hear from her before we head back."

Michael nudged her with his hip.

She smiled and nudged him back.

"Three more days with you?"

"If I don't drive us off a cliff."

"Always a possibility."

"Don't diss the driver, or you might not get a lift back to London. And then you won't be able to take up the starring role in that sexual health tour you've signed up for."

Two days ago, Steph had been wondering how she could work Erin into that schedule. Whether they could meet on tour. Now, getting far away from Scotland and putting herself on the road where she couldn't mope seemed like the best course of action. It was that, or do some more fake girlfriend work, and she couldn't face that again. Not so soon after round one.

She gave him a smile, then a sigh. Even if she was heartbroken, at least she had work. You couldn't have all your big-ticket items sorted, could you?

"Okay, I'll try to cheer up if you try not to kill us. Do we have a deal?"

Michael gave her a grin and they shook on it.

"Shall we get to our hotel and get a drink?"

"That's the best offer I've had all day."

* * *

The hotel bar was terribly swish, all marble tables, brass fittings and art deco style. Steph loved it.

Michael asked for the whisky menu, then glanced up. "Do you know anything about whisky? It's still a mystery to me. I like Jack Daniels, but I think they might slap me if I order that."

Steph reached over and took the menu from his hands. She ran a finger down the list, and stopped when she got to Jura. So did her heart.

The whisky she'd drunk with Erin.

Steph so wanted to see her again, to explain everything. If nothing else, to thank her family for what they did under terrible circumstances. More than anything, she wanted to know Erin was okay. Was she back in Edinburgh? But as Michael kept telling her, she had to give Erin space. If drinking Jura was a way to connect, so be it. She ordered two large glasses from the bartender, and they arrived quickly.

Michael twisted the crystal glass in his hands.

"Listen, I know your situation is eating you up. Can I give you a few words of wisdom? From one who knows?"

Steph tilted her head. "Since when have you ever been wise?"

"I'll ignore that comment."

He made sure he had her attention before he continued. "The first fake boyfriend job I did when I started the agency was for a man called Charles. He was tall, dark, and quirkily handsome, but I thought nothing of it. It was my first time. I went in and acted my little heart out. I put my arm around him. I hung on his every word attentively. I did everything we agreed beforehand. But when he laid the first fake kiss on me, it felt anything but fake. It felt like the most unfake kiss of my life, which didn't seem at all fair given everything that had gone before. I'd kissed my share of frogs and princes, right? But Charles was next level.

"We kissed for real later that night, we had sex and it was even better. We played at being boyfriends for a whole week in the Mediterranean, and then we said our goodbyes. I was sad, but I figured I'd get over it. This came with the territory. Charles was a music producer, and he worked at his studio in Mallorca for half the year. Our lives were so different. And yet, we'd shared so much in that week. You know how it is."

Steph nodded. She very much did. "It's like a month of dating all squashed into one intense portion of time."

"Exactly. A week later, Charles invited me to come back to his villa, as his guest for a long weekend. But I had another job booked. I couldn't say yes. Plus, where would it lead? Like I said, we led very different lives with very different schedules. I told him no." Michael took a deep breath. "He called again the following week and told me he couldn't stop thinking about me. That he'd like to try to make a go of it. That we could perhaps try to make our schedules work. He was prepared to try to mould our lives together because he felt it was worth it."

"And you didn't?"

His shoulders drooped. "I felt exactly the same, but I couldn't see how it could work practically. Plus, I'd just started the business and it needed my attention. I told him it wasn't practical. But my stone-cold heart broke in two that day, and I've never stopped thinking about him."

Steph stared. He'd never shared this story before. But then again, when he dropped out of the acting world, she hadn't seen him for months. She'd assumed it was because he was starting his own business. But now, she saw he'd been derailed by something else. Something he hadn't quite envisaged. Falling for someone when you weren't at all prepared.

"And that was why you constantly turned down my invitations to come out when you first started the company?"

He nodded again. "I threw myself into work to try to take my mind off it. But the more I worked with other clients, the more I realised what a gift Charles had been. We hit it off almost right away, and we just got each other, you know? I kissed a fair few other clients, but none of them were like kissing Charles. I had no trouble acting like a fake boyfriend for any of the others because it's what I was." He shook his head and took a deep breath. "But with Charles, nothing was clear cut. From the moment we kissed, I came alive, and I couldn't quite comprehend it."

"Why did you never tell me this before?"

He shrugged and twisted his whisky in his hand. "I couldn't change it, and it was too painful. I still feel it today. He's probably moved on, even if my heart hasn't."

Steph furrowed her brow. Michael was a player, a man about town. Not someone who fell so hard, so quickly.

Then again, neither was she—until now.

"I wish you'd told me sooner. There was me thinking you didn't understand." She cocked her head. "When you told me not to sleep with her, were you trying to warn me?"

"Maybe a little. But don't get me wrong, I slept with a couple of others, too, and there were no fireworks. No heart trouble."

"I think I've taken heart trouble to a new level."

Michael's eyes crinkled around the edges as he smiled. "You definitely have." He sat forward, taking her hand in his. "But the reason I'm coming clean now is I don't want you to make the same mistake if the same thing has happened to you. From what I've seen this week, it might have. Only you truly know. And yes, even if you get over the obvious, the practicalities might make your match too complex still. However, I turned Charles down because of geography. If that's what's holding you back with Erin, don't let it. London to Edinburgh isn't insurmountable."

If only that were the only obstacle.

Steph stared at her old friend, then moved towards him. She wrapped both arms around his broad shoulders and kissed his cheek, then hugged him hard.

As she did, Michael let out the longest sigh she'd ever heard.

"I can't believe the same thing happened to you."

"Minus the borrowed heart bit."

Steph smiled against his cheek, breathing in his very male smell, all soap and musk. But underneath, he was just as broken as she was. "Sounds like both our hearts have been put through the wringer by our fake dates." She held him at arm's length.

He nodded, his eyes shiny. "Just promise you won't dismiss it. I don't want to see you in two years' time with a sad face because you didn't at least try, okay?"

Steph licked her lips, then gave him a nod. "Okay." She paused. "But with you, Charles made the move. I have to wait for Erin to do the same, right?"

Michael nodded. "And there's the rub."

Chapter Twenty-Five

Alex sat on the deck of Lodge One, coffee in hand. His frown hadn't changed since he'd arrived, and his coffee was largely untouched.

"I still don't get it, though. Hiring a fake girlfriend. Where did you even find such a thing?"

"Morag."

He put his coffee on the table. "She just happened to have Steph hanging around in her shed? She's a bit kooky, but that's odd even for her." He paused. "I'm just sad you felt the need to do it in the first place."

"After everything that's happened, I'm sad I did it, too."

He ran a hand over his stubbly chin. "Are you? Because without Steph, I'm not sure we'd have had the weekend we did. Nadia's been dead for 20 years and we've never confronted our parents about it. Then Steph walks in and bam! Things get done. It's almost like she's channelling the spirit of Nadia. Does that sound strange?"

Erin shivered, then nodded. She'd had too many of those shivers of late. But she hadn't tasted candyfloss since Steph left.

"It's crossed my mind, but I pushed it aside because that makes the fact I slept with her even weirder."

"You need to stop thinking like that. You didn't sleep with Nadia."

"Easy for you to say."

Alex sighed, then gave her a soft smile. "You can beat yourself up about this all you like. All I'm saying is, Steph was a tonic for you *and* the whole family. So don't walk away from her unless you want to."

Erin crossed her arms over her chest. "She was only ever for the weekend, Alex. She was a hire car. Yes, I got an upgrade, but she always had a return date."

He sipped his coffee. "You're being stubborn and ridiculous, and getting in your own way about this. You know that, right?"

"I know you're annoying."

"Back at ya." He stuck out his tongue.

Erin had to smile. *Brothers.*

"My point is, do you want your time with her to be up?"

Erin gave an exasperated sigh. "Yes, no, I don't know! It's not that easy. She's not just some woman who I met and slept with, and then it didn't work out for some reason. The end. She's someone who I met, hired, slept with, shared stuff with, developed feelings for, and then I find out she has my sister's heart. That's not something I can process quickly. Plus, I asked Mum and she said she'd rather not meet any of Nadia's donors."

"You can't always get what you want."

"You think I don't know that? You're talking to the queen of not getting what she wants. I wanted a hassle-free girlfriend who'd fall for me and my family."

"Two out of three ain't bad."

"Are you just going to quote song lyrics at me today?"

Alex laughed. "This coffee's cold, by the way. And song lyrics often make a lot of sense." He wagged a finger at her. "Wendy was talking about it last night, and she thinks it's a sign. You could see it as things not quite going according to plan. Or you could see it as fate drawing you together. Steph has Nadia's heart pumping blood around her body. Who better to be her girlfriend than you?"

It was something she'd thought about all last night. Was it a sign they were meant to be?

"Would you sleep with a girl who had Nadia's heart?"

"I'm not sure Steph would be interested." He gave her a cheeky grin. "Honestly? I don't know. But I think the likelihood would be increased if she was someone I'd got to know, someone I liked, and someone who I could see something happening with. I get why you're hesitant because it is a bit weird when you say it at first. But then, Wendy might have a point. Bottom line, I don't think the fact that she's got Nadia's heart should stand in your way. She's not Nadia. She's way taller for a start. She's very much Steph, and that's what you have to hold on to."

She got what he was saying. But there was still a nagging doubt in the back of her mind. Yes, Steph was very much her own woman. But she wouldn't be here without Nadia. Her twin sister was inside Steph. The light that shone from her face when she smiled that Erin had so admired? It was there because of Nadia. The warmth of her skin? Nadia's doing. The way she kissed Erin like nobody else ever had in her entire life? Nadia was still in the mix. Could she separate the two?

"I'm not sure if you're being wise, or just not putting yourself in my shoes."

"You're overthinking it, which you always do. It's a character fault. You slept with her this weekend, right?"

Erin nodded. "I did." Blood crept to her cheeks. When Steph had straddled her, looked down on her like she wanted to eat her alive, Erin had been nothing but satisfied. She wanted that again so desperately. Now she'd popped her cork, maybe she could go out on the town and meet other women. Kiss them. Have sex with them. She tried to picture it, but her mind just pulled up Steph. But wasn't her theory correct? Just like they said on radio shows when a guest accidentally mentioned a brand, 'other products are available'. Didn't that go for women, too?

"And was it terrible?"

A broad smile landed on her face. She couldn't help it. "It was not." The opposite, in fact. But she wasn't going to elaborate. He was still her little brother.

"That's got to count for something." He grinned, then leaned forward. "Plus, I think you're leaving out the other factors that should influence your decision here."

"Which are?"

"She's smoking hot, she's into you, and your family like her. When has that happened in the last decade?"

He had a point.

* * *

Later that day, Erin sat on the edge of the pool, feet immersed. The surrounding hills were a mix of slate grey, moss, and midnight blue, the sky the colour of a baby blanket.

She flicked her toes in the water, and it took her right back to Saturday night. To Steph with her tanned, delicious skin. It had been the first time Erin had asked about her scar. The first time she'd really seen it up close.

Steph had said it was a heart thing she'd had when she was younger. She hadn't lied. But she hadn't told the full truth, either.

Erin closed her eyes as the familiar jumble of Steph-flavoured feelings streaked through her. She kept thinking about her mum's face. The way she'd walked off when Erin had told her, the way she'd avoided her ever since. They'd only just pulled the family back together again.

Erin couldn't blow it up for Steph.

Someone close by clearing their throat made her look up.

Dad. He looked tired. Sometimes, Erin forgot he was 65. That he wouldn't be around forever. Not that age equalled being closer to death. If Erin knew anything, it was that you could die at any age. Nadia had taught her that.

He ran a hand over his stubble, just as Alex had earlier. Her dad's dark hair had turned greyer these days, but the similarities with him and Alex were more evident every time she saw them together. "You mind if I join you?"

This was new. Dad never came to speak to his kids. It was always Mum that did the dirty work, and Dad who stood behind and nodded his agreement. Talking wasn't his strong suit. He'd said more meaningful things to Erin in the past day than he had in the rest of her lifetime. He'd always been great with facts, figures, certainties. That's why he'd gone into medicine. Over the years, he'd learned the reactions people expected. Unscripted feelings weren't his strong suit.

Erin shook her head, then jumped up, flicking water

from her feet. Her dad wasn't a pool person. He'd built it for his family. Building, he could do. Regular maintenance was his problem.

"I'll come over to the house if you like. I could do with a drink."

He nodded, waited for her to find her flip-flops, then they walked in silence.

He sat on the outdoor terrace, now so quiet compared to the weekend. The marquee was gone, as was everyone else. It was as if none of it had ever happened.

Erin got them both a beer from the small fridge her parents kept under a wooden awning at the front of the house, then sat next to him.

Her dad hitched his navy-blue shorts, then picked at the label on the beer bottle. He stared out to the loch, shimmering in the late evening sun. "Crazy weather we're having."

"I ordered it especially for the weekend."

He laughed, then crossed one leg over the other.

"Doug said he had plenty of sunburn victims in the surgery today." Doug Philips had taken over her parents' practice when they retired.

They sat in silence for a few moments, the only sound a shout from the High Street. It sometimes carried up the hill.

"I wanted to apologise."

She blinked. Of all the words Erin had expected, those were not the ones. "You do?"

"I think we need to. For making you think you had to hire a girlfriend." He shook his head. "I can't imagine where you go about finding a girlfriend now the Yellow Pages aren't an option. May I ask?"

"The internet. You can get most things on the internet these days."

"I suppose you can." He turned to her. "But I hate that you thought you had to. You are enough. You've always been enough."

Erin's heart twisted inside out. "That's not how it's seemed since Nadia died. It's why I left. I couldn't take the pressure. It felt like every time you looked at me, I reminded you of what you'd lost." Should she say anymore? She made a quick decision. This was a new era in their family. "I often wondered if you'd have preferred Nadia to live and not me. She had a boyfriend when she died. She was the more gregarious."

Her dad shook his head. He put down his beer and took her hand in his. "We never *once* thought that. If we ever looked at you in a funny way, it's because we wanted to make sure you were still there. We lived in dread of you dying, too. Yes, you reminded us of Nadia, I won't deny that. You're her twin. That's always going to happen. But when we looked at you, we only ever saw our beautiful, talented daughter. We *always* wanted you, nobody else. You and Nadia looked alike, but that's where the similarity ended. You were your own people."

Goosebumps broke out on Erin's skin. What a few days she was having. She was surprised the see-saw of emotions wasn't making her sick.

"We were, and we still are, even though she died. But by not bringing her up, you rejected her. In doing so, you also rejected me." Erin took a deep breath. Some of these thoughts she'd never verbalised before. She'd known them theoretically, but never expressed them out loud. But every single one of them was true. She and Nadia were different, but they were also forever linked.

Which is what made the Steph situation so incredibly hard to unpick.

But she couldn't think about that now.

This was about her and her parents. One step at a time.

"I know. I hate hearing you say that, but I know. We've done a lot wrong. You and Alex were brave to confront us. Now, we want to make it right. Which is why I came to find you. I know you've got a lot of things going on right now with Steph, but I wanted to let you know that the choice with Steph is yours, and yours alone."

Erin twisted around to face her dad, taking her hand back from him. She frowned. "That's not true though, is it? Mum said she resented her. That she'd rather not know her. In trying to do the right thing by bringing a girlfriend, I unwittingly brought the one person who could hurt the family."

Dad gave her a sad smile. "This family has been hurting itself for years on its own. Steph being here or not isn't going to impact that."

"But what about Mum? What about you?" Erin turned her palms upwards as she asked.

"Mum will get over it. What she said was a snap reaction. She didn't know the full story then. If you've developed feelings for Steph and you want to take it further, you have our blessing. You don't need it, of course, but you have it."

Was he telling the truth? Trusting her parents to do the right thing was going to take some getting used to. But she had to start somewhere. When Erin glanced up, her mum walked up behind her dad. She put her hands on his shoulders.

She wasn't wearing any makeup which was so unusual. Patsy Stewart was always made up, always ready for whatever the occasion demanded.

Today, she stood unmasked. Raw. Natural.

She stared at her daughter. "What your dad says is right. We want this family to heal. If Steph is a part of it, we'll cope."

Shockwaves flowed through Erin. Her mind couldn't keep up with all the changes this week. If she was flummoxed before, she was doubly so now. "I don't know what's happening with Steph. She left in such a rush. I don't know how either of us is feeling, apart from dazed and confused."

"I won't lie. Your dad and I were both spooked by it at first. Who wouldn't be? But then we stood back and asked, what would Nadia think? I think she'd be thrilled that her heart went to a woman who could make you happy."

"I hardly know her."

"But you *want* to." Her mum pulled out a chair and sat next to her dad. "I saw the way you two were. The way you danced. The way you looked at each other. That was a spectacular piece of acting if it wasn't real, on both sides."

All that was true. She had felt something for Steph she hadn't felt in an awfully long time. But there was still a major obstacle in the way for Erin, even if her parents had come to terms with it.

"I never felt the same as your mum. I found solace knowing Nadia's death helped others from the start. Meeting Steph helped me." Her dad looked her direct in the eye. "If you like her, don't let the donor thing stand in your way. It's a bump in the road. But if she becomes part of the family, it means Nadia is back with us in some way. That makes it extra-special."

Erin scrunched her face. "Not extra weird?"

"Only if you make it so." Her dad splayed his big hands. "I'm a doctor, so I'll give you my medical opinion. An organ is just that. It's a body part. If yours fails, you can hopefully get a replacement. None of it changes who you are as a person. When Nadia died, the person she was did, too. But she was able to help Steph, and that's incredible. It's not Nadia's heart anymore. She gave it to Steph."

It didn't change the fact there was still a part of her dead sister inside her most recent lover. "Who says she wants anything to do with me? We hardly presented as the model family at the weekend."

Her dad smiled as he stared out to the water. "I'd say that's for Steph to decide."

Her mum stood up and held out her hand to Erin. "Come on," she said. "Let's go inside. There's something I want to show you. We bought new frames today, and I need to decide where to hang all the photos of my children. All three of them."

Erin took a breath, then took her mum's hand.

Sometimes, you had to put your doubts to one side, and take a leap of faith.

Her family were sticking themselves back together. Slowly, but surely.

They thought they could get over the fact that Steph had Nadia's heart.

If only Erin could be so sure.

* * *

Erin poured a coffee from the pot, then sat on the sofa and stared out at the loch. She cupped its warmth, even though she didn't need it. It was comforting, and she could definitely do with that.

She couldn't sit on this sofa without thinking about Steph. She stroked the cream fabric, soft under her fingertips. Steph had slept right here. Erin had fucked her right here. She'd thought about moving into the main house when Steph had gone, but quickly reversed that notion when she realised she needed space after everything that had happened. Time to think, process, and reflect. It always took a while for Erin to work through her thoughts and feelings, and her parents were normally the same. Not this time, though. They'd scattered Nadia's ashes, agreed to therapy, and now Nadia was back on the walls of the main house.

Erin put a hand to her chest and pressed down. Her sister had always been in her parents' hearts, and now she was where she should have always been: in their daily lives. Her parents had said that if Erin's daily life involved Steph, they'd handle it. That Erin's happiness was important to them, especially after their past behaviour. They wanted to make it up to her, even if Steph came as part of the package. Erin wondered how they could be so sure. But then again, they didn't have to see her naked. See that scar. Be that close to a part of Nadia.

She took a deep breath and clutched her mug tighter.

It'd been a handful of days since Steph left, but it felt like it just happened. Erin could still feel her in the lodge, and she couldn't deny it was one of the reasons she wanted to stay, too. She didn't believe in love at first sight. At least, she hadn't, until she met Steph. But the fairy tales she read never came with a punchline like hers. Maybe they should have, to prepare Erin for precisely this moment.

She hadn't progressed as her family had. She was still stuck in the moment when Steph had dropped her bombshell. Erin could still picture the tortured look on Steph's perfect face, and she couldn't make herself move past that moment.

She still didn't know what she wanted to do. Her head said one thing, her heart said another. And Nadia's heart that was beating inside Steph's body? Well, that was a whole other layer to the puzzle.

She'd phoned Morag last night to get her view on the Steph dilemma. Morag had been speechless on the other end of the phone, probably the one and only time it'd happened in their history. Your lover having your dead twin's heart would do that, as Morag had told her. Her best friend had advised Erin to stay put and sort everything out before she came back to Edinburgh. To see Steph, whatever her decision. They'd left whatever they had in limbo, and Morag's verdict was they both needed closure so they could move on with their lives.

Erin ground her teeth together. Instinctively, she knew her friend was right, but she also wanted to bury her head in the sand and let someone else make this decision. Her life had always had obstacles, ever since Nadia died. Nothing ever came easy. For once, she'd like something to be plain sailing. This wasn't it.

She got up and put her mug on the counter, then gripped the edges and stretched her back. She'd done this when Steph was here, and Steph had proceeded to kiss the small of her back where her T-shirt had ridden up. That was what she wanted back. Physical touch. Their ease together. Godammit, she'd never had that with *anyone*. But was it enough to overcome everything else?

Erin straightened up, then picked up her phone and scrolled to Steph's number. Her finger had hovered over the delete button last night after a couple of wines, but she was glad she hadn't. Erin was a wild mix of wanting to expunge Steph from her life, but also wanting her back here, Steph's body pressed against her own, Steph's strong fingers pulling her close.

She tipped her head towards the ceiling. She wanted what they'd promised each other. She wanted it *so badly*. But would she forever be thinking of Nadia when Steph was around? Would it actually be weird with her family, despite what they were saying? There were so many ifs and buts and she didn't have an answer. All she knew was, it was an impossible decision, and things could go wrong whatever decision she made.

She stared at Steph's number. She didn't want to call, but she had to. Perhaps setting a deadline would force Erin to make a decision? Maybe as soon as she saw Steph, things would become clearer. She'd know what it was she wanted. What she could live with, or without. Giving herself this week hadn't helped, so something had to change.

Her heart thumped in her chest. Just the thought of Steph made it do that. But then her mind chimed in: *A lover with your sister's heart? What kind of twisted shit is that?* Steph had called it a mindfuck. Erin wholeheartedly agreed. But she couldn't stay in limbo forever. She had a life and a job to get back to, a family to glue back together again. All of those things still had to happen. She just had to decide whether they included Steph, or not.

She steeled herself, clutched the phone, then pressed Steph's number.

Okay universe, you've fucked me around enough this week.
A little slack would be welcome, today.

Fuck, she hoped it went to voicemail.

Chapter Twenty-Six

They spent their last full day climbing hills, then driving the A9. When they eventually arrived at their guest house in Dornoch, they were greeted by the owners—prime candidates to star in a remake of *The Good Life*—along with their pair of over-enthusiastic black Labradors. Trevor shooed them out into the garden, then came back.

"Sorry about that," he said. "Their bark is worse than their bite."

Trevor and Sheila seemed to be under the impression she and Michael were reliving their honeymoon. Mainly because Michael had told them that, and also because they'd booked a room with a king-size bed, so the owners naturally assumed they were a couple.

"Lovely to see you!" Sheila wore dungarees and those felt slippers Steph was constantly served ads for on Instagram. "Been anywhere nice today?"

"We drove down from John O'Groats, went to Dunrobin Castle, and then had a picnic by the water." He fluttered his eyelids Steph's way. "Just like we did on honeymoon 15 years ago."

He was *such* a bugger.

Sheila shook her head. "Fifteen years. You two don't look

old enough to have been married for that long. You've got such baby faces!"

Michael gave an exaggerated shrug and slung an arm around Steph's shoulders. "When you know, you just know, right?"

Steph dragged him away before he could do any more damage, then walked up the stairs to their room.

"I can see your eye roll even though I'm walking behind you."

She turned, giving him a look. "I should hope so. We've been married 15 years; you should know me by now." She raised both eyebrows, then led them into the room.

First things first: she had to get out of her clothes and take a shower. Today had been a good distraction. It turned out, walking Scottish scenery took your mind off your problems. There had been a moment, though, where she slipped on some loose rocks and nearly slid off the hill. Steph's heart had kicked in her chest. She'd hauled herself up the side of the hill, staring at the surroundings, as Nadia worked hard to keep her alive.

Nadia.

She'd often wondered about her heart donor. What kind of person she was. Now she knew. Nadia had been someone to reckon with: a certified badass. Steph liked that. That afternoon, sat on the hill, she'd almost felt Nadia telling her to be the same. To take a chance. To live her life. Steph had always shied away from strenuous exertions. But maybe the biggest strain she could put on her heart was falling in love. It might have already happened.

Michael clicked his fingers.

Steph jumped.

"Where were you?" He stared at her. "On second thoughts, don't tell me. You were probably dreaming about the moment where Erin is going to turn up here and declare her undying love for you." He put a hand on his hip. "What was she wearing? A Wonder Woman costume?"

"My daydreams don't generally involve cosplay." But now she couldn't think about anything else.

"Get in the shower, then we can have a great last night before we head back tomorrow. I've got a big meeting, and you've got your sexually transmitted disease to rehearse for." He sniggered as he said the last part.

"Whatever. At least I'm still doing the job of my heart." She wasn't sure that was true, but she had to say something.

Michael gave her a grin. "Whereas I'm doing the job of my bank account."

Ten minutes later, she stepped back into the bedroom, making sure the green bath sheet wrapped around her was secure.

When she did, Michael jumped off the bed like he'd been electrocuted.

She gave him a puzzled look. "What is it?"

Michael stared at her, then held up his phone in his hand. "I just got a call."

This was not news, he'd been getting them all day, even on the top of Scottish hills. Michael's phone had super-reception. "And?"

"It was from Erin."

Steph exhaled. Her whole system revved at the mere mention of her name. "Why did she call you?" Was she after a replacement fake date after her first one turned out to be faulty? Steph's chest heaved as she considered all the permutations.

"Because she couldn't reach you on the phone. You turned it off, remember? You said you wanted to spend the final day not taking photos, just actually being present?"

She had said that. What a berk.

"What did she say?"

Michael set his mouth in a straight line before he answered. "She said she wants to see you. I told her we were going home tomorrow. So is she. She's suggested meeting for a coffee at a services on the way. I told her you'd confirm by text."

Hot, dangerous hope flowed through Steph. This was what she'd wanted for the past five days since they last saw each other, wasn't it? Nadia was Erin's sister, and it was up to Erin to get in touch. Now she had. Did she want to see if things could go further, or did she just want closure? Steph wouldn't know until she spoke to her.

She pulled back both her shoulders and felt her backbone click. "I don't need to call her back?"

He shook his head. "She said to confirm by text."

"How did she sound?"

He raised his shoulders and gave her a despairing look. "Like a woman." He held up his hands. "I don't know how she normally sounds."

Steph scowled, then picked up a cushion and chucked it at Michael's head.

He let out a high-pitched squeal. "It's not my fault you were in the shower! I told her you'd message back, so I'm going to give you some space to do that while I take the longest shower in human history." He kissed her cheek as he walked by. "And once that's done, I'm buying you the largest glass of wine they have. Okay?"

She had a feeling she'd need it.

* * *

Steph hadn't eaten breakfast this morning, much to Trevor and Sheila's consternation. Now, as the signs told her that Balhaldie Services were within spitting distance, she thought she might vomit. Instead, she took deep breaths, checked her watch again, and bounced her knee in the footwell. Michael glanced her way, but she kept her eyes facing forward. Conversation wasn't what she wanted right now. Focus was her friend. That focus was pulled into sharp clarity when a black boxy building with a Starbucks logo appeared in the distance.

"This is it." Michael pulled into the car park, which was empty save for two other cars.

One of the two other cars was Erin's white Toyota.

Now Steph *really* felt like she might be sick.

"The Starbucks that could play a huge role in your future. Whoever thought that would be a sentence coming out of my mouth?" Michael cut the engine and reached across to take Steph's hand. "Just remember, whatever happens here, I'll buy you dinner when we get to England."

Steph flipped down the sun visor and checked her hair in the mirror, then reapplied her lipstick. She was as ready as she was going to be for a meeting she had no control over. Was this a make-up or break-up chat? Could you even break up when things hadn't truly got started? She wasn't sure, but this felt bigger than any other break-up chat she'd ever had.

She glanced at Michael, her fingers stroking the door handle. She didn't want to leave, but then, she did. "You'll wait here?"

"I promise I won't leave without you."

When she got into the Starbucks, Erin was already there. She stood up when she saw Steph and waved a hand.

Steph's stomach lurched but she managed to propel her feet forwards. Good start.

Even though she was sure Erin had been agonising over this meeting, she was still radiant. She wore a black shirt Steph hadn't seen before, and her short hair looked adorable. It didn't help Steph quake any less. Especially when she clocked her Marilyn beauty spot. She wanted to kiss it all over again.

"Hi. Thanks for coming." Erin's words were stilted, but she paired them with a smile. It didn't quite reach her eyes, but it was a start. "Can I get you a coffee?"

Steph shook her head. "I'll get it."

Minutes later, she sat opposite Erin with her flat white. She wasn't sure she'd drink it, but it was something to do with her hands.

Erin reached into her bag on the chair beside her and pulled out a can of Irn Bru. She put it on the table and slid it across to Steph. "Just in case you haven't tried it yet."

Steph's stomach flipped. She'd bought her a can of Irn Bru. That had to be a good sign, right? "I haven't, so thank you." Did you bring presents for someone you didn't want in your life? Steph's mind combed her life.

Sometimes.

She wasn't going to dwell on that.

"It's good to see you." She tried to pin down Erin's gaze,

but it wasn't easy. Was she pleased to see her? She couldn't quite get a handle on the vibe. On the speaker behind her, The Clash's 'Should I Stay or Should I Go' blared out. Steph rolled her eyes at the music gods, clearly having a good old joke this morning.

"Good to see you, too." Erin's fingers tightened around her cup.

Steph flexed her toes in her trainers. Was Erin telling the truth? She spied flecks of paint around her fingernails where Erin hadn't quite managed to clean the excess off. "You been having a busman's holiday?"

Erin held her fingers up. "I helped mum and dad clear out the relaxation room yesterday, and we gave it a little spruce up. Now Nadia's not there, it can be used again."

She winced, like she'd said more than she intended. Then Erin glanced down at the table, then back up to Steph.

"How was the rest of your week?"

"Surreal after my time with you," Steph replied. "I'd been looking forward to that part of the trip with Michael ever since we arranged it, and it's been great visiting all the places we came to in our youth."

Erin's gaze slipped to Steph's mouth as she spoke.

Heat flared inside Steph, but she continued. "When I took this job, it was a way to visit Scotland again. A place close to my heart as you know." She breathed deep. "I never for one moment thought the job would turn into the most important part of my trip. Or rather, the people I met. How are your family doing? How did they react when they found out I was the recipient of Nadia's heart?" Steph frowned. "I assume you told them? About everything?"

Erin gave an uncertain nod, and her face paled. "I did. They were stunned I hired you. They were even more stunned that you had Nadia's heart. My mum's coming around. My dad took it surprisingly well. As did Alex. Better than both my mum and me. Perhaps it says something about how the sexes view these issues? But everyone's had a bit more time to get used to the idea now."

"For me, too." Just the thought catapulted Steph back there. Back to scattering the ashes, hearing Nadia's name and knowing instinctively what that meant.

"I helped my Mum and Dad rehang Nadia's photos. Not too many, it's not a shrine, but Nadia's part of our story again."

That hit Steph in the gut. "She's a part of my story, too."

Erin was silent for a moment. "She is."

Steph's muscles clenched a little more. The stuttering nature of their connection didn't make her hopeful. Her heart ached with the finality of it all. Walking in here, she'd allowed herself to dream. Now, if Erin intended to drop the bomb, Steph wished she'd hurry up. Or should she save her the trouble and do it herself?

Erin took a deep breath.

Steph braced herself.

"I couldn't have done any of this without you appearing in my life, though. Changed my family. It all happened because you shook things up."

Steph's feelings, punch drunk and slumped on the floor, staggered to their feet. Had she been too hasty with her forecasts of devastation?

"I'm glad to have helped. Seeing as I also hindered things, it's good there was a balance."

Erin gave a gentle laugh. "Definitely more help than hindrance. For me, and for my family. I wanted to see you to say thank you for that."

Steph sat up and took the lid off her coffee. Steam rose up. It was still too hot. She looked down and traced the inside seam of her jeans with her index finger. Was that the only reason? They'd only been in the Starbucks for ten minutes, but already she'd had more highs and lows than she normally had in a month. It was par for the course for their relationship so far.

Erin didn't say anything. What was Steph missing? She decided to be brave.

"I missed you this week."

Erin tapped her foot on the floor. "I know," she said, paper-thin. "I missed you, too. I wanted to see you." She stared at the table.

Something wasn't right.

"Wanted?"

Erin shook her head. "It's complicated. I have my family's consent to see you. They'll all get over the Nadia connection. But I don't know if I can."

Spikes sprang up in Steph's throat. She could hardly breathe.

"Half of me wants to reach across the table and kiss you, but then the other half remembers the reasons I can't." Erin hung her head.

Panic rose in Steph. "Can't you focus on the first half? Because that part is pretty strong in me, too." She looked at Erin's fingers, within reach, but also off limits. When had that happened? This felt desperate now. "Saturday night meant something. We *had* something. I don't skinny dip with just anyone." If this was slipping away, Steph wasn't going to let it go without a fight. "Didn't you feel it, too?"

Erin raised her gaze to Steph. Her eyes shone. "Of course I did." Her voice wobbled as she spoke.

Fuck it.

Steph reached over and placed a hand on Erin's arm. "Then can't we try to make this work somehow? I mean, I know it will be difficult at first, what with both of our work schedules, but once my play is done, I could see if I could get more work further north." She struggled to keep her voice from wobbling. Sure, she'd never said exactly how she was feeling, but surely Erin knew from all they'd shared. *Surely, she knew.* She'd prepared herself to walk away, for Erin to reject her. However, now she was here, it was the absolute last thing she wanted. She was going to do everything in her power to fix this. She wasn't going down without a fight.

Erin gazed at her, then shook her head. "Aren't there too many obstacles? Isn't that trying to tell us something? I paid for you."

"I've asked Michael to refund you. I don't want your money. It should be in your account by now."

Erin squeezed her eyes tight shut and shook her head. "You didn't need to do that." She sunk her fingers into her hair and sighed. "But it's not just that and you know it. We live in different countries. My family. *Nadia's heart.* The list goes on."

Weren't they all just excuses? Was Erin scared, like in all her other relationships?

Michael's words from the other day rang in Steph's ears. "Don't let practicality stop you following your heart."

It was easier said than done. Practicality had a lot going for it. Her heart was the issue.

Steph shook her head. "It could be a test of how much we want it."

"Or it could be the universe telling us to see this for what it was. A momentous weekend in many ways, but that's it?"

Anger rose in her. Erin was throwing them away. "What about us? Don't you think there's something there that could be great?"

Erin wouldn't look her in the eye. "I'm not sure."

Something caught in Steph's throat. She wanted to adjust the reception on her antenna, because this scenario was not playing out as she intended. This was not how she'd pictured their reunion going. No smiles. No hugs. No kisses. She couldn't entertain the thought of never kissing Erin again. It would be a crime. Their kisses had been too good. Far from embracing that, Erin had chosen to put her heart on ice.

"Seriously? You're writing us off before we've even started? Why did you even want to see me?"

"Because I owed you that much. I'm thrilled you've led a good life, and I'm pleased that Nadia helped you do that. But if I got into a relationship with you, Nadia would always be in it, too. I'm not sure I want that."

Steph's brain blared red. "How about if it worked the other way? Your sister could bring us together, bind us in such a unique way." Steph drew back her shoulders and shifted in her seat. She couldn't quite believe that Erin was just prepared to chuck in the towel. That she wasn't even prepared to listen.

Perhaps she'd misread the situation when they were together. Perhaps she'd been in a bubble, and it had now burst. But even as she thought that, she dismissed it. What they'd experienced together had been all sorts of real. The realest thing she'd done in her entire life. Why couldn't Erin see they could use this to their advantage? That they could be great? Steph stared at the can of Irn Bru, mocking her. She pushed it aside.

"You know, I told you I might learn something on this job. Turned out, I learned more than I could possibly have imagined. That you should trust your gut and follow your heart. Don't be afraid of change." She shook her head. "It seems like you've learned nothing. I can't force you into something you don't want, so I'll walk out of here and you'll never hear from me again. But you want to know what I think?"

She stared at Erin's addictive face. Her blue eyes. Her soft skin. Nothing had changed. Steph still felt the same. But Erin wasn't prepared to acknowledge that she might, too. Steph had to make her see.

"You're running away again. Using Nadia as an excuse. If I let every setback I ever had dictate my life, I probably wouldn't be here. When do you plan on living your life? What age are you going to wait for, Erin? Are you scared now that all the familiar obstacles have been torn down, so you need to put up some new ones?" Steph knew this was harsh, but Erin had to hear it. She stabbed her index finger to her own chest. "Your sister gave me a second chance at life, and I took it." She paused for added effect. "Now, Nadia would want you to take yours, too."

Steph took one last look at Erin. There were so many strong arguments, but she didn't want to listen. Steph had to be true to her word. She got up, turned, and walked out, leaving her coffee, Irn Bru and Erin behind. She didn't look back.

She'd come into this open and full of what might be. But Erin hadn't. Why had she instigated the meeting in the first place? That was the mystery to Steph.

She pushed open the door and walked out onto the car park, the gravel crunching underfoot. It reminded her of Loch View House. She shook the image from her head. The Highlands used to be a special place. Not anymore.

Michael got out of the car as she approached, but she shook her head.

"I was just going to get a coffee and come and say hi." He gave her a puzzled look.

She shook her head. "Not in this coffee house. You'll have to wait until the next one. Right now, you need to drive so I can get as far away from here as humanly possible."

Chapter Twenty-Seven

It was good to get home and back to some level of normality. At least, that's what Erin kept telling herself.

Over the next few weeks, her parents got a therapist recommendation and went to three sessions. Erin was impressed. They reported it was hard work, but they were going to continue. Erin couldn't ask for any more than that. She drove up to see them in June but made sure to stay in the main house. The lodge raised its eyebrows when she walked by, but Erin kept her head down. That weekend with Steph had been a mirage in her life. An aberration. A blip. It was time to get back to normal when she visited the Highlands and she was going to do just that.

Meanwhile, back in Edinburgh, work was full-on, and Erin couldn't love it more. When she wasn't painting and decorating, she ran. She pounded Edinburgh's streets, and tried to put everything out of her mind. But every time she turned on the radio, they seemed to be playing heartbreak songs. Every time she thought about Nadia, her sister frowned. In everything she did, Steph was there. In every brushstroke. Every van ride. Every mug of tea she drank.

But Erin had made the right decision. The only decision for her and her family. She'd put a note on her calendar to sign up to a dating app. Now that she'd dipped her toe back into the water, she might be ready for the real thing. Because that's what Steph had been. A bridge back to the dating world. Nothing more.

Erin ground her teeth together and kicked a stone on the pavement. She had this argument with herself most days. She was ready for Steph to get out of her head and out of her life, but she was proving stubborn. It had been nearly two months since she last saw her, but she was still very much alive inside her.

The thought of never seeing her again, never hearing her voice made Erin's stomach churn.

Like it was doing now.

Her phone beeped in her back pocket, and she took it out. A notification flashed up, telling her today was the final day of Steph's school tour. Erin swiped it from the screen, then exhaled. She raised her eyes to the overcast sky. It mirrored her mood.

She'd put those dates in before the dreadful Starbucks day when there was a possibility they'd be together. When the thought of Steph in Carlisle meant Erin could drive two hours to see her. She still could, but she was pretty sure Steph would blank her. She'd been harsh at Starbucks, she knew that now, but it'd been too raw. Would she change her mind if she had to do it all again?

She still wasn't a hundred per cent sure, but she'd be less black and white. Particularly when she had to look into Steph's eyes and tell her they couldn't have a relationship. What had felt so sure, so certain two months ago now seemed on shakier ground.

She took a deep breath. It didn't matter now. It was too late, even if she might change her mind.

She'd even been on a date with another woman. A friend of a friend of Morag's named Chrissy. She'd been lovely. A perfectly acceptable date. Astute, disarming smile, own teeth, solvent. Someone Erin should have been ideal for.

But Chrissy had one failing that Erin didn't want to face: she wasn't Steph.

Morag was still pissed off with Erin. They'd had words the night before. Erin hated the colours their new clients had chosen, describing them as "pukey pink" and "vomit violet". Morag had told her they painted homes whatever colours clients wanted. She'd also told her that nothing was right in Erin's life at the moment, and that was because she wasn't facing up to her feelings. Morag had basically reiterated what Steph had told her two months previous. That she was running away and using Nadia as an excuse.

Erin could almost see her scowl as she pulled up in their work van and slammed the door. Morag put a hand on her hip as she landed in front of her, dressed in standard blue overalls and white T-shirt. "Good morning, sunshine!" Her sarcasm reverberated in the air. "Ready to play nice today with the clients paying our wages and tell them we love their colour choices?"

Erin cracked a half-smile. It was the best she could do. "I've been practising my play-nice phrases all morning."

"Grand. But just to be safe, let me do the talking on this one, yes? You just smile, nod and look like a cool lesbian."

"That, I can do." Erin put the tips of her index and middle fingers to her forehead and gave Morag a salute.

Morag rolled her eyes.

Their clients today—Tracy and Rachel—had just bought their first home together. To say they were happy about it getting painted by women would be an understatement. They answered the door together on Morag's first knock, and their bright white smiles almost bowled her over. "We've been waiting at the door, we're so excited!" they both said at the same time.

Erin gave them her best grin, still only operating on 65 per cent. "We are, too."

They walked in, and the pair showed them through to the lounge. Their flat took up the ground floor of one of Edinburgh's many tenements. The rooms were vast, with high ceilings, and this flat hadn't seen a lick of paint in at least a decade. It was more than enough to keep Erin and Morag busy for a couple of weeks.

"Can I just say, we're both so thrilled you're doing this. We couldn't think of better decorators to make our dreams a reality."

Morag gave them a grin. "We hope we do your dreams proud, don't we, Erin?"

Erin nodded, then gulped. In the corner of the lounge, propped up against the wall was a huge hand-painted canvas. The painting depicted a Ferris wheel, and two women on it, laughing. But it was what was in the women's hands that drew Erin to the image. They were both holding huge pink swirls of candyfloss on sticks. She gulped. She hadn't tasted candyfloss since Steph left, no matter how much she thought about Nadia. Here was a painting that was the pure essence of Nadia. A fairground, with candyfloss. If Nadia had lived to be an adult, this was the painting she'd have hung above her mantlepiece.

But she hadn't lived. She would never hang a painting.

But Steph could on her behalf.

Something glowed hot above her ribcage, and Erin swayed on her feet. She frowned, then rubbed her chest. She stared at the floor to regulate her breathing. The two women were still talking about their vision for the room, but their words spun in the air around Erin.

She glanced at Morag, who was nodding at the clients like a pro, but Erin knew she was side-eyeing her, too.

Erin gulped, then knew she needed air.

"I'm just going to…" she began, then bolted from the room. The tiled hallway was blurred under her feet as she yanked open the olive-green front door, clutched the front gate, then vomited on the Portobello pavement outside. Erin's head throbbed, and every muscle she owned shook as she retched a little more. Her vision swam as if she was underwater. All this from a painting? Erin squeezed her eyes tight shut and waited for it to pass. When she eventually turned her head back to the lounge, Morag and the two women stared at her through the large bay window. Erin put up a hand and gave them a weak smile.

Seconds later, Morag was on the pavement beside her. "What the hell was that?" she whispered, then put an arm around her. "I know their colour choices are bad, but vomiting before they've even opened the paint tins is a bit much."

Erin shook her head. She went to speak, but she couldn't. She went to say the word 'candyfloss', but couldn't. An image of Steph by the pool, licking candyfloss from her fingers assaulted Erin's mind. Then one of them dancing, cheek to cheek. Then Steph on the beach, eating her bacon sandwich, giving her that grin. The one that still made Erin's stomach swoop right this second.

This job was a sign. Being sick when she saw that painting was a sign.

She had to see Steph again, didn't she? She had to go back and question her choices. She'd known her decision would come with consequences, but now she had to make a change. Because life without Steph wasn't proving that good.

Erin was living it on autopilot. She was living a half-life. She'd told Steph she didn't think she could be with her because she had Nadia's heart. But it was the *complete* opposite. Erin had walked on eggshells ever since her sister died. Just when her family had changed, she'd thrown herself back into the same turmoil all over again. It made no sense. She had to move on. Nadia would *want* her to. Nadia was never coming back, but Steph could. It was only now Erin realised that was what she wanted.

What had Steph said? "Nadia gave me a second chance at life, and I took it. She'd want you to take it, too."

She still didn't have the taste of candyfloss in her mouth. She wanted it back. Suddenly, Erin knew exactly who held the key to getting it. Steph might slam the door in her face. But she had to at least try.

Chapter Twenty-Eight

The sexual health play ended up being way more fun than Steph had anticipated. It turned out, playing Chlamydia had more ups than downs. Plus, chatting with a bunch of teenagers every day had given Steph much-needed optimism for the future. These kids appeared to have their lives sorted way more than Steph had at their age.

It'd also been two months since she'd left Scotland. The same amount of time since she'd heard a word from Erin. She'd put what happened with them to the back of her mind, consigned to the box marked 'experience'. Steph had walked out in an attempt to retain at least some of her dignity, leaving Erin and her can of Irn Bru behind.

She'd even gone out to the local gay bar in Preston the night before and chatted up a woman. It had felt good. Nice to be back out there, even if her heart wasn't wholly in it. The woman had asked for her number, but Steph had shaken her head. She'd left for Carlisle the following day. The last stop on their two-month tour that had taken in the whole of England. There was no point trying to stay in touch with a stranger, especially when they lived so far apart. She'd tried that with Erin, and look how that had ended.

Only, Erin had never been a stranger, had she? She'd left

a mark on Steph's life from the moment they'd met. One that Steph was struggling to wipe off. Mainly because she didn't want to.

The first few weeks after she left, Steph had been so angry with Erin for just throwing them away. However, that anger had soon been replaced with what ifs. With sadness. With wondering how she could win Erin back. Should she bombard her with flowers? Write her a poem? Text Erin her feelings? But all of those smacked of desperation, and that was no way to win Erin over. So she'd done nothing. It had been very un-Steph-like, but it had been the right thing to do. So many nights, she'd nearly caved and contacted her. But she hadn't.

However, being in Carlisle meant she was that bit closer to Erin, so she was on Steph's mind. Their final performance this morning had been to a hall of 500 teenagers, and it had been raucous and real, just like the others. She loved talking to these kids, and she loved their energy. Maybe she should retrain to be a drama teacher. Over the past weeks, Steph had felt like she could truly reach these young people. Her acting career hadn't really panned out as she'd anticipated, but she could teach them a lot about how to act, being resilient, never giving up. That was the life of an actor. As the thought flickered in her veins, it sprang to life in her mind. A smile crept onto her face. Maybe that was the next move. Teaching. She had a degree. Could she put it to good use and get a job that didn't require auditioning every five minutes? That would be a real bonus.

Her fellow cast member, Jody, clicked her fingers in front of Steph's face and made her jump. She nearly fell from her bar stool in the process, which wouldn't have been a good look. All around her, lights blinked, and people whooped with Friday-night energy. It was the end of the week, and for them, the end of a very successful run.

"Girl, you were away with the fairies then. But you had a dreamy look on your face. Who were you thinking about and when do I get to meet her?"

Steph smiled and accepted the tequila shot Jody held out. It was her third in the last hour. This was what wrap parties looked like, and she was more than ready for it. Being on the road was gruelling, as was living out of a suitcase. But it had been exactly what she needed to take her mind off Erin. Plus, could it have unlocked a new work avenue for her future?

"I was just thinking I might become a drama teacher." The words tasted good on her tongue. *Right*. "I was also thinking about the one that got away."

Jody raised an eyebrow in reply. "You made a delicious Chlamydia, and you'd make an even better teacher." She didn't break her stare. "But tell me more about the second part, please."

Steph shook her head. She'd thought about confiding in Jody so many times on this tour, but something had held her back. Jody had asked how her fake-date gig had gone at the start, but she'd stopped asking when Steph kept changing the subject. Steph regretted saying anything now. Those thoughts were best left in her rear-view mirror.

"Nothing to tell. I had an amazing long weekend with a woman, but she decided it couldn't go anywhere else, so it was a holiday romance of sorts." She could still smell Erin's perfume if she concentrated hard enough. "But the very best kind."

"Where was this holiday?"

"Scotland."

"Up there?" Jody pointed a finger to the ceiling. "Is this the one Michael set you up with? The fake date job?"

"What has he said?" She rolled her eyes, and they downed their shots.

Jody made the tequila face at her. "Before you entertain visions of punching him, you should know he told me a bare minimum. Just that you might be a little sore about it, but not to bring it up until you did." She smiled. "Tell him I've been true to my word."

"You wouldn't stop asking me at first!"

"I stopped after five times."

"That must have almost killed you." They'd shared a room for the whole tour.

"You have *no* idea." Jody gave her a wink. "But now you've brought it up, and you can still smile despite evidence to the contrary, why don't you see if she's around? You've got an open train ticket that's good for another few weeks, so you don't have to come back to London with us tomorrow." She paused. "If this woman can put a smile on your face, I'm all for it."

"It's too late." Erin was close, but also very far. "It was two months ago, and she hasn't contacted me. The ball was in her court, and she didn't play." Steph exhaled. "As my mum always says, you win some, you lose some."

But Jody wasn't satisfied with that. "Michael told me you'd say it was too late."

Steph's eyes widened. "Michael should have kept his mouth shut."

"Giving up isn't your best look. Ask yourself, what would Chlamydia do?"

Steph snorted. "She'd go after what she wanted." The role she'd played for the past two months had been the complete opposite to Steph.

"Can't you take a leaf out of her book? Like we told the kids this morning, you can learn a lot from sexual diseases."

"I'm really not sure where you're going with this."

Jody shook her head. "Neither am I." She grinned. "But what I am sure about is you can take elements of her philosophy and run with them. To seize the day. To show up uninvited. Be a little irritating. Not traits to build your life around, but sometimes they're necessary. Where's the harm in sending a text to this woman to let her know you're still thinking about her?"

"The harm will be to my ego when she doesn't message me back."

"If that happens, you're still in the same place you are now. Then, at least you know." Jody tilted her head. "How dreamy was this holiday romance?"

"We fucked in a swimming pool." Steph's clit gave a tingle of approval.

"You fucked in a… message the damn girl! You'll still be in her memory too, trust me." Jody stared, then held up a finger. "Question: how do you have sex in a pool in Scotland? It's a fabulous country, but it's hardly Ibiza."

Steph gave her a satisfied smile. "It was the weekend I was there. Perfect weather, perfect woman."

"That does it." Jody picked up Steph's phone from the bar. "Message her please. If you're thinking about her, she's probably thinking about you."

"Ever heard of unrequited love?"

Jody rolled her eyes. "That shit from Shakespeare plays and movies? It doesn't apply here; I can feel it. We've been on the road for the past two months and you've given me jackshit about your love life. Not a bean. Whereas you know all about my tortured soul. All of sudden you give me this titbit and you light up. Literally." She squinted at her. "I mean, it could be the tequila, but I doubt it." She waved a large hand with gold fingernails all around Steph's face. "You're lit, you know? In all the ways it's possible to be." She keyed Steph's passcode into her phone. Another thing that happened when you were away on tour with people forever: passcodes became everyone's property.

"What's her name?"

Steph smiled. "Erin."

Jody began to scroll.

Suddenly, Steph couldn't believe she'd opened her mouth. She got up from her stool and reached for her phone, but Jody just held it aloft. Unfortunately, Jody was the tallest cast member. Plus, she wore heels. Of course she did.

"Jody." Steph sobered up abruptly as Jody held the phone above her head and typed something into the message window. "You better not be texting her. I will never forgive you."

"You might in the long run."

"I'm warning you."

Jody turned, gave Steph a sweet smile and placed the phone in her hands. "All done." She leaned forward and kissed Steph's cheek. "You know, one thing I learned in the first part of my life when I was stuck in the wrong body was that men just do shit. Half the time, it's stupid, and half the time, it's genius, but they don't stop to consider the consequences. They just do it. Women, on the other hand, think everything through too much. You'd have talked yourself out of it, so I just did it for you. You're welcome."

Steph skidded to her messages. Jody hadn't been kidding. Sure enough, there was a message to Erin.

I'm in Carlisle and free this weekend if you fancy meeting up. It would be lovely to see you. Steph. xxx

It could have been worse.

"I'm going to kill you."

Jody signalled to the bartender to refill their tequilas, then placed it in front of Steph and shook her head. "No, you're not. You're going to drink this, and then we're going to dance. It's the last night of tour, and this is a party. Time will tell if your party has an extension." She held up her tequila. "To you and Erin."

* * *

If Steph ever had any doubt that tequila was the devil's work, the next morning served as a stark reminder. She cracked open an eye, then promptly shut it. Nausea swilled around her body. Somewhere, she could hear singing. Who the fuck was singing? She pulled the duvet down, then cracked open the other eye. Once her head was out in the real world, the singing was even louder.

Jody. She loved to sing; said it woke her up in the morning. She especially loved to do it when she needed an extra boost. Although, Jody didn't seem to suffer from hangovers the way everyone else did. She said it was because she'd suffered enough in life already, so she'd been spared those.

A dart of remembrance hit Steph right between the eyes.

The message to Erin. She shut both eyes and squeezed them tight. Erin had rejected her once, and she was sure that tally was about to double. Pieces of last night came back to her now. She and Jody had checked the phone over and over for a reply, but it hadn't come. The message had been read, but Erin had chosen not to reply. So they'd had more tequila. It had seemed like a great idea at the time.

Steph turned and flung a hand out, stroking the bedside table until her fingers found her phone. She grabbed it, then took a moment to focus on the screen. Her fingers were fat as she keyed in her passcode, then saw the tell-tale notification at the top. She had a message. She flicked to her messaging app and held her breath. She opened it; it was a reply from Erin.

Holy fucking shitbags.

She clicked, tensed, and focused.

There were words. Sentences. Full stops. A question mark.

What a surprise to get your message. A good one. I'd love to see you. I know you said you'd come to Edinburgh, but I could equally come to you? Or we could meet halfway? x

Damn it, Jody had been right. This was one of those times when being stubborn and annoying paid off. Turned out, Chlamydia was good for something.

Steph sat up, ignoring the nausea that threatened to drown her, and took a breath before replying. She told Erin that no, she'd come to Edinburgh. It felt like the right thing to do. Erin replied almost instantly suggesting they meet in the Malmaison where they'd first met. Steph agreed, then she collapsed back onto the pillow with a stupid smile on her face. Erin wanted to see her, too.

"Good morning, gorgeous. How are you feeling?" Jody was wrapped in a hotel robe, and giving Steph the same beatific smile she'd given her every morning for the past two months.

"Like I want to throw up, but I've also had a reply." She waved her phone in the air.

Jody shrieked. "And?" She clapped her hands together and sat on Steph's bed. "Does she want to see you again?"

Steph tried to play it straight, but she'd never been much good at that. Instead, she burst into a smile to rival Jody's. "We're having lunch tomorrow."

Jody flung herself onto Steph, letting out a high-pitched squeak. "I knew it! I fucking knew it!" She burrowed her head into Steph's neck, before pulling back. Then she raised her famous eyebrow. "You, my dear, are getting laid tomorrow."

Steph shook her head. "It's lunch."

"Lunch with benefits."

Steph grinned. "Whatever. It looks like I'm going to Scotland today."

"Looks like." She leaned over and kissed Steph's cheek. "I've only got one thing to say. Good luck, and don't fuck it up."

Chapter Twenty-Nine

Erin recognised Steph's loose, languid lines as soon as she saw her. Her scalp tingled as she stood up. This *had* to go well. She couldn't fuck it up like she had last time. She had to remember how futile life had been since Steph walked out of it. How she'd been living on half-speed. Morag had told her as much before she left. She needed to get her life back on track, and only Steph could help.

As Steph walked across the bar, her hair spilt down her head in autumnal shades. Erin couldn't quite believe she'd let her leave the first time. This woman, this sculpted form of brains and beauty who had only had eyes for her. Did she still? Time would tell. Why had no production or theatre company snapped her up, given her a leading role in a blockbuster? She was clearly a superstar. But if they had, she wouldn't be here in this bar. She was grateful for that. The same bar where Steph had role-played picking her up when they'd first met. Where Erin had stuttered and blushed. So much had happened since then. Could Erin unpick what had been said? She hoped she got the chance.

When Steph got closer, her pace slowed. Doubt covered her features. Erin's heart went soft. That was her fault, so now she had to take the lead. She got up from her sofa and gave

Steph the warmest smile she could muster. "Good to see you. You look incredible." And she did. She looked luminous. It was all Erin could do to keep her words calm, belying the fact nerves swamped her system.

Steph's eyelids fluttered and her cheeks flushed. "Thanks." She sat on the sofa.

Erin sat back beside her.

They both ordered gin and tonics, then settled back, assessing one another.

If this was an interview, Erin had already fast-tracked Steph in her mind. Whatever obstacles that had gone before had disintegrated as soon as Steph walked in the door. Erin had needed time, and time had healed. Now, she wanted Steph: everything about her. Her perfect skin, her styled brows, her sharp mind. Most of all, she wanted her bravery and her kindness. And yes, she wanted her heart. Erin never thought she'd say that, but it was true. When Steph was in the room, she lit it up. Could everyone else see it, or was it just Erin?

She breathed in Steph's familiar smell and concentrated hard on making herself irresistible. Erin had pondered long and hard on what to wear today, wondering what colour went best with anxiety and pressure. She'd decided on her jade-green jumpsuit because she remembered Steph's reaction to it on night one of their Highland fling. How Steph's eyes had undressed her as soon as she put the jumpsuit on.

"Thanks for getting in touch. It was brave. I was going to contact you, too." She wasn't going to tell Steph she'd thought about it for real just after she was sick on a pavement in Portobello. That was strictly on a need-to-know basis.

Steph screwed up her face. "I'll be honest, it wasn't me who sent the text."

"It wasn't?" This had shades of their first meeting, when both their best friends had pushed them into the fake date.

Steph shook her head. "I told my friend Jody the story of us. She said I was too close not to message you when I still clearly had feelings."

"I'm glad she did."

Steph gave her a soft smile. "I probably wouldn't have been brave enough, after how it ended last time. You were pretty clear what you wanted."

Erin exhaled. "I know."

"It was a very long drive back to London."

Erin screwed up her face. "I'm sorry I put you through that." She stared at Steph's chest. "I'm really fucking sorry for it all. I know you're a warrior, but even warriors have their limits. The whole Nadia thing just threw me for a loop. Just when we were all finally moving on, you being such a visual representation of Nadia seemed a little too much to take."

Steph nodded, understanding in her eyes. "It was a lot for everyone involved." She paused. "Have things changed?"

Erin drew a breath before she replied. What had changed? To all intents and purposes, nothing. The facts were still the same. Steph was still a challenge, from top to toe, beginning to end. But somewhere along the line, Erin realised Steph was a challenge she didn't want to live without. Nadia had been her twin, but also a challenge. Maybe Steph was sent to remind her to start living again.

"Nothing, but also everything. When I went home, nothing was the same. It was like while I was away, someone had come in and rearranged all the furniture in my life and in my mind. That someone was you. You made me see things differently. You challenged me." She stared at Steph's gorgeous lips. "That you looked like a fucking rockstar while you were doing it wasn't a bad thing, either."

Steph smiled, and it reached her eyes. "A rockstar? So long as it's Pink and not Iggy Pop, I'll take that."

Erin let out a bark of laughter. "Definitely more Pink. Although I think you outshine Pink." She shook her head. "I don't know how this can work. But what I do know is I haven't stopped thinking about you. Seeing you now, it's the first time I've smiled in two months. You were right. I need to start living again. I need to take a chance. And if you're still willing, I'd love to take a chance with you."

Erin reached over and took Steph's hand in hers. She couldn't wait any longer. She ran the pad of her thumb across Steph's knuckles.

Steph shivered on contact.

That was a good sign, right? She hadn't pulled away, at least.

"Please don't say you've moved on, that you've met someone else in the past two months. If you have, would you consider dumping them?"

Steph eyed her. "I'm not sure how my fiancée will take it, but I'm sure she'll understand it's for the best."

"Sounds like she's an understanding woman."

There was a beat as they both weighed up where this chat was headed.

Eventually, Steph leaned in, her eyes wide, her pupils dark. Her eyes dropped to Erin's lips.

"You're really fucking maddening, you know that? Are you sure about this? You're not going to change your mind and freak out? Because I've still got your sister's heart. That's non-negotiable. I can't give it back."

Erin's own heart rippled. She'd be lying if she said she was 100 per cent on board. But she was on board enough to want to give it a try. That had to be enough for now.

"If you'll take the leap with me, I promise to give it my best shot. And not to freak out." She stroked the side of Steph's face with her fingertips. "Also, it's your heart now. We signed the paperwork."

"Let's call it a timeshare."

Steph leaned in and pressed her lips to Erin's.

Her kiss was exactly as Erin remembered. The kind of kiss she could build on. The kind she wanted to come back for again and again.

After a few moments, Steph pulled her lips away, then pressed her forehead to Erin's.

Erin shook as Steph's intense stare pinned her in place.

"Before we do anything else, I just need you to promise: no more heartache? I've had enough of that, one way or another, to last a lifetime."

Erin took a deep breath, then nodded. "I promise. You were right when you said I need to start living my life—and I want to start living it with you."

Erin pressed her lips back to Steph's. Erin's eyelids fluttered shut. She was instantly back at her parents' party when they'd danced together, and kissed, and the whole world had stopped. It was happening again.

Their gin and tonics arrived. The waiter cleared his

throat as he set them down, blushed and left. Erin bit down a laugh.

Steph stared at Erin. "Are you sure this is what you want? Because I can't start and stop again."

Erin ground her teeth together, then stood up. "You want to take these drinks and see if we can get a room here? I told you, no more heartache on my watch. But if you don't believe me, let me show you how sure I am."

* * *

They got to the room, and Erin fumbled for the key card. The ice in their drinks clacked against the glass as they dumped them on the dresser.

In seconds, Steph had Erin up against the wall, the textured wallpaper raised against her fingertips. Steph pressed her hips into her, then crushed her mouth to Erin's. Erin groaned. Steph's lips were so hot and loaded, they should be illegal.

Erin was so ready, too. She'd been ready ever since they'd met.

"Up against a wall is new, isn't it?" Steph nibbled Erin's neck. "We've done it in a swimming pool. On a sofa. Even in a bed, how old fashioned of us. But never against a wall."

A slow fog descended in Erin's brain. She couldn't form any words. But she had a fondness for all the ones that fell from Steph's lips.

In moments, the zip on her jumpsuit was down.

Erin took a huge breath in as Steph's hand connected with her skin, her fingers warm and soft.

"The first time I saw you in this jumpsuit at your parents' place, I knew I was in trouble." Steph rained hot kisses down

Erin's neck, and then back up to her ear. Her lips settled there. "And we need to talk about how it makes your cleavage look. But not right now." Backing up her words, Steph swept her tongue up Erin's cleavage.

Erin's mind stuttered and she closed her eyes.

Just as Steph's tongue had spun her inside out, now it was the turn of Steph's fingers, warm, strong, and long. If Erin thought this was going to be drawn out, she was wrong. This was going to be like a lot of their encounters. Quick, satisfying, and bruising, in the very best possible way. They had all the time in the world for slow.

Steph thrust a thigh in between Erin's legs to push them apart, then her fingers slipped inside Erin's underwear in seconds.

Erin's insides ran nuclear-hot. Then, as Steph slid two fingers into her and began to slowly fuck her, Erin willingly imploded. She wrapped a leg around Steph's thigh, then pressed her hips forward. The pressure was exquisite. Erin's breath caught in her throat as they moved as one. She inhaled Steph's perfect skin, that covered every inch of her perfect body. Perfect for Erin, nobody else.

This was the first time they'd had sex on a level playing field. Erin wasn't paying for Steph's time anymore. There was no ticking clock. Erin hoped this was the start of a new chapter, not just a footnote of the last. They hadn't spoken about it, but it was implicit in their actions. Last time out, Erin had cut the cord. This time, they were both here of their own accord. It was fast becoming Erin's happy place.

Steph pulled back her head and traced Erin's bottom lip with her tongue.

Erin's mind slid sideways. When she opened her eyes, Steph stared straight at her.

A bullet of desire hit Erin's centre and she wondered if it were possible to collapse on the spot. For her muscles to dissolve in an instant. Not for the first time, Steph had dismantled her. But Erin had complete faith she'd put her back together again, and that she'd be better for it.

Then Steph's mouth and fingers were everywhere. On Erin's earlobe, her clit, the hollow at the base of her neck, her G-spot. Steph ran hot, fiery, and hotter still.

Erin pushed her head back against the wall, as her own internal walls pulsed. She couldn't hold out anymore, and she didn't want to. With a groan to be proud of, she came while Steph's fingers thrust into her with gentle precision.

Steph moaned, a drawn-out sound of her own in Erin's ears.

"You're killing me," she told her, as Erin's eyes squeezed tight shut. "But I want to taste you, too. With you on top."

Erin wasn't sure which way was up and which way was down, but Steph stripped off Erin's clothes and lowered her naked body onto the bed. "You're so fucking beautiful, you should come with a warning."

Shockwaves reverberated through Erin, but she managed a smile. "Sweet talker."

When she opened her eyes, Steph was naked. She kissed her way up Erin's body, then urged her on to her knees.

Steph's stare was so intense, Erin couldn't look away. She placed her knees either side of Steph's cheeks, and Steph grabbed hold of Erin's hips and settled her in place. When Steph's hot breath hit Erin's centre, she didn't have a word in any language to describe the feeling. When Steph's hot tongue swept up and through her, Erin flew. Steph's skills went beyond any she'd encountered before. Or maybe that's because Erin felt more for her than she had for anyone before. Steph was different, and she had been from the start.

Letting Steph call the shots and opening up to her was new to Erin. She'd rewritten her rulebook, and she was reaping the benefits. Steph wasn't the only one to have a change of heart. Right now, riding Steph's face, it was like Erin had stepped outside herself, and was watching a different person. It was going to take some time to get used to this new her, to this new way of being. One of surrender, of going with the flow, of acceptance. At her parents' place, Erin had let Steph in, but that was only step one. Now, Erin had confirmed her interest. She'd signed up for real. It was going to take guts to stay the course, but she owed it to herself. She owed it to Steph. She definitely owed it to Nadia.

But she wasn't going to think about her sister now. They might be twins, but some things were just for her. Like this moment.

Steph slipped two fingers back into Erin.

Erin made a noise that former Erin might have been embarrassed by. Not present Erin. Instead, she ground into the moment, into the slickness of Steph's touch. As Steph secured Erin with her free hand on her hip so she didn't fly away, Erin threw back her head and came like she never had before. Came for all the past versions of herself who'd never felt like they could. Tonight was a love letter to them all, to Steph, and to Nadia.

This Erin *could*.

"Oh fucking hell, yes!" Erin roared as Steph brought her to the precipice once again, then tipped her over the edge.

Every part of Erin throbbed in the best way. Steph's hand squeezed her buttock, and Erin smiled. She wiggled her arse, as Steph swept her tongue for the final time. Erin let out a groan a grizzly bear would be proud of, then laughed.

Underneath, Steph laughed right into her.

Erin saw stars.

As she came down from her climax, her heart wobbled. She stopped to rest her forehead on the wall for a good ten seconds.

Steph kneaded her butt, then lightly pushed her backwards.

Erin unglued her head and tried to arrange her face into something approaching normality. She wasn't sure if she managed it. She stared down into Steph's big, brown, bottomless eyes. She could easily drown in them. Every time they were together, there were no lifeguards on duty. It was every woman for herself.

She slid down Steph's body until she lay flat on top of her, their faces level. Then she shook her head. She should move more, but she was incapable. Her body was boneless, slammed. She used to know things before today. Erin had a degree, ran her own business. But now, all she knew was Steph. Steph's tongue on her, taking her to new heights. She never wanted to move again.

"I really fucking missed you. I missed this. Us."

Steph shook her head. "Is it crazy after we only knew each other for such a short time?"

Erin smiled. "I kept saying that to myself. But every time I did, I came up with the same answer. I just had a feeling this was right."

"I know, I was there. It happened for both of us."

"I'm so glad. If you'd have turned up today just to throw it all in my face — which you'd have been within your rights to do after my performance at Starbucks — I would have taken it like a champ, then sobbed for the next three years."

Steph laughed, then grazed a hand up and down Erin's backside.

Every part of Erin reacted. It was who she was now.

"We might have to visit another Starbucks and have a coffee where we don't split up. Create new Starbucks memories."

"I don't know; the coffee's not all that."

Steph's laugh stuck in her throat, and she nuzzled her face into the hollow of Erin's neck. When she recovered, she placed a sticky kiss onto Erin's collarbone, then exhaled.

"You're quite something, you know that?"

"I'm glad the hot actor thinks so." She sighed. "I'm also glad I'm not paying for your time anymore." She paused. "That sounds bad."

Steph smiled. "I hope I gave good value."

Erin kissed her lips. "The very best." She sighed. "When do you have to get back to London?"

Steph stared into her eyes.

Erin waited for her bliss bubble to be burst.

"Not anytime soon. My ticket is good for another month, and I don't have any work happening for a bit. If you want, we could get better acquainted. Plus, I might have some plans where we could be in closer proximity. Plans that might mean me moving here to teach drama." She paused. "I've only just started thinking about it, but it might work. But only if that's what you want, too."

The hesitation in Steph's voice made Erin's insides sigh. She'd sown the seeds of doubt in the first place. Now it was her job to rip them up and start afresh.

"Of course that's what I want." She rolled off Steph, then she grasped her hand in hers. "I haven't spent the past couple of months working through all my shit to see you disappear." Erin took a deep breath, then rolled onto her side, and planted her cheek into her palm. "As you know more than anyone, I can be monumentally stupid. Blindsided. Dictated to by a ghost. But one thing I know for sure is I want you in my life." She ran her fingertips over Steph's chest. "You, and your heart. The heart that very much belongs to you. Nobody else."

As she spoke candyfloss flavour filled her mouth. Erin grinned. Her sister picked her moments, didn't she?

"Anything I should know now I've told you I don't want you to leave?"

Steph knitted her brows together. "Let's see. I've got hardly any money, I hate dusting, but if you want anything from the top shelf of the supermarket, I'm your woman."

"Sold." Lightness flowed through Erin as she pressed a kiss to Steph's warm lips.

Steph gathered her in her arms and stared into her eyes. "You sure? This is a very big U-turn from two months ago. Can you handle me and everything that comes with me?"

Erin paused before she nodded. "I can't predict the future, but right now, my answer is yes. Yes to you moving here, yes to giving us a shot." She ran a hand down Steph's cheek. "I'm just glad you came back and stopped me from making the biggest mistake of my life." She paused. "You know what else?"

"What?"

"My family are going to be delighted. They loved you. Patsy, Duncan, Alex, Wendy. All head over heels for Steph."

"Even after everything?"

Erin nodded. "*Especially* after everything. You gave us all the push we needed."

Steph paused. "I sent your parents a thank you note. After my transplant. Via the trust. I hope they got it."

"You did?" Pure sunshine flowed through her. "They never said. Then again, they're not that great at communicating. But that could all be about to change, thanks to you." She snagged Steph's gaze, then took a breath. "I think I owe *you* a thank you note more. We all do. It's not just my family who are crackers about you. I think I could fall in love with you, too." She'd never said truer words in her life.

"You think?" Steph's breath and stare were hot on her face.

Erin nodded. "I do."

"That's settled it, then. I'm moving to Scotland. The heart wants what the heart wants." She kissed Erin's lips. "After all this time, my heart's finally coming home."

Epilogue

Five months later…

"I'm jealous of your Christmas plans, have I told you that?" Morag let out a huff, then took a sip of her sauvignon blanc. The Falcon was busy on this Saturday evening, the December crowds in full swing. Tinsel lined the shelves behind the bar, and the bar staff were in the mood, too, sporting Rudolph jumpers. Outside, the dark Edinburgh night pressed black against the windowpanes.

"You've got good plans, too. Aren't you going to Tim's family?" Erin asked.

Freddo the chocolate Lab scuttled past, clearly on his way to a fallen crisp. He was the dog for crisp emergencies.

Morag shivered. "Exactly. His family live in a tiny village in Ayrshire. It's not the Highlands with a pool, is it?" She sighed dramatically. "It's a shame your brother's married."

"It's not. I work with you all day long. If you were going out with my brother, it might be a bit much." Erin gave her best mate a grin.

"This is the thanks I get for delivering you the love of your life." Morag lifted her eyes to the ceiling.

"I believe that was me," Michael butted in. "But you made

292

the enquiry, so let's say it was a joint effort." He raised his merlot to Morag, and she tapped her glass to his.

"Definitely a joint effort," Steph squeezed Michael's knee. "But now, the love bug has even caught up with Michael. Did you know the king of the fake dates got back in touch with his first fake date, and he's flying out to Mallorca for Christmas to spend it with Charles?"

Erin gave him a wide smile. "Our baby's all grown up." She'd only known Michael a short time, but they'd already become firm friends. Steph had told her the Charles story, and she knew it had been on Michael's mind ever since they got back together. With Steph's help, he'd emailed Charles and got a very positive reply. He was flying to Mallorca the next day.

"Everybody has more exciting Christmas plans than me." Morag pouted. "He's going to Spain!"

"It'll probably rain," Michael said, with a straight face.

Morag gave him the finger.

They all laughed.

Erin sat back and shook her head. "You know, I remember sitting in these very seats with Morag earlier this year. I'd just decided I was going to skip my parents' party because I didn't have a date and I felt like a loser. Then Morag came up with a hare-brained plan that involved hiring a fake date."

"That sounds crazy." Steph gave her the smile she reserved just for her. The one that made her insides flip. Like now.

"And you nearly didn't follow my advice," Morag added.

"I'm very glad I did."

Because it had all worked out, hadn't it? Despite the many bumps in the road, Erin and Steph were now a solid item, living together happily. Steph had moved to Edinburgh as promised, but she was still getting used to the Scottish winter. She'd spent the first couple of months working alongside Erin and Morag, but she had an assistant job lined up in January, in the drama department at a local college. She was even pondering going back to school to do a teaching qualification and make it official. Plus, she'd started an online workshop and course for the same thing, and it was going well. For the first time in a very long time, Steph was in control of her work and not the other way around.

"Have you seen her family since the summer?" Michael asked.

Steph nodded. "I went back up for Erin's birthday. Also Nadia's birthday, of course. It was nice they could all be together again without any baggage."

"No secrets, no shame," Erin said. "It was quite the moment." And it had been. This Christmas would be the first one her family were spending as a family where Nadia would be a topic of conversation. Where her photos would be on show. Where her parents would be more relaxed than they had been in years. Erin hadn't believed the change when she'd seen them in September. Her parents had greeted both her and Steph with bone-crushing hugs.

"My mum's coming for Christmas as well," Steph said. "She arrives this week. It will be her first time to meet Erin."

Michael sat back and folded his arms over his chest. "From relationship-phobic to full-on commitment. Families meeting. Big steps, ladies."

"When you know, you know," Steph replied. "Plus, our families have an extra-special bond, don't they? My mum's really looking forward to meeting the family that saved my life."

In the end, the one thing that Erin had stumbled on hadn't been quite the block she'd first imagined. Now, she loved that Steph had Nadia's heart. It had brought them closer. One of her favourite things to do was lie in bed and listen to it beat beneath Steph's warm skin. When she was that close to her twin and the love of her life, she felt the most content ever.

Plus, she always tasted candyfloss.

THE END

Want more from me? Sign up to join my VIP Readers'
Group and get a FREE lesbian romance,
It Had To Be You! *Claim your free book here:*
www.clarelydon.co.uk/it-had-to-be-you

Did You Enjoy This Book?

If the answer's yes, I wonder if you'd consider leaving me a review wherever you bought it. Just a line or two is fine, and could really make the difference for someone else when they're wondering whether or not to take a chance on me and my writing. If you enjoyed the book and tell them why, it's possible your words will make them click the buy button, too! Just hop on over to wherever you bought this book — Amazon, Apple Books, Kobo, Bella Books, Barnes & Noble or any of the other digital outlets — and say what's in your heart. I always appreciate honest reviews.

Thank you, you're the best.

Love,
Clare x

Acknowledgements

I hope you enjoyed reading *Change Of Heart*, a story with all the emotions and buckets of feels. Here's hoping the humour and heart had you rooting for Erin and Steph!

The idea for the story came to me after watching the jewellery show 'All That Glitters'. On it, a woman's life had been saved by her friend when she donated her bone marrow. The woman thanked her by commissioning a beautiful brooch. It triggered something in my brain about what would happen if you met the family of your donor. What if you then fell in love with someone in that family? My wife and I fleshed out the idea on a driving holiday around the Scottish Highlands, and we also had a sandwich on that special beach that Erin and Steph visit, where we nailed down the plot. The book was born in Scotland, so it couldn't take place anywhere else. I hope I managed to convey just how beautiful the Highlands are. If you want to visit the real-life Caribbean beach, head to Achmelvich Beach on the west coast. It's a hidden treasure.

Huge thanks to my Scottish friends Elaine & Rachael for their shocked reaction to the storyline when I outlined it on a day trip to Cromarty. I knew then, whether you loved it or not, it would be a story that caused conversation, which is never a bad thing.

Thanks as always to Angela for her first read and encouraging comments. Also to my fantastic advanced reading team for their eagle eyes. This one had a few more niggles, and you picked them all up. I couldn't do this without you, so you get all the plaudits!

Lashings of praise to my wonderful team of talented professionals who make sure my books look and read the best they can. To Rachel Lawston for the standout cover. To Cheyenne Blue for the fabulous editing and excellent blurb handholding. And to Adrian McLaughlin for his typesetting prowess and general loveliness. Plus, a special cheer for my wife, Yvonne, for helping me come up with the story in the first place, and for reading the draft by a pool in Portugal and telling me it made her cry. I don't normally want to do that, but in this case, it was perfect!

Finally, thanks to you for buying this book and supporting me on my writing journey. I loved creating this story, and my next novel will be a standalone romance too. I hope you stick around for that, and plenty more books in the future. Thanks for making my dreams of being a professional writer come true.

If you fancy getting in touch, you can do so using one of the methods below:

Website: www.clarelydon.co.uk
Email: mail@clarelydon.co.uk
Instagram: @clarefic
Facebook: www.facebook.co.uk/clarelydon
Twitter: @clarelydon

Also by Clare Lydon

Other Novels
A Taste Of Love
Before You Say I Do
Christmas In Mistletoe
Nothing To Lose: A Lesbian Romance
Once Upon A Princess
One Golden Summer
The Long Weekend
Twice In A Lifetime
You're My Kind

London Romance Series
London Calling (Book One)
This London Love (Book Two)
A Girl Called London (Book Three)
The London Of Us (Book Four)
London, Actually (Book Five)
Made In London (Book Six)
Hot London Nights (Book Seven)
Big London Dreams (Book Eight)

All I Want Series
All I Want For Christmas (Book One)
All I Want For Valentine's (Book Two)
All I Want For Spring (Book Three)
All I Want For Summer (Book Four)
All I Want For Autumn (Book Five)
All I Want Forever (Book Six)

Made in United States
North Haven, CT
16 February 2022

16153561R00183